EMPIRE OF REBELS

The Lord King & The Lady Queen

Tarik Bouchnayf

Copyright © 2024 by Tarik Bouchnayf

All rights reserved.

No portion of this book may be reproduced in any form without written permission from the publisher or author, except as permitted by U.S. copyright law.

CONTENTS

1. Chapter 1   1
2. Chapter 2   10
3. Chapter 3   17
4. Chapter 4   26
5. Chapter 5   37
6. Chapter 6   47
7. Chapter 7   53
8. Chapter 8   64
9. Chapter 9   69
10. Chapter 10   79
11. Chapter 11   87
12. Chapter 12   94
13. Chapter 13   103
14. Chapter 14   114
15. Chapter 15   121
16. Chapter 16   129

17.	Chapter 17	139
18.	Chapter 18	147
19.	Chapter 19	155
20.	Chapter 20	165
21.	Chapter 21	173
22.	Chapter 22	181
23.	Chapter 23	190
24.	Chapter 24	199
25.	Chapter 25	211
26.	Chapter 26	217
27.	Chapter 27	227
28.	Chapter 28	233
29.	Chapter 29	244
30.	Chapter 30	251
31.	Chapter 31	266
32.	Chapter 32	272
33.	Chapter 33	282
34.	Chapter 34	289

CHAPTER 1

Aznek stood in front of a majestic white oak tree, seemingly ordinary in appearance despite its towering height of eighty feet. Its massive canopy extended far and wide, with its lower branches parallel to the ground. The tree trunk boasted such breadth it could effortlessly house five adults within its hollowed core.

Though Ali and Leah had offered reassurance, the queen hesitated to proceed with the ritual. Her gaze shifted between Ali and Leah, seeking their affirmation. With a nod from both of them, she turned her attention to Arsalan, who wore a comforting smile and uttered, "I wish I could spend the rest of my life there!"

Arsalan's words resonated deeply with her, instilling a sense of resolve. Finally, she reached a decision and placed both hands on the Blessing Tree, focusing her thoughts on her utmost desire: to see her son, Alexander, seated on the Solumy throne, to rule over a world unshackled by tyranny.

As her surroundings blurred and spun around her, a deafening silence engulfed her, and her heart pounded in her chest. Then, everything faded into darkness as she lost consciousness.

After a while, Aznek opened her eyes and found herself in a place entirely different from where she had been before. She stood within a vast enclosed area, similar to a cavern in Solum, yet uniquely radiant as if standing atop a sunlit rooftop.

Aznek stood on her feet, bewildered and trying to comprehend the situation unfolding before her. Suddenly, a shadowy figure materialized in front of her. The man stood tall with flowing golden hair and piercing blue eyes, his form emitting an otherworldly luminescence akin to the glow of the moon.

Recognition flooded over the queen as she fell to her knees, tears streaming down her face like a torrential downpour. "Uncle Rajab!" she exclaimed through her sobs, her voice choking.

"I reside in a realm far superior to yours now, Aznek, and I am no longer known as a king," the man replied, his voice resonating with wisdom. "Instead, I am a Thinker, entrusted with guiding you on your arduous journey."

Aznek's mind flashed back to the teachings of Ali, who had taught her about the existence of the Thinkers. They were men who dedicated their lives to goodness, and upon their demise, the Creator granted them eternal life, allowing them to guide those who walked the path of righteousness.

Gathering her strength, Aznek rose from her kneeling position and asked her question to the enigmatic figure. "Why have I been brought here?" she said.

"You have been brought here to discover the truth about yourself and the world in which you reside," the Thinker responded, his eyes shimmering with ancient knowledge.

Resolute, Aznek extended her hand, gently touching the surface of the rock. In an instant, the scenery surrounding her morphed into a familiar setting—the walls and doors of her residence in Solum remained. Everything was intact, but the furnishings had changed, exuding an unfamiliar aura.

A woman's anguished scream pierced through the air, capturing Aznek's attention. She hastily made her way toward the sound, bursting into a bedroom to find a woman lying helplessly on a bed, flanked by three attendants. Two of the women were dressed in servant's attire, while the third wore an elegant red gown.

Aznek introduced herself, but her presence was met with indifference. It was only when she glanced at her own reflection in the mirror that the queen realized the truth— she was invisible in this realm. She could not see her own reflection.

Despite her lack of corporeal form, Aznek sensed an inexplicable connection to the woman lying on the bed. Though unfamiliar to her, a profound empathy struck her, urging her to observe and understand what was happening.

As the tension in the room escalated, another man made his entrance, dressed in a regal blue robe adorned with the emblem of the Solum kingdom— three trees.

The three women immediately dropped to their knees, their voices merging as they uttered in unison, "Your Grace!"

Aznek swiftly deduced his identity—the King of Solum. The woman in a red dress addressed him urgently, voicing her concerns, "Where is she? If we delay any longer, my sister and her unborn child may not survive."

The king took a deep breath before responding, "Her condition is exceedingly delicate. My trusted healer has informed me that only a midwife from the Turban tribe can safely guide her through childbirth!"

One of the servant women interjected, bowing her head, "Your Grace, I do not mean to doubt your judgement, but our midwives are trained by the most esteemed healers. How could a woman from an isolated tribe surpass their expertise?"

"My dear friend, the King of Turba vouched for this woman's exceptional skills!" the king explained.

Before he could finish, another servant interrupted, her voice trembling with urgency, "Your Grace, the midwife has arrived!"

Without hesitation, the king commanded, "Bring her in immediately!"

The midwife entered the room, accompanied by an eight-year-old boy. Aznek's heart skipped a beat as she felt an undeniable familiarity emanating from this boy. With soft, cascading black hair, warm brown eyes, and an infectious smile, the boy's striking handsomeness captivated the queen, drawing her gaze irresistibly towards him.

However, the woman in the red dress abruptly stood, her tone firm and resolute. "The boy cannot remain here!"

Ignoring her protest, the midwife approached the patient, gently placing her hand on her forehead. She then addressed the king, her voice calm and assured, "Your Grace, your wife is ready to deliver. You must leave the room."

The king offered a gentle smile, replying, "Of course, I will entrust my queen to your capable hands."

The woman in the red dress erupted in anger, exclaiming, "How dare you order a king around?!"

Unfazed by the outburst, the king maintained his composure. "It is quite alright, Lady Guenever," he remarked, before turning his attention back to the midwife. "What is your name?"

"My name is Halima, and this is my son, Ali," the midwife responded, introducing herself and the young boy.

Aznek's mind raced as she made the connection, realizing why the boy had seemed so familiar—he was the rebels' leader, Ali.

The king clasped Ali's hand and together they exited the room. Inside, Halima firmly grasped both of the queen's hands, her voice soothing and reassuring. "Your baby's positioning isn't ideal, but fear not. I have performed deliveries like this many times. With your cooperation, you will soon lay eyes upon your child. All I ask is that you keep pushing."

The queen nodded, and her sister tightly held her hands, providing comfort and support. The labour reached its peak, and Halima's hands moved with a seemingly magical grace. She applied gentle pressure to the queen's abdomen, her hands spreading and massaging, as if weaving a spell of ease and progress.

Aznek, filled with curiosity about Ali's childhood, stepped outside the room in search of more insights. Meanwhile, the king, filled with both excitement and anxiety, eagerly awaited the sound of his baby's first cry. In an attempt to distract himself momentarily, he engaged Ali in conversation.

"Ali," the king began, his voice tinged with anticipation, "as you grow older, what do you aspire to do? What dreams lie within your heart?"

Expecting the boy's reply to centre on aspirations of becoming a triumphant knight, the king found himself pleasantly taken aback by Ali's response. "I want to be a Lord King, like his grace Tamim," he declared.

Delighted by the ambition expressed at such a tender age, the king inquired further. "And why is that?"

Ali's reply was simple yet profound. "My mother told me so."

Before their conversation could continue, the joyful sound of a baby's cry erupted, igniting every fibre of the king's being. Without hesitation, he hurried back to the room and knocked gently.

Lady Guenever swiftly swung open the door, her face radiant with happiness. "Congratulations, Your Grace! You have a beautiful daughter, and your wife is fine!"

Overwhelmed with joy, the king rushed to his wife's side, tenderly kissing her hand. He then turned to Halima, gratitude pouring from every word as he thanked her for her invaluable assistance.

After Halima provided instructions to the attending servants, she began packing her belongings, preparing to depart. Lady Guenever approached her, a genuine apologetic expression on her face. "I apologize for my earlier outburst," she said sincerely.

Halima clasped her hands, a warm smile gracing her lips. "I would have reacted the same way for my own sister," she replied.

Lady Guenever extended a generous invitation. "I would like you to be our guest for the next three days! Will you?"

Halima bowed her head respectfully, grateful for the queen's generosity. "That is incredibly kind of you, Your Grace but I must depart. Our leader's wife, Lady Fatima, is due to give birth in the coming days and I must be present"

Aznek was startled as she quietly whispered to herself, "That's the birth of Nisay!"

Another servant entered the room, holding a letter in her trembling hands. She promptly handed it to the king and swiftly exited.

As the king read the letter, his complexion grew pale, alarming Lady Guenever. She hurried to his side with concern etched across her face. "What is it, Your Grace?"

Ignoring her question, the king approached the bed and requested from the servants to leave.

Lady Guenever's voice was filled with worry. "Please, tell me what's happening?"

Clutching his wife's hand tightly, the king revealed the grave news. "The emperor is advancing with an army!"

Attempting to rise from the bed, the queen's determination was met with resistance from her husband.

"It seems he has learned everything!" he said, his voice heavy.

A tear escaped the queen's eye as she implored, "Do whatever is necessary for the safety of our child!"

"Of course, my love," the king said, turning his attention to Halima. "This little girl represents not only the hope of Solum but also the entire world. She bears the royal bloodlines of Solum, Turba, Topraki, and Token."

Halima remained silent, absorbing the weight of the revelation, while the king continued, "She poses a genuine threat to Ceres, which is why the emperor seeks her demise!"

Interrupting with confusion, Lady Guenever asked, "But why?"

"King Tamim held power with his three royal bloodlines, leveraging him to become the Lord King," the king explained. The Queen tried to rise from the bed and screamed in pain.

"My daughter must survive!" she pleaded, gripping her husband's hand. "Do whatever it takes to protect our heir!"

With a tender squeeze of her hand, the king reassured her, "I am proud of you, my love!" He then turned to Halima, his gaze unwavering. "I will dispatch my soldiers with you. Take her to the King of Turba. He is a dear friend, and I trust he will provide sanctuary."

Halima glanced at the queen, who, despite the torment she endured, displayed an unwavering determination. "I need my daughter to be safe."

Halima then turned to Lady Guenever, who beamed at her, silently encouraging her to accept the weighty responsibility of this mission.

"I would be honored to protect her with my life!" Halima replied, "But the Kingdom of Turba is not necessarily safer than your own kingdom. It is riddled with spies, and it won't take them long to discover the existence of your daughter."

"She speaks the truth," Lady Guenever added.

The king couldn't deny their concerns, and Halima continued, "Your Grace, I may not possess the political acumen that you and Lady Guenever possess, but I have a suggestion to offer."

Desperate for guidance, the king pleaded, "The politicians have betrayed my kingdom. I yearn for counsel from honorable individuals. Please, Lady Halima, speak your mind!"

"The safest haven, for the time being, would be the Kingdom of Token," Halima proposed. "It is the only kingdom that remains untainted by corruption."

"I couldn't agree more," the king replied, "but I have a strained relationship with King Rajab due to his brother. Convincing him will be no easy task."

As Aznek listened intently, her teeth gritted, and she couldn't hold back her words any longer. "Father, you have always been a source of problems!" she exclaimed.

A smile crept across Lady Guenever's face as she interjected, "We don't need to convince the king."

All eyes turned to her, awaiting an explanation. "His brother had fallen in love with one of the girls from the brothel here."

"Get to the point, Lady Guenever," the king urged.

"We can compel the girl to falsely claim that your baby is his daughter."

Aznek's jaw dropped in astonishment, her emotions swirling uncontrollably as she realized where the conversation was heading. The pieces of the puzzle were falling into place, and a mix of surprise, excitement, and a touch of apprehension washed over her. She struggled to contain her overwhelming emotions, knowing that the unfolding revelation would have a profound impact on her and those around her.

She wiped away her tears, collecting herself, and redirected her attention to the King of Solum, who was engaged in conversation.

"King Rajab's brother was ousted from my kingdom a mere seven months ago, plenty of time for him to have impregnated the girl."

Lady Guenever smiled, "That works perfectly!"

Aznek observed in sheer amazement, tears cascading down her cheeks. She comprehended the profound sacrifice her mother was about to undertake, relinquishing her child and the destiny of Solum. Still, her mother's priority was the safety of her daughter. Halima, with a comforting tone, assured the queen, "Your decision is just, Your Grace. Now, what name shall we bestow upon her?"

Realizing that this was the only path to save his heir, the king's smile broke through his tears. The room filled with sorrow as everyone wept, even Lady Halima. And to set the tone, the king turned to Ali.

"Ali, what should we name our daughter?"

"Let's name her after the first queen of Turba, Aznek," Ali suggested.

The king smiled at him, nodding. "Aznek it is."

The invisible Aznek remained frozen in her place, taking in the sight of her beautiful mother and noble father. She longed to embrace them, to feel their warmth. Ali approached the baby and gently placed his index finger in her tiny hand. The baby squeezed his finger, and he turned to his mother, tears streaming down her face.

Looking back at the baby, he vowed, "Queen Aznek, when I grow up, I promise to protect you."

Through her tears, the invisible woman replied, "I know you will, my friend."

CHAPTER 2

Leah woke up from a beautiful dream, wishing she could linger in its embrace, where her husband Ali had forsaken his role as a Thinker. Despite understanding the significance of such a privilege, she couldn't help but complain.

Concerned for her son, Leah hurried to the next room in her tent to check on him, only to find his bed empty. It wasn't time to panic yet, but a surge of worry still propelled her into action. Gripping her two daggers, she stormed out of the tent, calling out, "Noah, Noah!" in a frantic voice.

No one replied, and Leah, barefoot, stepped on the remnants of thistles scattered on the ground, their prickly leaves grazing her feet. She cared far more about her four-year-old son than the discomfort.

She ventured into the woods, calling out her son's name repeatedly, but received no response. Frustration grew within her, turning into panic. She knew that Ceres would stop at nothing to lay hands on his grandson. Fortunately, she discovered her boy practicing with a stick under Ali's guidance.

"Are you trying to kill me?" Leah screamed at Ali, who halted at the sound of her voice. He remained silent, approaching her with open arms for an embrace. Leah's anger subsided momentarily as she let go of Ali and grasped Noah's hands.

"How many times have I told you not to leave the tent without informing me?" she yelled.

"You were sleeping, and you always get angry if someone wakes you up," Noah innocently replied.

Leah burst into laughter, turning to Ali. "You've taught him well." Ali smiled, and Leah added, "Let's go home and have breakfast"

Before she could depart, Ali pointed to two partridges on the ground. "Let's eat here! for old times' sake."

Leah smiled, and Ali interjected, "But first, let me tend to your bleeding feet. You're still the highborn lady, after all," he said with a wink.

Following Ali's suggestion, they prepared the birds and satisfied their hunger. But this time, Leah couldn't hold back her thoughts.

"You miss them, don't you?" she remarked.

"What do you mean?" Ali responded.

"Stop pretending. They were your friends. And you know what? I miss them too," Leah admitted.

Ali inhaled deeply. "It's strange how our world works. During the war, we were united like a family. But ever since Aznek accepted the truce with Ceres, it feels like our friendship has been cursed."

"Are you telling me you miss the war?" Leah questioned.

"I miss wielding my sword, but like anyone, I despise war. I just don't trust your father and the four kings. Sooner or later, they will betray us."

"But you were the one who advised Nora and Aznek to sign the truce," Leah countered, "And it was the right decision. We couldn't stand against the four kingdoms and the empire."

"But the truce cost us Sofia and Arsalan," Leah said, her head lowered.

Ali asked, "Any news about her?"

"No, ever since she left Solum, nobody has heard anything about her."

Ali suddenly held Leah's arm and whispered, "Did you hear that?"

In an instant, Leah sprang to her feet, grabbing her son and returning to Ali, who remained lying against a tree. "What was it?" Leah said.

Ali smiled, trying to dismiss it. "No, I think I just didn't sleep well."

However, his intuition had been spot on. Just as his family turned to walk away, ten masked men emerged from the trees, arrows poised in their bows.

"If you move, you're dead." one of the masked men warned.

Leah turned to Ali, a defiant smile on her face. "Your wish is granted. You will finally get to use your sword."

"Let's hope it doesn't come to that," Ali replied, assuming the men were mere bandits. He turned to them, "I have no gold. The best we can offer you is a meal."

Laughter erupted from the masked men. "We know who you are, and we're willing to spare your lives if you hand over the child," said one of them.

Leah instinctively reached for her dagger, but Ali held her hand, calmly addressing the threat.

"Since you know who we are, you must be foolish to think that you can snatch my child from me with just ten men," Ali stated.

"You're right. Thanks for the tip," the leader of the attackers turned to his comrades, commanding, "Shoot them both."

The men eagerly embraced the command, ready to release the first arrow. However, before they could, arrows seemingly materialized out of thin air, piercing the soldiers one by one until only two remained.

Ali turned to Leah and asked, "Who do you think it is?"

Leah shrugged, "Roulan and Sai?"

But she was mistaken. A young man with long brown hair tied in a ponytail emerged from the trees, brandishing a sword. He was accompanied by a brunette girl in her twenties, who held two daggers.

The young man addressed the remaining bandits, a hint of anger in his voice. "We spared you for our blades," he said, then turned to his companion and added, "Let's go."

The brunette girl displayed incredible skill with her blades, rolling and hurling her daggers at her opponents. The masked men laid dead on the ground.

The young man became visibly furious and confronted the girl. "I didn't need your help."

The girl replied, "I didn't want to take the risk and lose the love of my life."

Ali and Leah remained in their place, observing this remarkable couple.

The girl approached Ali and Leah and asked, "Are you okay?"

Ali smiled. "Thanks to you, we are."

"Of course you are," the young man interjected, anger still present in his voice. "You bring your wife and child to a dangerous place and don't care about the consequences."

Ali suppressed a smile and stood up. "You're right, and we couldn't be more grateful." The couple remained silent, and Ali continued, "We would love to invite you to our humble home."

"We have more important matters than sitting in a tent and eating," the young man replied abruptly.

The girl interjected, "Ashil, this is not the proper way to speak to people." She then turned to Ali and Leah. "He doesn't mean that. We're just in a hurry."

"He's a very brave man, and we completely understand," Leah said, smiling. "However, we would like to help you."

"That's kind of you. Like Roulan and Sai, we took an oath to not rest until the empire falls."

Leah exchanged a knowing smile with Ali, and she asked Ashil, "That's a noble quest. May the Creator bless you. But why are you risking your lives?"

Ashil replied with pride in his voice, "Ever since we made this oath, the Creator has showered us with blessings, granting all our prayers except one."

Leah smiled and asked, "And what is that?"

"Meeting with the rebels' leader, Ali, and fighting alongside him," Ashil answered.

Ali took two steps forward, facing Ashil. "Well, young man, Ali is honored to meet you, and he couldn't be more grateful for saving his family."

Ashil stared at Ali, processing the words he had just heard. Then, he dropped his sword and knelt down on one knee. Tears filled his eyes as he looked up at Ali. "Lord Ali. tell me I'm not dreaming."

Watching from behind, Zaya cried uncontrollably. She wiped her tears and looked at Leah. "If he's Lord Ali, that makes you..."

"Yes, I'm Leah," Leah confirmed. "And you? What is your name?"

"I'm Zaya, and this is my husband, Ashil," she whispered as she knelt.

"Ashil, Zaya, please stand up," Ali said gently. "If you want to be by my side, never kneel before anyone."

With smiling faces and tear-filled eyes, Zaya and Ashil stood up.

"Since you have found who you were looking for, would you accept our invitation?" Leah asked.

Zaya and Ashil exchanged glances and nodded.

"But first, we need to bury these bandits," Ali said.

Zaya's expression turned surprised, and Leah noticed. "What is it?"

"These are not bandits; they are soldiers from the empire."

Ali found it hard to believe at first, but then spoke in a firm tone to both Zaya and Ashil. "The two of you have to tell me everything, right now."

Without hesitation, Ashil began to explain, "We are from a tribe called Alinians..."

Leah interrupted, "You mean the same tribe as the man who helped Roulan kill Ramessess?"

"That was David, but he's not our leader."

Zaya interjected, "Our leader is my mother, Lady Umali. She has placed her whisperers in all the kingdoms and the Empire. We were her eyes within the Union."

Leah inquired, "And what have you learned?"

"Ceres and the four kings are preparing an attack on Solum and Token. But Ceres' plan was to weaken the two kingdoms by eliminating all the rebels," Ashil said, "These soldiers were here to kill both of you!"

Ali turned to Leah. "All of our friends are in danger. Leah, you take Noah with you and go to Queen Aznek." He turned to address his new friends, "Zaya, Ashil, you go with Leah. My family is in your capable hands."

Ashil placed his right hand on his chest. Leah, however, hesitated. "What about you, Ali?"

"I'm going to Token. I need to warn Nora and Nisay," Ali replied.

Ali knew that Ceres would eventually break the truce. It was only a matter of time. He remembered when Solum had survived the attack from the five kingdoms five years ago. Queen Aznek and her council had anticipated a retaliation from Ceres, but instead, they received a letter signed by Ceres and the four kings, proposing a truce.

Initially, many had been skeptical, except for Queen Aznek and Ali. They understood that Ceres needed time to regroup and consolidate his power after losing his prime advisor and Helena. His empire was weak, and he wanted to reorganize without drawing too much attention to the rebels.

Aznek and Ali were aware of Ceres' true intentions. He wasn't interested in peace, and as soon as he had gathered enough forces, he would break the agreement and strike Solum. Despite knowing this, Aznek had decided to accept the truce. Her people had just survived a devastating attack and lost over a thousand soldiers. War was the last thing she was prepared for, and Ali was the only one who agreed with her.

It had taken time to convince the rest of the group, but Sofia and Arsalan had refused to be persuaded. As a result, they had left the kingdom and ventured elsewhere.

Ali foresaw daunting times ahead, his confidence in Queen Aznek's capable leadership calming his concerns for Solum. Yet, the shadows over Token, where Nora and Nisay struggled, were far more ominous. In their recent conversation, Nisay had voiced unease about two council members, a sentiment that Nora didn't share.

"If Ceres intends to strike back, he will start with Token," Ali murmured to himself, fully aware of the risks that lay ahead.

CHAPTER 3

Nora stood before her husband, dressed in a white tunic under a green, suede vest embroidered in golden colors. Nisay admired her, smiling brightly.

"You're making me very uncomfortable," Nora complained.

"I can't help it," Nisay replied.

"It's as if it's the first time you've seen me." Nora retorted.

Nisay didn't respond. Instead, he walked towards her and gently held both of her hands. "If you don't believe me, come and see yourself in the mirror."

Nora released his hands and briefly brushed his cheek with a smile. Then she said, "Today is a significant day, King Nisay. Let us proceed to our council."

Nisay's smile faded as he responded, "Are you sure you want to do this? I support your decision, but I have a bad feeling about it."

"It's the only way to secure our kingdoms," Nora said.

Though Nisay harbored doubts, he chose to conceal them and accompanied his wife to the council meeting.

The generals were already gathered as the gates opened and the royal couple entered. All the chiefs stood as their queen entered.

"Please be seated, chiefs," Nora said, taking her place.

"You both look radiant today, Your Grace," Prime Advisor Emil remarked.

Nisay had never been fond of Emil and had opposed his appointment as the prime advisor. However, Nora believed Emil was the right fit for the position.

Emil gave his report with a smile. "Your Grace, the kingdom has never been better. Our treasury is brimming with gold, and we have enough schools to accommodate not only our own children but also those from other kingdoms. We now have over a hundred healers." He paused, "The glory of your father is restored."

Nora felt a sense of pride upon hearing the positive report, but deep down, she knew she could never fully trust the stability of her kingdom. Like Ali, she understood that it was only a matter of time before Ceres would break the oath he had made.

Standing up, Nora gestured for the generals to remain seated. "My father used to tell me that a good king is not only one who takes good care of his kingdom, but also one who can foresee the future."

Curious, one of the generals said, "And what about it, Your Grace?"

Nora continued, "Four years ago, we used to send fourteen boxes of gold to the Union as tax payments, and then we suddenly stopped. Do you think Ceres is kind enough to let go of all that gold?"

The Chief of Finance, Tom, tilted his head. "Maybe the death of his prime advisor and daughter taught him a lesson."

Nisay interjected sharply, "If our previous chief of finance, Lord Arber, were alive, he would have removed you from the council."

Although Nora didn't appreciate Nisay's response, she chose not to display her disagreement before the council. Instead, she pressed on as if The Chief of Finance hadn't spoken.

"If Ceres, along with his allies, decides to wage war against us, they will crush our kingdom," Nora explained.

Emil nodded in agreement. "Your Grace, I couldn't agree more. Our best course of action is to strengthen our military, while the truce remains."

"That would be a viable approach if we had no other choice."

Emil inquired, "Do we have any other options?"

"Well, after much contemplation and seeking counsel from King Nisay, I have decided to forge an alliance with Her Grace, Queen Aznek."

Emil was taken aback. "Your Grace, she is already our ally."

Nora revealed her plan. "We will swear allegiance to her."

Emil exclaimed, "This is madness!"

Nisay's voice grew stern as he intervened, 'Watch your words, Lord Emil; you're speaking to the queen!'"

Emil leaned back in his seat, his tone softened. "Forgive me, Your Grace. I merely spoke out of concern. The people of Token have a deep-seated loyalty to your dynasty and may not easily accept bending the knee to another."

Nora responded softly, "It's not just about Token. Once they learn about her true identity, all the other kingdoms will swear allegiance to her. She is the rightful ruler, the Lady Queen."

Emil's eyes widened. "But she's a bastard. How does that make her a Lady Queen?"

Before Nora could reply, the council chamber's gate swung open, and a guard entered with a letter in his hand. Nisay turned to Nora and whispered, "I hope my worries are unfounded."

Nora opened the letter and read its contents silently. *Ceres is on the move. Prepare your defenses.*

Deciding to conclude the council, she announced, "That will be all, my lords. We will reconvene tomorrow."

The queen and king departed, retreating to their private quarters. Once inside, Nisay turned to Nora and said, "My darling, this is not good. Did you discuss our plan with Aznek with anyone else?"

"Except for Emil, no," Nora replied.

Nisay shook his head in disappointment. "You've got to be kidding me!"

"I trust him!"

"We'll see about that," Nisay muttered under his breath.

Nora felt as though her husband was mocking her and responded with increased severity, "I am your queen, and you owe me complete obedience."

Nisay was taken aback by her words, realizing he had unintentionally provoked her. Recognizing that his wife was not in a state to have a rational discussion, he decided to give her some space and retreated to another room.

"This is not the first time you've walked away in the middle of a discussion!" Nora exclaimed, chasing him to the door.

"You want to make it my fault now?" Nisay said, feeling a mix of emotions. "*Why?*"

Nora stopped in her tracks and stared at him. Her face softened. Without responding, she embraced him tightly.

***

The next morning, Nora decided to pamper her husband. She woke up early and prepared a breakfast of fruits and juices, bringing them to his bed. Brushing her hand over his hair, she woke him up with a soft voice. "My love?"

As he opened his eyes, Nora placed her index finger on his lips and said, "Have you ever seen a queen preparing breakfast?"

Nisay looked at her lovingly and said, "A beautiful queen serving a shepherd? How is that possible?"

After enjoying their breakfast together in bed, Nora was confident that the tension between them had dissipated. She invited Nisay to get dressed, and they walked hand in hand to the council chamber.

While making their way down the corridor, they noticed an unusually high number of guards. There were five rooms separating their chambers from the meeting room, and each room had at least twelve guards stationed outside its door.

Nisay tightened his grip on Nora's arm and asked, "Did you request this increase in guards?"

Nora looked at him, confused, and replied, "I was about to ask you the same question." She stopped near the second room and approached one of the guards, demanding, "You, who ordered all this extra security?"

One of the guards stepped forward, placing his right hand on his chest. "Your Grace, we thought you were aware of it. Lord Benjamin, the military chief, requested it."

Nisay inquired, "What is your name, soldier?"

"I am your humble servant, Ajlin, Your Grace."

"This is the rightful ruler of Token. If anything happens to her, the kingdom will fall. It is our duty to protect her with our lives."

Ajlin laid his hand upon his chest and declared, "My life belongs to my queen and king!"

As they continued their way to the council chamber, Nisay forcefully kicked open the door and locked eyes with Emil, his voice a blend of anger and concern. "You had better clarify why you're fortifying security without obtaining the queen's consent, or the next blade may find its mark within your heart."

The prime advisor finally spoke up, admitting that he had given the command to Benjamin. He glanced at the queen, silently urging her to rein in her husband. However, Nora firmly asserted that Nisay was the king and had valid concerns. She walked towards her throne, taking her seat.

Emil waited for them to settle into their seats before responding cautiously. "The commoners are deeply discontented with your decision, particularly the act of pledging allegiance to a person of questionable lineage," He noticed the fury kindling in Nora's eyes and hastened to clarify, "Please understand that I do not intend to disrespect your cousin. I am merely relaying the sentiments expressed by the common folk."

"This information was never meant to leave the council," Nora declared, "Who among us leaked this crucial information? It must have been one of you."

Emil's lips curved into a knowing smile as he responded, "It was me."

Nora's anger flared, and she yelled, "Why on earth would you do such a thing?"

Emil's voice mirrored her tone as he responded, "And who do you think you are? Outlaws lurking in the woods, proclaiming yourselves as kings and queens." Emil spat and contorted his face in disgust. "Your reckless deeds have cast shame upon our kingdom, and now you have the audacity to attempt to enslave us for the illegitimate queen?"

Nora screamed in outrage, "Lord Benjamin, seize this traitor!"

Benjamin, however, burst into laughter. "You're the real traitor here."

Emil clapped his hands, signalling the opening of the gate. In a swift motion, over twenty soldiers marched in, brandishing their spears.

Nisay and Nora stood frozen in shock, their faces pale.

"By the orders of His Highness Ceres," Emil shouted, "I hereby arrest both of you as traitors!" He pointed at Nisay and Nora. "Soldiers, apprehend these traitors!"

The soldiers swiftly moved forward, carrying out Emil's orders with resolute determination. The room descended into chaos as the truth unveiled itself – treachery.

Nora exchanged a meaningful glance with her husband, silently conveying her unspoken plan. In unison, they drew their swords, ready for the impending confrontation.

"Soldiers!" Nora's voice rang out. "I am the queen, and I command you to lay down your weapons. Consider this your final warning."

Two soldiers hesitantly approached, only to swiftly fall under the lethal strikes of Nisay and Nora's daggers. The king and queen engaged in a fierce battle,

Nora seized a spear from a soldier, using it to dispatch both him and another adversary with her swift swordplay. Just as a third soldier attempted to attack her from behind, she deftly turned, her crown in hand, and impaled the soldier's chest with one of its sharp edges.

Meanwhile, her husband was defending himself against multiple opponents, wielding two swords with remarkable dexterity. With each opening, he eliminated another assailant. None of the twenty soldiers could lay a hand on the king and queen.

Nora turned her attention to Emil, a fierce determination burning in her eyes. "Now, where is Ceres to shield you from my blade?"

Emil, still seated, made no effort to rise. More soldiers began pouring into the room through the doorway.

Nora turned to Nisay, urgency in her voice. "We cannot overpower them all, but we can escape! The secret door."

Nisay's memory was jogged. There was a hidden door beneath the throne. Without hesitation, they sprinted towards it and delivered a forceful kick, expecting to reveal an escape route from the castle. To their dismay, the secret door was sealed shut.

Nora turned to Emil, seething. "I swear, you will pay for this."

"Drop your weapons and do not test my patience!" Emil retorted.

Nisay whispered to his wife, "For now, let us focus on staying alive."

Together, they braced themselves for the incoming onslaught, prepared to fight their way out if necessary.

Nora simmered with rage, her mind consumed by thoughts of exacting revenge on Emil. However, she couldn't ignore the fact that he was too cunning to make such a move without careful preparation. Reluctantly, she acknowledged an unpleasant truth within herself. *'I have lost my kingdom to traitors.'*

In a moment of surrender, Nora dropped her weapons, and Nisay followed suit. Two soldiers approached them ready to restrain them. The first soldier moved towards Nisay, who offered no resistance as he allowed himself to be chained. The second soldier was none other than Ajlin, the very one they had encountered prior to the council. He grinned at Nora and spat out his words. "Give me your hands, whore."

Without wasting a moment, Nisay swiftly seized Ajlin's head, his right hand pressing against the back of the soldier's neck while his left hand grasped beneath Ajlin's chin. With a quick twist, Nisay turned his hands in opposite directions, snapping Ajlin's neck. Lifeless, Ajlin fell to the ground.

Nisay raised his bloodied hands, addressing the remaining soldier with a fierce glare. "That is the fate that awaits those who disrespect the queen!"

The soldier, taken aback by the brutal display, hesitated for a moment before stepping back, clearly unsettled by Nisay's act of retribution.

Nisay raised his hand, and the soldiers promptly shackled him along with Nora, confining them within a carriage cage. Both of them surmised the destination of this carriage: the Empire.

CHAPTER 4

Sai placed his hand on his wife's belly, waiting patiently for any movement. Roulan watched him with a smile, her eyes fixed on his face. After a while, Sai felt a gentle pulsation beneath his hand.

Sai withdrew his hand, astonishment evident on his face.

Roulin laughed quietly at him. "That was your child's fist."

"Really?" Sai said, his disbelief evident. He placed his hand on Roulan's belly once again, determined to nurture his child's strength. He declared, "I will make his fist the strongest one of all."

"Does that mean you prefer a boy?"

Sai shook his head, clarifying his stance, "No, of course not. When I see remarkable women like you, Nora, and Queen Aznek, I would be a fool not to like a girl of my own blood, just like you ladies."

Roulan gently reminded Sai, "Don't forget about Sofia." Her voice wavered as she spoke.

There had been no news or sightings of Sofia since the truce was signed between Queen Aznek, Nora, and Ceres, binding their kingdoms together – for four years. Roulan longed for news.

A servant knocked on the door, and Roulan invited her inside. The servant informed Sai that the queen wanted to see him.

Sai squeezed Roulan's hand and said, "Wish me luck."

Roulan placed her hand on her belly. "We do."

Sai proceeded to the council chamber with a young man named Stephen by his side. As they entered, they both bowed respectfully before the queen.

A warm smile graced the queen's face as she greeted them, instructing them to rise. Her attention turned to Sai's companion, and she inquired, "Is this Stephen?"

Stephen's eyes welled up with tears, and Sai supported him, placing a comforting hand on his arm. "Yes, Your Grace, he is my best student."

Sai paused briefly before adding, "In fact, he is no longer a student."

The queen rose from her seat with grace and determination, striding purposefully toward the assembled group. Her voice carried a regal authority as she addressed them. "In the wisdom passed down by my uncle, I learned that swords are wielded to conquer a kingdom, while the mantle of science ensures its prosperous maintenance. Knowledge holds the key to our triumphs, but let us not embrace its corrupted forms."

"Your Grace, how can science be corrupted?" Sai asked, unsure of what she meant.

"Science, much like religion, is meant to ensure the safety and well-being of our world. However, when they are misused or abused, they have the power to cause destruction."

Both Stephen and Sai listened intently, hoping for further clarification. The queen turned her attention to Stephen and asked, "What do you believe is the purpose of science?"

Stephen replied respectfully, "Your Grace, science is meant to improve our lives. It helps us discover new treatments for diseases, construct sturdy homes to shield us from the elements, and find more efficient methods of agriculture."

A smile played on the queen's lips as she then turned to Sai. He responded, "To advance in our lives. In the past, people had to migrate multiple times a year in search of warmer lands. However, with advancements in science, such as the invention of warmer walls, our way of life has changed."

The queen nodded in agreement." Exactly. As long as we maintain realistic expectations, science remains a blessing. However, the moment we start expecting miracles and boundless riches from it, our world will suffer."

Before the scientists could delve deeper into the discussion, Queen Aznek interrupted and said, "Let us proceed. I am eager to witness your masterpiece."

The three of them embarked on a journey, riding three miles outside the castle until they reached a place known as Solum's Mouth.

Ancient people gave the place its name due to its unique geographical characteristics. Solum resembled an isolated landmass, akin to an island, surrounded by water on all sides. The mouth of Solum served as the only connecting point to the neighboring lands.

Sai had envisioned utilizing Solum's Mouth as a strategic advantage to trap any potential enemies. To stop them before they even reached land.

The queen, however, had her doubts. "What about our friends: the merchants and visitors? If we set traps at Solum's Mouth, they would face difficulties entering our kingdom. What if they get hurt?"

Stephen stepped forward. "That's why we call Sai a mastermind. He has devised a system with triggers. When any horse steps into Solum's Mouth, arrows will be launched toward the castle, signalling our team of archers. They will then assess the nature of the visitors, and if they prove to be enemies, our archers need only to sever the cords that hold our secret weapon underground."

Sai smiled and replied, "Stephen likes to make things sound fancy. It is simply wicks connected to the orange eggs that would be buried underground."

Interrupting Sai, Aznek realized the destructive potential and exclaimed, "So, all we need to do is light the wicks, and everyone at Solum's Mouth will be burned to their bones?"

Both Stephen and Sai nodded.

Curious about the timeline, the queen inquired, "How long will it take to set up?"

"Around two months, Your Grace," Sai said confidently, hoping to impress her.

However, the queen's response was firm. "You have one month."

Stephen and Sai exchanged a knowing smile, but before they could speak further, the sound of approaching hooves reached their ears.

Sai immediately shouted, "To the horses!"

They rushed to the spot where they had tied their horses, only to find them missing. The queen looked at her companions, with Stephen panicking and unable to speak.

"This can't be good," Sai declared.

The sound of hooves grew louder, indicating the riders drawing nearer. Sai's instincts kicked in, and he yelled, "Run!"

Aznek and Stephen didn't question Sai's directive, sprinting into the nearby woods. However, Sai knew they wouldn't be able to outrun their pursuers for three miles without getting caught. He quickly formulated a plan.

As they ran, Aznek asked, "Why aren't we heading to the castle?"

"No time to explain, Your Grace," Sai replied, focusing on their escape. "But I have a plan to save you."

Aznek glanced back and saw about thirty mounted soldiers galloping toward them. After running for a few hundred feet, they reached a bridge and came to a halt. Sai placed a hand on Stephen's shoulder and spoke with determination.

"You go with the queen!" Sai commanded.

Aznek turned to Sai, concerned, and asked, "What about you?"

"They will catch us if we keep running. Go and call for help," Sai ordered, understanding the consequences. "Besides, I am a rebel. They will only arrest me. Ali will come for me, as he always does."

Both Stephen and the queen hesitated, but Sai urged once more, "Go now!"

His companions swiftly ran across the bridge. Sai positioned himself at the entrance, unsheathing his sword, ready to face the approaching soldiers. He stood his ground, unwavering, as if the thirty soldiers were mere specs of dust. They were led by a bald man, taller than Ali, with piercing green eyes, a long red goatee, and a distinctive appearance marked by bushy eyebrows and side-whiskers.

"You must be Sai," the leader of the soldiers sneered, laughing. "I was told you were smart, but I'm disappointed. Did you really think you could stop us from reaching your queen?"

Sai remained silent, his attention shifting to ensure the safety of his queen and Stephen, who were now off the bridge. Without hesitation, he swiftly severed the cords holding the bridge, causing it to collapse entirely except for the one remaining rope above. Sai didn't bother cutting it, knowing that no one could use a single rope to cross a hundred-foot bridge.

Turning back to face the bald man, Sai spoke calmly, "Looks like your owner will be mad at you. I wonder, what kind of punishment do you think Ceres has in store for his loyal hound like you?"

The bald man smiled. "You're a clever man, I'll give you that," he said, then he turned to his soldiers. "Kill him!"

Three soldiers eagerly drew their swords, ready to engage Sai in combat. As they charged at him, Sai swiftly retrieved two daggers and flung them with precision. His two opponents fell to the ground, incapacitated, while the third required three strikes from Sai's sword to meet his demise.

Applauding Sai's display, the bald man remarked, "Nice work, Sai. Not only a scientist but also a skilled fighter."

"I will kill all your men and then you," Sai declared through gritted teeth, glaring at the bald man.

"Why waste time? Let's settle this right now." Drawing his sword, the man added, "It's important for you to know the name of the man who will kill you. I am Kanoot."

On the other side of the bridge, the queen watched the unfolding events, silently praying that Stephen would arrive with reinforcements before it was too late.

***

Leah, accompanied by Zaya and Ashil, had just arrived at the castle of Solum. As they were granted entry, Leah immediately recognized one of the commanders who approached her with enthusiasm.

"Lady Leah, what a pleasant surprise!" the commander exclaimed.

Leah offered a smile and replied, "Thank you, Lord..."

"Sam! I'm Sam. I fought alongside you and Ali," he reminded her.

"Of course, Lord Sam. You're the prime advisor now. Please forgive me; It has been a long journey."

Sam assured her, "I'll have the servants prepare your room right away so you can rest."

Leah thanked him then explained, "I wish I could rest, but there is no time – I must speak with her Grace immediately."

"Forgive me, my Lady, but the Queen isn't here."

Leah took a deep breath and urgently asked, "Please tell me she didn't leave the castle alone!"

"As a matter of fact, she didn't. She went with Sai and Stephen," replied Sam.

Leah turned to Ashil and his wife, commanding them, "Come with me!"

Without questioning her, they prepared to leave. But when Leah's ears caught a familiar voice, she turned to find her old friend, Roulan, approaching her.

Roulan hadn't seen Leah for years, but the worry in Leah's expression alarmed her. "What's going on, Leah?"

"Sai and the queen are in danger. We're going after them."

Before Roulan could respond, Leah noticed Roulan's pregnant belly and said, "Go and rest. I'll handle this."

Roulan adamantly refused, stating, "There's no way I'm letting you go without me."

Knowing she couldn't waste time arguing, Leah did not fight Roulan's determination.

After riding for about a mile, they encountered a young man running towards them. It was Stephen. Recognizing Roulan, he hurriedly approached her and exclaimed, "Lady Roulan, please hurry! They're at Bridge Ilsi!"

Without a word, Roulan spurred her horse forward, and Leah urged her companions to keep pace. Stephen interjected, "There are many of them!"

Leah instructed, "Take my horse and go back to the castle and get help. Join us as soon as possible."

Stephen quickly turned his horse back toward the castle while Leah pressed forward. They rode towards the bridge where the queen stood, helpless to aid her loyal scientist, and praying for assistance.

The queen observed Sai facing off against Kanoot. As he attacked with his sword, Sai skilfully blocked the blow with his own blade. However, Kanoot swiftly retaliated by delivering a punch to Sai's face, followed by a powerful kick. Sai fell to the ground but managed to retain his grip and rose back on his feet.

Aznek's voice filled the air, desperate and pleading. "Whoever you are, spare his life! Name your terms. You shall have what you want!"

Kanoot disregarded the queen's pleas and taunted Sai. "I didn't know a queen would care so much for you."

Sai remained silent, determination shining in his eyes. He quickly rose to his feet and lunged at Kanoot, swinging his sword, but he quickly twisted Sai's wrist and made him drop his weapon.

Seizing the opportunity, Kanoot tightened his grip around Sai's neck. Sai's face turned bright red, his legs kicking uselessly in the air.

But it was futile. The man held Sai's neck too tightly, and with a swift motion, he thrust his sword into Sai's abdomen. The tip emerged from Sai's back. Kanoot then flung Sai to the ground and departed from the scene."

Amongst the chaos, he heard a familiar voice screaming his name. He turned his head to catch a glimpse of the love of his life one last time.

Roulan stood next to the Queen and Leah, on her knees, tears streaming down her face.

Leah was overwhelmed, unsure of what to do. The bridge was destroyed, and the number of soldiers seemed insurmountable. Desperate for an alternative, she asked, "Is there another way to reach Sai?"

Zaya informed her of another bridge about half a mile away. Leah was about to instruct her companion to go there, but something caught her attention, leaving her stunned.

Roulan took hold of the last remaining rope from the bridge and wound it tightly around her fist. Leah rushed towards her, attempting to stop her, but she was too late. Roulan, with sheer determination, leaped off the cliff, using her feet to shield herself from the rocks below. She started climbing the rope, disregarding the blood on her hand, even in her eighth month of pregnancy. Miraculously, she reached the other side, finding the soldiers gone. However, nothing else mattered to her except her husband.

Roulan cradled Sai's head in her trembling hands, her voice choked with emotion as she pleaded, "Sai, Sai, please stay with me." Tears streamed down her face, her heart heavy with the weight of impending loss.

With great effort, Sai opened his eyes, a flicker of determination shining within them. His voice was gentle, yet filled with an unwavering resolve as he spoke softly, "I know that our love cannot simply fade away without a proper goodbye."

Roulan, her voice quivering, continued to implore him, her grip tightening as if trying to anchor him to the world they shared. "Please, Sai, don't leave us. We need you. I need you."

A faint smile graced Sai's lips as he mustered the strength to respond, his words laced with love and tenderness, "I love you, Roulan." With those precious words, he turned his head ever so slightly, his gaze drifting towards the distant horizon.

Those three simple words hung in the air, etching themselves into Roulan's heart forever. Overwhelmed with a mixture of grief and profound affection, she leaned in and placed a tender kiss upon Sai's forehead, her lips lingering as if to imprint their love upon his very soul. With a whispered prayer, she found solace in the belief that his spirit would find peace in the realms beyond.

Leah and the rest of the group swiftly crossed the alternate bridge, reaching the other side where Roulan was gripping Sai's hand tightly.

Aznek's face was etched with sorrow and empathy. They all understood the magnitude of the loss and the strength it would take to move forward.

Each friend offered their own silent support, their presence a testament to the unbreakable bond that had formed among them. In this moment of shared grief, they stood together, ready to face the challenges that lay ahead and to honor Sai's memory.

Leah placed a comforting hand on Roulan's shoulder. She stood up, embracing Leah while tears continued to flow. "He's gone, Leah. The love of my life is gone!"

Leah remained strong for her grieving friend, "My dear friend, he died defending his queen. He is a hero, just like Keita and Alighieri."

Roulan didn't respond, but instead, she walked towards the queen and asked, her voice flat, "How did this happen?"

"Sai sacrificed himself to protect me. And I swear I didn't ask him to do it," the Queen explained, her voice filled with grief. Roulan held her right hand, offering comfort and support.

"He did what he believed was right. He had faith in you," Roulan replied, her voice trembling with emotion.

"Your Grace, it's not safe here. We need to return to the castle," warned Ashil, the urgency evident in his tone.

But before they could react, Kanoot reappeared, accompanied by an even larger group of soldiers. They positioned themselves, arrows aimed and ready to be released.

"Move a muscle, and I will order them to shoot," Kanoot threatened, his voice laced with malice.

Roulan paid no heed to the warning and hurled a dagger towards Kanoot. He skillfully evaded the attack and dismounted from his horse.

Exhaustion weighed heavily upon Roulan, but her thirst for vengeance overshadowed any concern for her well-being. She charged towards Kanoot, sword in hand.

However, Kanoot proved quicker and delivered a powerful kick to her belly. Leah rushed to her side, immediately checking on her friend and assessing the severity of the blow. Pain seared through Roulan's body, a terrible ache gripping her.

Kanoot laughed triumphantly, commanding his soldiers to arrest everyone present. Zaya and Ashil prepared to fight back, ready to defend their companions, but the Queen intervened, issuing a firm order for them to stand down.

CHAPTER 5

A man lay in a strangely unique place, where no one had ventured and ever returned to tell the tale to his loved ones.

His limbs were motionless, and his heart had long ceased its beat. The man was unsure if the place was dark or if he had been rendered blind. Suddenly, his ears caught the sound of footsteps nearby.

He attempted to move but found himself immobilized, as if bound, yet he felt no physical restraints upon him.

Memories began to flood back—a sword piercing his chest, a woman weeping by his side. He could not recall her name or his connection to her.

His lips remained sealed, unable to utter a single word.

'Am I dead?'

A booming voice resonated throughout the space, declaring, "Yes you are, Sai, son of Jaya!"

Though darkness still shrouded him, his lips were freed, and his recollections flooded in—Roulan, Ali, his queen.

"Get me out of here. I am not dead! I can hear footsteps approaching. They're my friends!" he said.

The thunderous voice spoke once more, "Yet, here you are, returning to the soil from which you were made!" said the voice, "Sai, who do you believe brought you into existence?"

"The one true God, who has no parent or heir, the creator with no beginning or end," said Sai. But as the words left his lips, a sudden realization struck him. He had never been taught these words his entire life.

"I don't remember learning these words!" he exclaimed, his voice filled with confusion and disbelief.

"And even if you had learned them, you would not have been able to speak them. For your heart had dominance over your mind," explained the resounding voice. Then, a different voice addressed him, saying, "You have done well, Sai of Jaya. Welcome to the realm beyond life."

Suddenly, Sai's vision expanded, revealing a breathtaking panorama. What should have been soil beneath him was an expansive and wondrous green landscape. Trees devoid of trunks surrounded him, each boasting vibrant colors and bearing unique fruits. He glanced downward to discover an extraordinary ground, transparent as glass. Through it, he could discern rivers, their hues shifting from orange to honey-like shades of brown.

He rose to his feet and approached a colossal mirror to catch a glimpse of his reflection. To his surprise, he appeared unchanged from his previous life. However, the garments adorning his body were entirely different—a silk white robe peppered with sparkling coral.

"Am I in heaven?" he muttered to himself.

"No, you are not, Sai, son of Jaya." responded the two voices, now taking the form of two men whom Sai recognized. One was black and bald, while the other possessed golden hair and a fair complexion.

"Keita, Alghieri!" Sai exclaimed.

Alghieri turned to his companion and remarked, "Indeed, those were our names."

Keita smiled and faced Sai. "Welcome to the realm beyond life, Sai. A small slice of heaven."

***

Ali remained oblivious to the unfolding events in Token and Solum. The mastermind he had counted on opposing the empire had been brutally assassinated, and his wife, along with their friends – including the two queens – had been abducted. As if that wasn't dire enough, Nora's realm had once again succumbed to the rule of usurpers, adding another layer of darkness to the situation.

Uninformed about these events, Ali set out towards Token with the intention of alerting Nora and Nisay. Ali was acutely conscious of Ceres's capricious nature, and he meticulously considered every conceivable outcome as he travelled.

About two miles away from the kingdom, he climbed a tree to gain a vantage point on Token. From there, he observed a small group of Token soldiers stationed about half a mile from the castle.

While nothing seemed amiss, Ali chose to exercise caution and silently observe their activities. Listening intently, he detected no cause for alarm.

"Hello, folks. Mind some company?" Ali called out after a while.

One of the soldiers chuckled, "Depends on whether you're a friend or an enemy."

"I always prefer the company of kind-hearted people," Ali replied.

Another soldier chimed in, "And who the hell are you?"

Deciding not to reveal his true identity, Ali opted to assume an alias—Demir from Toprak.

The soldiers laughed and welcomed him. "Toprakies are good people. You can join us."

Ali took a seat, and another soldier inquired, "What brings a Topraki to this doomed kingdom?"

Ali feigned surprise and asked, "Why do you curse your own home?"

Laughter erupted among the soldiers, leaving Ali silent.

"We are from the Empire," one soldier revealed.

Ali maintained his composure and forced a laugh.

The soldier continued, "We have reclaimed Token from the harlot who dared to call herself a queen. The prime advisor has arrested her and her husband."

"And they're on their way to the empire," another soldier added smugly, "I would give anything to attend their execution."

Ali felt a seething rage building within him, a desire to kill these soldiers for their callousness. However, he forced himself to remain composed, knowing he needed to gather as much information as he could. He asked, his voice tense, "What about Queen Aznek and her allies?"

"It's over, the emperor has won," one of the soldiers declared, "The Queen and the rebels were arrested by Kanoot."

Ali fought to control his mounting anger. He needed to find a way to escape from these soldiers. They were merely pawns in a larger game.

"And Leah had been captured as well," one added, "I bet Lord Kanoot would enjoy himself on the road."

The soldier's words pushed Ali's fury to its limits. Without hesitation, he swiftly drew a dagger and plunged it into the first soldier's neck, ending his life in an instant. Standing tall, he faced the remaining soldiers, eight in total, as they unsheathed their swords.

Normally, Ali would give his opponents a chance to walk away, but not this time. Instead, he swiftly dispatched two soldiers before they even moved towards him. The remaining soldiers closed in, thinking they could punish him for his audacity. However, Ali moved with the speed and agility of a scorpion, evading their strikes and taking them down one by one, whether with his sword in his right hand or his dagger in the other.

He swiftly dispatched five more soldiers, leaving only one trembling soldier standing before him, holding his sword with both hands.

"Do you know who I am?" Ali asked, his voice cold and commanding.

The soldier nodded, his voice barely audible as he mumbled, "Lord Arsalan."

"No, I am his friend Ali," Ali replied, his voice filled with determination. "I will spare your life so that you can inform whoever is in charge in Token. Tell him that I am coming for him, and that if he wants to live, he ought to run. Fast."

The soldier said nothing and quickly fled toward the castle, while Ali mounted a horse and galloped away.

With his mind racing, Ali contemplated his next move. Tracking them to the empire would be exceedingly risky, considering the number of soldiers under Kanoot's command. He briefly considered heading to Solum and gathering a group of soldiers, but he couldn't shake the fear that corruption had also taken root there.

Ali hadn't felt so alone in a long time. Two of his closest friends were gone, his family was on their way to an unknown fate, and the Queen he believed in had been usurped. He longed to reach out to Arsalan for assistance, but it had been years since he had last seen him.

Determined to find a way forward, Ali rode onward, his path uncertain but his resolve unwavering.

***

"I've got a bad feeling, Nora," Nisay expressed his worries as he sat chained inside a locked wagon being pulled by two horses.

Nora held his hands tightly and said, "Don't worry, our friends will find a way to rescue us."

"I think this has been well orchestrated, and I bet they have Queen Aznek in their clutches."

"Stop it!" Nora whispered, her voice filled with desperation, "Why are you being so pessimistic?"

"Because I think we need to find a way to escape. Otherwise, Ceres and his allies won't hesitate to execute us," Nisay said.

Nora sighed, realizing the gravity of the situation. "You're right, but how can we do it with these chains and over thirty soldiers surrounding us?"

Nisay surveyed their surroundings, observing the scattered soldiers everywhere. He refused to give up, his mind racing with ideas. Suddenly, the sound of approaching hooves reached their ears. Nisay looked at Nora with a glimmer of hope and said, "are you thinking what i'm thinking?"

Nora didn't reply immediately. Instead, she gripped the bars of the wagon, straining to catch a glimpse of the approaching figures. Her hopes were dashed.

It was the Unionists, led by a tall, bald man.

Nora couldn't contain her anguish as she let out a scream upon seeing her friends in chains, being pulled by horses. Roulan was barely moving, supported by her friend Leah. The queen's face was marked with bruises, as were the faces of a young couple beside her.

The bald man dismounted his horse and approached Nora and Nisay. "Queen and King of Token! It is an honor to meet you!"

Nisay stepped forward within the confines of the cage and spoke with unwavering resolve, "Many cowards like you were excited in the beginning, but their heads ended up on our spikes."

"I don't know about that," Kanoot replied, laughing, "But it's over now. You are all in my custody, and soon I will have Ali and Arsalan."

Kanoot turned to his soldiers and ordered them to lock up the Queen and her friends in the same cage as Nora. The soldiers eagerly complied, relishing in their cruel task.

Nora's eyes fell upon the blood between Roulan's thighs, and fear gripped her heart. She stood up and rushed to Roulan's side, holding her gently until she could see clearly. "What is it, Roulan?"

Roulan, seemingly in a state of shock, didn't respond or react to anything around her, like a statue frozen in time. Nora turned to Leah and her friends.

Nisay, attempting to lift Roulan's spirits, reassured her, "Don't worry. Ali and Sai will come for us."

Roulan lifted her head, tears streaming down her face. "Sai is dead. Kanoot killed him."

Nisay covered his eyes with his hand. He and Sai had become very close over the past three years. As for Nora, the loss of the mastermind was like losing a family member, but she couldn't allow herself to cry. Her focus was on Roulan, her best friend, who had lost the love of her life.

Nora gently placed her hand on Roulan's knee and spoke softly, "May he rest in peace."

Leah interrupted their moment, saying, "Nora. Roulan was kicked in the belly, and she's been bleeding. Can you check on her?"

Nora shook her head, expressing doubt. "I'm uncertain if I'm capable. Matters such as these require the skills of a healer."

"I can help," Zaya volunteered, her voice determined. "My mother is a skilled healer, and she's taught me extensively."

Nora didn't hesitate to accept the assistance. She turned to her husband and the young man, Ashil, her tone unwavering as she instructed, "Both of you, avert your gazes."

Zaya examined Roulan and issued a warning, "This is not good. We need tools, or she could lose her child and possibly her own life."

Roulan finally spoke in a pleading tone, "Please, Nora, do something for my baby. I don't care about my life, but my child has to live."

Nora embraced her friend and assured her, "You and your child will live."

Queen Aznek stood up and addressed one of the soldiers, saying, "You, call your repugnant leader. I need to speak with him!"

"You're no longer a queen to give me orders," retorted the soldier, and without hesitation, a dagger pierced his back. Queen Aznek extended her gaze to see Kanoot approaching with a smile.

"That's what happens to those who disrespect the Queen of Solum," Kanoot remarked sarcastically.

Aznek met the leader's eye. "I have no time for games. Our friend is wounded, and she might lose her child. Take us to a healer!"

Kanoot rolled his eyes, "And why would I do that?"

"For gold. I will give you whatever you want," Aznek offered.

Kanoot approached the cage and spoke firmly, "You've lost everything, and you have nothing left to give."

"I still have my allies," retorted Aznek, her resolve unwavering. "And if you claim to be a true king of Arena, challenge one of them."

Kanoot rubbed his chin, considering her words. "You're already doomed, why would I accept a challenge from any of your comrades?"

"To salvage your dignity!" Aznek replied, her gaze sweeping over some nearby soldiers. "Do you think they will continue to respect a leader who cowers from facing a rebel? What kind of leader does that?"

Aznek pressed harder, her words cutting deep. "Don't worry, Ali isn't among them."

Her words struck a nerve with Kanoot; his face turned red, and he clenched his teeth. "Choose your best champion!"

Both Nisay and Nora stood up, suggesting that they should face Kanoot. However, Aznek had another idea.

"Leah, what do you think?" she asked.

Leah eagerly welcomed the command, but Nora and Nisay disagreed. "Queen Aznek, she's a mother," Nora protested.

"And Ceres' daughter, the one they couldn't kill," Aznek countered.

Leah was released from the cage and handed a sword, ready to face Kanoot.

Kanoot spun his sword around his wrist, poised to confront Leah. He addressed her previous statement with a chilling tone, "Your queen made a valid observation. I'm unable to kill you. However, I can assure you of one thing—I will inflict torment upon you, and your screams will resound, reaching Ali's ears no matter where he might be. And I will enjoy it." He paused, "I suppose you don't understand why.?!"

Leah brushed aside his words, adopting a stance ready for combat.

Kanoot provided the answer anyway. "Vlad was my brother."

Leah, her defiance unwavering, spat on the ground and retorted, "That's fitting. I'll send you to him."

"Show me what you've got, Your Grace!" Kanoot taunted as Leah charged at him.

Kanoot's reflexes were lightning-fast, and his kick landed on Leah's chest before her sword could reach him. However, Leah's relentless strikes gave him no respite, leaving him no opportunity to counterattack. Though he was physically stronger than her, her hits were unyielding. In a surprising move, Leah unleashed a powerful punch to his face followed by a swift kick that sent him crashing to the ground.

Quickly recovering, Kanoot stood up, prepared for Leah's next assault. As she charged toward him, he cunningly threw soil into her face, obscuring her vision.

Seizing the opportunity, Kanoot struck her with a kick. Leah fell to the ground, momentarily stunned. Before she could regain her footing, he pressed his foot against her right hand and held his blade to her neck.

"If only you weren't his highness's daughter, I would have enjoyed myself before cutting off your head," Kanoot sneered, then ordered his soldiers to tie her to a nearby tree.

CHAPTER 6

Kemal delicately skewered a piece of juicy steak with his fork, ready to savor the succulent morsel. However, his dining experience was abruptly interrupted by a resounding knock on the door. Annoyance flickered across his face as he turned his attention to the guard who had entered.

With a hint of irritation, Kemal addressed the guard, his hand still hovering in mid-air. "You'd better provide me with a valid reason for interrupting my meal."

The guard fumbled nervously, barely audibly mumbling, "Your Grace, it's a message from His Highness!" He presented the letter with both hands, and Kemal's curiosity overwhelmed his annoyance. The dropped forked steak clattered onto the plate as he snatched the letter eagerly.

A smile of satisfaction slowly spread across Kemal's face, prompting his step-daughter to inquire. "What does it say, Father?"

"Sweetheart! We have captured the rebels and the two imposter queens," Kemal revealed, "I had a premonition that today would be a beautiful day. Great news keeps coming, and it won't stop here."

Summoning the guard back, Kemal barked an order, "The trial for the traitor will take place today. Go and inform the prime advisor immediately."

Kemal's step-daughter, waiting until the guard had exited the room, took hold of her stepfather's hand and pleaded, "Father, he's my uncle, the only remaining connection to my mother. Please spare his life!"

Kemal withdrew his hand, his tone resolute. "Izmir, he is a traitor, and he must face the consequences for his actions!"

"We don't know for certain!" Izmir protested.

"That's precisely why there will be a trial," Kemal declared with fervour, then softened his voice, "He is not the only thing left from your mother. You have me, and I want you to consider me as your father, alright?"

Izmir smiled and nodded, her gaze lowered. The King of Toprak instructed her to prepare herself and join him in the council. Following his instructions, she adorned herself in appropriate attire and made her way to the council chamber, where she was granted entry. All the chiefs rose from their seats, bowing in her presence.

She wore a smile as she approached her stepfather, who had reserved a seat for her on his right side. Kemal, instead of occupying his throne, took a seat on the left. The grand throne remained unoccupied, reserved for Judge Ayden, who arrived shortly after. Ayden was a short man with a clean-shaven face, dressed in a black robe and a white turban. Carrying a book in his right hand, he made his way toward the throne.

The king stood up and respectfully kissed the judge's hand. "Your honor, thank you for accepting to preside over this trial."

The judge smiled in response. "Your Grace, it is my duty to ensure that justice is served."

Taking his place on the throne, Judge Ayden raised his hand, signalling for the attendees to be seated. "Call the accused!" he commanded.

Soon, a weary-looking man in his sixties emerged, wearing a tattered gray robe. His face appeared pale, and exhaustion was etched in his features.

Izmir's heart ached, but she felt helpless in the face of the unfolding events. She could only pray that there wouldn't be sufficient evidence to condemn her uncle.

The two soldiers who had escorted the accused were about to leave, but King Kemal's voice boomed, "Not you, Commander Salim. The accused was once a formidable fighter. We need your presence here in case he attempts anything foolish."

Commander Salim placed his hand over his chest and nodded.

"Lord Murat," the judge addressed the accused, "In previous trials, numerous witnesses testified to your attempts to overthrow the king. These statements are recorded in my reports. Do you wish to bring forth these witnesses to testify in my court?"

"Your honor, only a fool enjoys hearing the same thing twice," responded Izmir's uncle.

"So, you admit to attempting to usurp King Kemal?"

A smile crept onto Murat's lips as he posed another question. "Your honor, what do you call an enemy of an enemy?"

"A friend," the judge replied.

Murat's smile widened as he posed yet another question. "And what about a usurper of a usurper?"

Izmir muttered to herself, "Please, uncle, don't do this!"

Rather than answering the question, the judge interjected, "This is a simple yes or no question."

Murat's smile remained as he replied, "Yes, your honor," causing Izmir to release a scream of anguish. The judge glanced at Kemal, who nodded, silently conveying, *It's alright.*

Though his heart was breaking, Murat stayed composed and spoke to his niece in a gentle voice. "It's alright. I am not ashamed of what I have done. I hope someone else will succeed where I failed."

The judge stood up, and all the attendees followed suit. "Well, this is not a matter that requires extensive deliberation," Judge Ayden declared with a firm tone. "Based on the complete confession we have heard and the testimony of the witnesses, I, Judge Ayden, hereby sentence Lord Murat to death."

Kemal displayed a sense of relief and turned to Commander Salim. "Commander Salim, escort this traitor to his cell and instruct the soldiers to prepare the execution grounds for tomorrow."

"I will die defending my kingdom, and I couldn't be prouder. The only regret I have is that I won't be here to witness your head being severed," Murat said defiantly.

Salim was about to forcefully remove the guilty man, but Kemal motioned for him to wait. "Lord Murat, didn't you hear? The rebels have been captured. It's over. We have won."

Murat smiled and said, "That's what you believe, and we both know it. Ali and Arsalan are still free, and they will strike back, as they always do." He then turned to Salim. "Commander, lead the way!"

Unable to bear the situation any longer, Izmir politely requested, "Your Grace, your honor, thank you for giving my uncle an opportunity to redeem himself. May I be excused?"

King Kemal offered her a comforting smile and raised his hand, granting her request to leave. As she departed, the judge addressed the king, expressing his concern. "Your Grace, she is a risk. You need to take care of her!"

The prime advisor and the generals concurred, but the king had a different perspective. He stroked his beard and stated, "She is naive and weak. I need her alive more than dead. In Toprak, women are not permitted to rule. Her blood poses no threat, but rather provides a possibility for forging alliances with stronger kingdoms."

***

Izmir locked herself in her room, overcome by sorrow and frustration, she wept for her uncle – the last surviving member of her family. The weight of her helplessness settled heavily on her shoulders, knowing that she could do nothing to aid him in his time of need.

Her father, King Solomon, had passed away when she was a mere six years old. At that tender age, Izmir lacked a true comprehension of death and its far-reaching implications. However, her mother, fully aware of the consequences of a king's demise, especially in a society where male heirs were paramount, understood the gravity of the situation. In the kingdom of Toprak, women were strictly forbidden from ascending to the throne: this harsh reality was deeply ingrained in the fabric of their society.

Desperate to ensure stability and continuity, Izmir's mother attempted to place her brother, Lord Murat, as the ruler. However, the law proved to be an insurmountable barrier due to his status as a bastard. It rendered him ineligible for the throne.

Kemal, a prominent advisor during that time, wielded great wealth and power. Recognizing the need for protection and a secure future for her daughter, Izmir's mother devised a cunning plan. She proposed the idea of marrying Kemal herself, envisioning him as a shield of influence until her daughter reached maturity and could bear a male heir. When the time was right, Izmir would ensure the continuity of her father's dynasty.

Her plan was progressing smoothly until tragedy struck. A servant overheard her discussing matters with her half-brother, Murat, and upon discovering her intentions, the newly crowned King Kemal took matters into his own hands and killed Izmir's mother.

Murat became Izmir's guiding light, instructing her to play the role of a naive girl who trusted and loved King Kemal as if he were her father. And she played her part convincingly – at least, for the most part.

The memories resurfaced, reminding Izmir of her solemn oath to avenge her family. However, she knew that for the time being, all she could do was wait for the right moment. And she was steadfastly confident that it would come.

Lost in these memories, Izmir drifted off to sleep, only to be awakened by her servant's voice calling her name.

"Your Grace, the king is here to see you," the servant announced.

Izmir rose from her bed and adorned herself in her robe. "Let him in."

Kemal entered the room, and Izmir greeted him with a smile. The king feigned concern for her well-being, and Izmir pretended to believe his deceit.

Kemal took hold of her hand and spoke, "I will ensure that you marry a king, so you can become a queen like your mother."

Izmir wished she could dig her thumbs into his eyes and claw at him, but she suppressed her rage, maintaining her smile.

"I need you to be strong and attend the execution," Kemal stated.

"He is my uncle," Izmir whined.

Kemal embraced her and spoke softly, "He was a traitor, and it is essential that you witness his execution."

Wiping away her tears, Izmir replied, "I will dress up and join you, Father."

CHAPTER 7

Leah found herself bound to a tree, her face bruised and battered from hours of relentless beatings by Kanoot. She and her friends were powerless to stop him, their pleas falling on deaf ears.

Exhausted and filled with fear, the queen watched as Roulan's life hung in the balance, while Leah endured torture. Aznek, despite her best efforts to negotiate with Kanoot, felt defeated. He was obstinate and refused to listen to reason.

One of the soldiers, who had observed Leah's kindness toward him during his training in the Union's army, couldn't bear to see her suffering. He approached her and offered her a drink from his bottle. Kanoot noticed and erupted in anger.

"Soldier! What are you doing?" he bellowed.

"She is his highness' daughter. We cannot let her die," the soldier replied.

Kanoot walked towards him, his voice now hushed. "His highness' daughter?" he questioned.

The soldier remained silent, and Kanoot continued in the same tone. "Who is in charge here, soldier?" he inquired, not allowing his subordinate to respond. With swift brutality, Kanoot drew his dagger and stabbed the soldier in the chest. The poor man collapsed to the ground, gasping for breath.

Nisay could no longer contain himself and clenched his fists, letting out a piercing scream that reverberated through the air. "Coward!"

Kanoot strolled leisurely towards the wagon. "Did you call me a coward?" he asked rhetorically. "I just defeated your best fighter."

Expecting to ignite a spark of ego within Nisay, Kanoot anticipated that he would claim superiority over Leah. However, Nisay was adept at the game of words.

"No, you didn't," he retorted. "She outmatched you and instead of fighting with honor, you resorted to dirty tactics. What kind of fight was that?"

"A fight that proved I can vanquish my enemy!" Kanoot declared.

"Why don't you prove that you're no coward?" Nisay challenged him.

Kanoot turned to his soldiers, laughing. "He's challenging me. What do you think I should do?" he inquired, amused. The soldiers chuckled, but none of them offered a response.

"I accept his challenge," Kanoot declared with a grin. He whispered something to one of his soldiers, who eagerly carried out his order.

Opening the wagon, Kanoot beckoned Nisay to step out. Nisay glanced at Nora, who held his hand tightly and spoke in a furious tone, "Bring down this coward."

Nisay offered her a reassuring smile and was ready to leap off the cage, but Aznek interjected firmly, "I don't doubt your skill. However, Leah was one of the best, and Kanoot had a sword to her throat."

Nisay nodded with determination and approached Kanoot, confident that he would slay him in front of his soldiers.

Kanoot addressed his soldiers, "If this arrogant man wins, set him and his friends free and let them go." He tossed a sword to the ground and beckoned Nisay to retrieve it.

"Are you not going to untie me?" Nisay asked.

Kanoot smiled. "You didn't ask for that. Remember, all you asked for was a sword. Here it is!"

Nora grasped the bars and screamed, "Untie him and fight like a real man!"

Kanoot locked eyes with Nisay and taunted, "Can you picture the look on her face when I present her with your head?"

Without waiting for Nisay's response, Kanoot lunged towards him, brandishing his sword and leaving no time for the Turban to retrieve his own weapon.

As Nisay evaded the strike by leaning back, Kanoot attempted to pierce him with his dagger, but to no avail. Nisay swiftly fell to the ground, rolled, and regained his footing.

Kanoot halted, wearing a smirk. "Not too bad. But I'm wondering how far you can go."

Suddenly, a voice bellowed from behind, calling out Kanoot's name. It was none other than Ali, the rebels' leader and Ceres' most wanted man.

"Ali, I was expecting you. In fact, I left signs for you to track," Kanoot declared with a laugh, before summoning his men.

Fifteen soldiers emerged from the surrounding trees, joining the initial fifteen soldiers already present.

Ali glanced from left to right, counting the overwhelming number of soldiers, and realized he was trapped. He and Nisay, trapped and outnumbered, could not single-handedly defeat all of Kanoot's forces.

He froze, his mind racing for a way to escape with his friends, but none seemed feasible.

"I promised his highness that I would arrest you and your friends," Kanoot proclaimed triumphantly. He turned his gaze towards the wagon, a sinister grin spreading across his face. "And you've made it so much easier."

Ali remained silent, and Kanoot continued, "Arsalan is still missing, right? You must be wondering. King Kemal is preparing a great surprise for him."

Ali's face remained neutral. He took a step towards Kanoot.

"Drop your weapon!" Kanoot screamed.

Ali didn't comply because he knew the consequences. The queen he believed in, the last legitimate heir, and all his friends would be executed.

Nisay contemplated making a move, but the archers would annihilate him before he even reached the first soldier.

Ali looked at the queen, who smiled and nodded sadly. *You fought well, but we have lost*, her face seemed to say.

Nora and the young couple wore the same defeated expression. Roulan and Leah remained unconscious.

Ali reluctantly dropped his weapons, and the soldiers couldn't believe their eyes. Despite Kanoot's command to arrest Ali, they hesitantly approached him.

The ordeal was far from over. A masked figure stealthily made his way towards the carriage, catching Nora's attention. Before she could react, the mysterious figure swiftly placed a finger over his lips, signalling for silence, and deftly unlocked the cage.

Kanoot and his soldiers remained oblivious to the intruder's presence until a barrage of arrows suddenly rained down upon them, originating from another one of the masked fighters. The chaos and confusion provided the perfect opportunity for Ali to seize his chance. Taking advantage of the distraction, he retrieved his sword and swiftly cut Nisay free from his bindings.

With remarkable agility and speed, the fighter systematically dispatched five soldiers within a matter of moments. Though Ali and Nisay were uncertain of their rescuer's identity, they joined the fray, engaging in the battle alongside Nora, Ashil, and Zaya.

Together, the group fought valiantly, their determination and coordination evident as they skillfully defended themselves against their adversaries.

Kanoot observed as his soldiers dwindled in numbers, realizing he had no choice but to mount his horse and flee.

Zaya, fueled by caution and curiosity, pressed her blade against the masked fighter's neck, demanding an answer. "Who the hell are you?" she said, her voice filled with both determination and suspicion.

Nora, recognizing the need for prudence, intervened by placing her hand on Zaya's sword, gently restraining her. With a steady gaze, she said, "We will soon find out."

Ignoring the identity of their savior, Ali rushed toward his wife, untying her and gently trying to rouse her from unconsciousness.

She opened her eyes and gave him a smile.

Nisay brought a bottle of water and handed it to Ali, who helped his wife take a drink. When she finished, she smiled and said, "You always succeed where we fail."

Ali held her hand. "This time, it wasn't me. It was this great fighter."

The masked fighter stood at a distance, seemingly hesitant to approach.

"Whoever you are, we owe you our lives," Ali addressed the mysterious savior.

Leah coughed and chided, "Shame on you, Ali. You don't recognize this fighter?"

All eyes turned towards the masked man, wondering about his identity. He was slimmer and shorter than Arsalan.

"You may come closer," Leah beckoned.

The masked fighter removed the mask, and a wave of joy washed over everyone's faces.

Nora was momentarily speechless before uttering the only word that escaped her lips, "Sofia!"

She rushed towards Leah and embraced her. Ali went to check on the two queens and the rest of their companions.

Roulan was lying motionless inside the wagon. Ali inquired of Aznek, "What happened to her? And where is Sai?"

The queen bowed her head, and so did Nora.

"Your Grace, what has happened?" Ali asked, concerned.

The queen met his gaze and replied, "I'm sorry, Ali. Kanoot killed Sai."

Ali's smile vanished. He closed his eyes, struggling to hold back his tears, but they flowed nonetheless.

"For what it's worth, he sacrificed himself to protect his queen," Nora offered.

Ali remained silent, grappling with his grief. Aznek then turned to him and said, "Roulan and her baby are in critical condition. We need a skilled healer, and unfortunately, we don't have one in Solum."

Ali's determination ignited, and he exclaimed, "She cannot die, nor can her child!"

Zaya coughed to capture their attention.

Queen Aznek recognized the urgency in Zaya's demeanor and encouraged her, saying, "Zaya, you are one of us. Speak!"

"My mother is a renowned healer. I believe she can help," Zaya suggested.

Ali turned to Aznek and proposed taking Roulan to Zaya's mother, but the queen did not agree. Instead, she turned to Nisay.

"I need Ali for something else. Nisay, you will go with Ashil and Zaya," Queen Aznek commanded.

***

Murat lay on the cold floor of his cell, counting down the remaining hours of his life. His heart ached for his homeland, Toprak, and his beloved niece. However, he was helpless and could only pray for her well-being and the survival of his Kingdom.

The guard opened the door to Murat's cell, and Salim, the same commander who had escorted him to the council, appeared before him.

Salim commanded the guard, "Leave us!"

Without questioning, the guard obeyed and left the area. Murat spoke up, "Commander Salim, you seem to be a decent man. May I ask you a favor?"

Salim stared at him and replied firmly, "There's no time for favors. Do you have any trusted friends?"

Murat was taken aback by the question. "What?"

"You heard me," Salim reiterated. "Do you have any trusted friends?"

"All my potential friends are arrested—the rebels and the two queens," Murat replied with a tone filled with desperation.

"So, you have no friends," Salim stated. "Listen to me carefully, I have around thirty men under my command. And today won't be your last."

"You mean...you're going to rescue me?" Murat asked, hope flickering in his eyes.

Salim didn't respond but instead chained Murat's hands and led him to the execution yard.

Hundreds of people had gathered, eagerly awaiting the sight of a traitor's head being severed. A tall soldier stood on the wooden platform with a long sword hanging at his waist. There was to be a beheading.

Izmir had no inkling that her uncle had a chance at survival. She believed that his time had come, but she refused to shed a tear. She didn't want her uncle's resolve to weaken.

Her uncle was relieved to see her there, for he had faith in her. He was confident that she would succeed where her mother and he himself had failed.

Izmir, with her curly red hair that cascaded just below her shoulders, was of average height. Her fair skin bore a few freckles on her nose, and her eyes shimmered like sea foam.

She gazed at her uncle, offering him a smile as if to say. She mouthed silently, "I'm proud of you."

King Kemal stood and raised his hand to capture the audience's attention.

"People of Toprak," he began, his voice resounding. "Justice is above all, even the king himself. Lord Murat has stood in multiple trials, and he has been found guilty." Yesterday, he confessed to his crimes of treason, and Judge Ayden sentenced him to death." He paused, "May the Creator forgive him!"

The executioner fetched his imposing sword, but King Kemal withheld the order. Instead, he added, his voice dripping with malice, "Lord Murat is not the only traitor here. Commander Salim is as well."

Salim locked eyes with one of his men who wore a smirk, and King Kemal proclaimed, "You thought you could escape the consequences of your treason."

Salim spat, and the king screamed, "Archers!"

Ten arrows were unleashed towards Salim, who swiftly knelt and rolled, skillfully evading every single one. As he rose to his feet, two arrows came hurtling towards his chest. However, Murat rushed forward and positioned himself in front of Salim.

"Lord Murat!" exclaimed Salim in shock.

Remaining steadfast, Murat replied, "Run and come later to save my niece."

Three more arrows struck Murat's chest, and he collapsed to the ground.

Salim leaped off the wooden platform only to be confronted by five soldiers. He swiftly retrieved two daggers and hurled them at his assailants before unsheathing his sword, dispatching the remaining three soldiers in a blur of swift strikes. He continued his desperate escape through the crowd, with the commoners too afraid to impede his path. Skillfully navigating, he managed to infiltrate the royal residence unscathed.

Over thirty soldiers pursued Salim, his every move fueled by determination to survive. He raced through the castle without a clear plan, until an idea struck him—one that carried considerable risk. He decided to hide in the last place the soldiers would search: the king's own quarters. Climbing the stairs, he made his way towards the king's room, with only a short distance left to cover. However, his progress was halted abruptly as an arrow pierced his back.

Turning around, Salim spotted five soldiers approaching him.

The pain from the arrow seared through his body, and fatigue weighed heavily upon him. Nevertheless, he drew his sword and spoke through gritted teeth, "I'm going to kill you!"

The soldiers charged towards him, but their ranks were swiftly reduced when two of them fell. Arrows pierced them from behind. The remaining soldiers turned to see the source of the arrows but were unable to identify the shooter before they expertly shot three more arrows, each finding its mark.

Salim felt a surge of delight and collapsed to the ground. Hot pain thrummed across his back.

The savior couldn't carry Salim due to his weight, but instead, pulled him into a nearby room—not the king's room, but a neighbouring one.

Realizing the urgency of the situation, the rescuer wasted no time and poured a bucket of water on Salim's face, jolting him awake. Salim initially panicked but quickly regained his composure upon seeing the unexpected savior who had saved his life. It was none other than Lady Izmir, the gentlest girl in Toprak.

Attempting to speak, Salim was interrupted by Izmir.

"There's no time for that. Stand up and follow me. I'm sorry, you're heavy, and I can't carry you."

Salim exerted his strength and followed Izmir. They entered her bedroom, where she swiftly moved a table and revealed a hidden hatch beneath the carpet. Without hesitation, Izmir opened it and motioned for Salim to descend the stairs that led to a cavern. He complied, and Izmir followed, carrying a bag in her hand.

The commander was filled with curiosity, eager for Izmir to explain herself. However, time was of the essence, leaving no room for lengthy explanations. Instead, Izmir instructed Salim to lie on his belly. She tore his shirt, leaving only a small piece of fabric covering the area where the arrow had pierced his flesh. Placing a stick in his mouth, she warned him, "It's going to hurt."

After counting to three, Izmir swiftly tugged the arrow from his back. Despite the pain, Salim remained silent, grateful for her assistance. Izmir took out a glowing blade and applied it to the wound, causing Salim to let out a scream.

"It's over, commander. Drink this," Izmir said, offering him a potion.

Attempting to sit up, Salim was gently restrained by Izmir. "You need to rest for a few hours before you walk away from this doomed kingdom."

Confused, Salim inquired, "Is this a tunnel?"

"Yes, my uncle told me about it. It will lead you to the woods, and from there, you'll be on your own," Izmir explained.

Standing up, Izmir added, "I wish I could take better care of you until you've regained your strength. However, I must leave before the soldiers discover the secret hatch in my residence."

"Why did you help me?" Salim asked sincerely.

"Because you tried to help my uncle."

"I'm sorry I couldn't succeed," Salim expressed his remorse.

Izmir offered him a warm smile and said, "You tried. Our intentions are more important than our deeds."

Izmir took the first step on the stairs, preparing to depart. Before she left, Salim summoned the courage to share a confession with her.

"Lady Izmir, I have something to confess to you."

Izmir turned, her smile unwavering, and replied, "I already know who you are, Lord Arsalan. Please convey my greetings to Ali and our friends."

With those parting words, Izmir continued her journey, leaving Arsalan to contemplate the unexpected twist of fate and the enduring bond that had formed.

CHAPTER 8

A Speaker had arrived at the Empire to investigate a peculiar sickness afflicting Ceres—a pus-filled bump forming under his back. Ceres laid on his belly, awaiting the verdict of the healers. After thoroughly examining his back for a while, the Speaker arrived at the same diagnosis as the Healer in the Union: a skin ailment known as the Boiling Skin.

Confused, Ceres sought further clarification and requested more details from the Speaker. The Speaker began, "Your highness, could you please sit down?" Ceres complied, hastily putting on his shirt, sensing the gravity of the situation.

"There's both bad news and good news," the Speaker began cautiously.

"What's the bad news?" Ceres inquired.

"Your highness, I'm afraid I don't know of any healers who can cure these boils," the Speaker admitted.

"What about the good news?" Ceres pressed, urging the Speaker to continue.

"The records show that this sickness has been cured in many individuals in the past," the Speaker revealed. "Though the treatment is not widely known."

"So there is a cure!" Ceres said, nodding, "You may leave now."

With the Speaker dismissed, Ceres retired to his office and proceeded to write four letters, sealing each one. He called upon his trusted messengers and entrusted them with the task of delivering these letters to his four allied kings.

Aware that his remaining days might be numbered, Ceres's servant entered the room, bowing respectfully. "Your highness, Lord Kanoot has arrived and wishes to speak with you."

Ceres nodded, allowing Kanoot to enter. Kanoot knelt before him, visibly proud as he proclaimed, "I bring you good news, my lord! I have slain the mastermind!"

Ceres's expression remained unchanged. "And what about the others?"

"I have captured them all, including the two queens. However, a masked fighter appeared like a phantom and eliminated my soldiers," Kanoot explained.

"So, you failed to keep them in custody?" Ceres stated with disappointment. He walked closer to Kanoot and continued, "I had taken advantage of the truce and devised an elaborate plan to quell the rebellion. But your actions allowed them to escape."

"My apologies, Your Grace. But the good news is that I inflicted a severe blow by killing one of their best assets, Sai."

Ceres maintained his stern demeanor and responded, "No! That is not good news. Instead, you have enraged the most dangerous man! May the Gods protect us from his wrath."

Kanoot attempted to interject, but Ceres raised his hand and declared, "Leave immediately and do not show your face until I summon you."

Leaving his office behind, Ceres proceeded to summon the council members and generals to join him. Shortly thereafter, they gathered to address the pressing matters at hand.

His face bore a pallid complexion, and his brows furrowed with worry. The newly appointed prime advisor stood and asked, "Your highness, may I speak openly?"

Ceres nodded, granting permission, then the prime advisor turned his gaze towards the generals before focusing on Ceres himself. "Your highness, while Lord Kanoot has failed in his mission, we cannot solely place blame on his shoulders."

Ceres remained silent, allowing the prime advisor to continue.

"Lord Kanoot was dealing with Ali, and we are all aware of the formidable capabilities possessed by that man," the prime advisor elaborated.

The financial chief, Roman, interjected, "Are we here to praise our enemy?"

The prime advisor turned to Roman, offering a smile. "I merely wanted to suggest that we should not judge Lord Kanoot based on one mistake. On the contrary, he successfully apprehended two queens and came close to eliminating the rebellion, were it not for an unknown soldier's intervention."

The military chief nodded in agreement and added, "Lord Ben is correct. Kanoot is a skilled and resourceful soldier. I propose that we maintain him in his current assignment, while perhaps administering a mild reprimand."

Ceres contemplated the suggestion, a sense of guilt washing over him. "After what I have already done to him, I suppose it could be considered more than just a punishment."

***

Kanoot stood alone, wielding a whip in his right hand, striking his own back with every lash. The pain was excruciating, but he welcomed it, wishing for it to be even more agonizing. Tears streamed down his cheeks as he continued to chastise himself, repeating, "I failed my emperor and the Gods."

He did not cease until he finally collapsed, succumbing to the pain and exhaustion. The following morning, he awoke in severe agony, as though his back had been stripped raw. Yet, Kanoot paid little heed to the pain. All he desired was forgiveness from Ceres.

Kanoot harbored a deep love for Ceres, viewing him as a father figure. When the rebels took his brother, Vlad, and ended his life, Kanoot swore an oath to avenge him. After Vlad's burial, Kanoot approached Ceres and Ramessess, pleading to be accepted into the military.

But both Ceres and Ramessess had refused, recognizing Kanoot's passion for science and his lack of proficiency with swords. Reluctantly, Kanoot left the empire behind. A year later, he reemerged in the Arena as an entirely transformed individual—his head shaved, his body chiseled, and his spirit hardened. It was there that he emerged victorious in the tournament.

At that time, Ceres was still reeling from the loss of Helena and Ramessess. Yet, Kanoot's appearance felt like a divine gift. Not only was he a formidable warrior and a military strategist like his late brother, Vlad, but he possessed a keen intellect akin to that of a seasoned politician.

Ceres recognized Kanoot's potential but exercised patience, initially assigning him smaller responsibilities such as training soldiers or representing the council in allied kingdoms.

While Kanoot found himself lost in his remorseful thoughts, the prime advisor entered unannounced. "Pull yourself together!" Ben grimaced.

Kanoot whimpered, "I do not deserve forgiveness, I have failed my emperor."

Ben motioned to Kanoot's attendants. "Take him to the healer," he ordered, before turning back to Kanoot and stating firmly, "Join His Highness and myself in the council, once you are done."

CHAPTER 9

Despite his overwhelming fatigue, Arsalan emerged triumphantly from the tunnel, his body aching and sore. Undeterred by his exhaustion, he knew he had no alternative but to forge ahead and reach the sole secure haven on Earth—Solum. The gravity of his mission weighed heavily on him, knowing that King Kemal would not make it easy after his audacious move.

Following the white arrows marked on the walls, Arsalan eventually reached a dead-end. He noticed a circle of light ahead, indicating a hatch, but it seemed out of reach. Arsalan hesitated, considering routes to reach it. The pressure mounted as the wooden torch in his hand dwindled, its flame gradually dying. Moreover, his water supply was running low.

"This is a secret passage. There must be a way out," he muttered to himself, determined to find a solution.

He approached the wall, using the dying flame of his torch to illuminate it, searching for any clue. Despite his efforts, there were no markings or signs to guide him. Frustration consumed him, and in a fit of anger, he threw the torch to the ground, releasing a resounding scream that filled the space.

To his surprise, as the torch hit the ground, the fire caught onto something and refused to be extinguished. Intrigued, Arsalan disregarded the pain and quickly reached out to the flame. It revealed a small rope, just a few inches buried in the ground.

"There's only one thing to do with this," Arsalan proclaimed loudly, mustering all his strength to pull the cord. The rope smoothly followed his tug, emerging from the ground and the wall.

A surge of joy coursed through Arsalan as he discovered that the rope led to the hatch. Without hesitation, he began to climb. Fearful the hatch might be locked, he pushed against it with his hand, and it effortlessly opened.

Emerging from the ground, Arsalan rejoiced in the sight of the sun and the lush greenery of the woods. His hunger gnawed at him, and his immediate plan was to hunt for anything that moved. However, fate took an unexpected turn. Instead of becoming the hunter, he found himself being hunted by five Topraki soldiers who had cornered him in the woods, their laughter echoing in the air.

"Coward and traitor," one of the soldiers sneered. "You thought you could act without facing the consequences"

Arsalan, unarmed, faced his impending execution without fear. His sole concern was to eliminate Toprakies.

"Listen!" he pleaded, "my fight isn't against you. I don't want to kill my own people!"

"Drop your weapon," one of the soldiers ordered, "His Grace and the emperor want you alive, rather than dead."

"So, your loyalty lies with a treacherous king and a dictatorial emperor," Arsalan retorted.

"Enough!" the soldier shouted. "Soldiers, capture this traitor alive!"

As two soldiers advanced toward him, one brandishing his sword, aimed directly at Arsalan's chest. The rebel reacted swiftly, evading the attack by dropping to his knees. With seamless grace, he seized the hand of the soldier holding the sword and redirected it towards the other soldier, piercing his belly. Retrieving the blade, he then twisted the first soldier's arm with a brutal snap, instantly breaking his neck.

The leader of the soldiers, undeterred by the fate of his comrades, ordered the remaining two men to kill Arsalan. However, before they could even lay a hand on him, Arsalan dispatched them, leaving them lifeless on the ground.

"It seems I'll be the one escorting you to His Grace," the soldiers' leader declared, rolling an axe in his hand.

Arsalan dropped the sword he had taken from one of the fallen soldiers and retorted, "I don't think you're handling that axe properly. I can hear it, and it's ashamed to be wielded by a traitor like you."

The soldier lunged toward Arsalan, but Arsalan quickly grabbed his wrist, applying pressure until the soldier relinquished his grip on the axe. Arsalan then delivered a fierce headbutt to the soldier's nose, followed by two powerful punches to his belly. Finally, he kicked the soldier to the ground.

Retrieving the axe from where it had fallen, Arsalan said, "I've missed you terribly."

The soldier, now on the ground, quickly rose with a dagger in his hand. But before he could hurl it, Arsalan hurled the axe instead, hitting his opponent smack in the middle of the forehead. The man fell to the ground with an audible thud, and when Arsalan peered over him, a single line of blood was trickling down his face,

***

Leah was granted entry by the guard into Queen Aznek's residence. Despite being turned down twice before, Leah persevered and sought an audience for the third time.

"Your Grace, thank you for receiving me," Leah said.

Aznek offered a warm smile. "You are both an ally and a friend."

Leah reciprocated the smile, her expression hinting at an underlying purpose. "But," she anticipated.

"Sorry, Leah, I am a queen. I have certain standards," Aznek responded, maintaining her regal composure. "I cannot grant you your wish."

"Sofia made a mistake!" Leah countered.

"She defied my orders and insulted me in front of my council," Aznek replied, her tone firm.

"If we had followed her advice and attacked the empire back then, Sai might still be alive!"

Aznek couldn't conceal her shock, and Leah realized the impact of her words. She sighed. "Your Grace, please understand, I do not mean to disrespect you. But Sofia, like all of us, made a mistake."

"Why do you so desperately want me to forgive her?"

"When my father discovered my relationship with Ali, he locked me in a room. I was abandoned by everyone, including my two sisters, Helena and Emily. Sofia was the only one who stood by my side, risking her own safety to fight for both me and Ali. And today, we would all be dead if she hadn't shown up and saved us."

Aznek remained quiet, weighing Leah's words.

"She made a grave error, and you have every right to banish her from your land. But I can assure you, she understands the magnitude of her mistake, and she deeply regrets it," Leah concluded, hoping to sway the queen's decision.

Aznek stood up and approached Leah, her gaze unwavering.

"The council will convene shortly. Let us proceed for now, and we can have a private conversation later," Aznek proposed.

Leah smiled and replied, "After you, Your Grace."

They made their way to the council chamber, silently acknowledging that further discussion could wait. As they entered, all the council members rose to their feet, paying respect to the queen. Aznek headed straight to her chair.

"My lords and ladies, we find ourselves in challenging times. Just a week ago, we lost a man who was anything but ordinary. Sai was a brilliant mind, possessing the courage of a gladiator. He was a husband, and soon-to-be father. When a man of his caliber passes, those who loved him are obligated to fulfill two duties." Queen Aznek paused, her gaze shifting to Ali, who returned her gaze with a comforting smile. The queen resumed her address.

"We owe Sai a proper burial, and we owe him the continuation of his work."

Prime Advisor Sam raised a hand, "To our hero, Sai."

The queen nodded approvingly at Sam, offering him a smile before taking her seat. She gestured for everyone to do the same.

"This is Sam, my prime advisor," the queen introduced, and Leah greeted him with a smile. "Thanks to him, the kingdom has remained steadfast."

Ali glanced at Sam and added, "Thank you for safeguarding our son, Noah."

Sam humbly responded, "He was my guest, and I merely fulfilled what Her Grace expected from me."

The queen then turned her attention to Sam and asked, "Why don't you brief us on what occurred during our absence, Chief Sam?"

The prime advisor stood and began to speak, addressing the gathering. "I anticipated a multitude of challenges in your absence, but thankfully, nothing significant occurred—except for this," Sam said, raising a letter in his hand. Without hesitation, he opened it and read its contents aloud.

"You have been chosen to serve the greatest power. Come to the mouth of Solum, and you shall receive suitable rewards."

Nora raised her eyebrows. "Did you go?"

Ali interrupted, his voice filled with conviction, "If he had, he would either be dead or seated on Solum's throne."

Sam smiled and continued, "I received two more letters bearing the same message."

The military chief of Solum spoke up, "We have a traitor who had access to the royal residence."

"Unfortunately, there are always weak hearts who sell their souls for gold," the queen lamented before instructing the guards to admit a guest.

A short man with shoulder-length hair and a goatee entered, bowing respectfully. The queen introduced him to the assembly. "Ladies and lords, this is Stephen, Sai's assistant and his most brilliant student."

Sam stood and added, "He is the one who will carry on Sai's legacy."

Stephen spoke with humility, "I can never fill Sai's shoes, but I promise to give my best."

Ali offered an encouraging smile, and the queen turned to Stephen, commanding him to explain the strategy for Solum's mouth.

The plan Stephen presented left everyone astounded, except for Ali, who maintained a composed demeanor. Aznek noticed this. She knew he possessed the ability to read between the lines and perceive what others could not.

"Lord Ali, is there something you wish to share with the group?" the queen inquired.

"Your Grace, someone exposed your location to our enemy. They attempted to exploit the person with the most power after you, aiming to corrupt our kingdom," Ali paused, his gaze shifting toward Sam, "Fortunately, he remained loyal to you and to the kingdom."

Sam smiled at Ali's words and remarked, "I wholeheartedly agree with Lord Ali. Everything we had planned prior to Sai's tragic death needs to be re-evaluated."

"Thank you, Lord Sam!" Ali expressed his gratitude before turning to the queen. "Your Grace, perhaps it would be wise to take some time to reflect and discuss these matters further."

Aznek understood the implication behind Ali's words. There might be a traitor among them, and he didn't want to voice his suspicion openly in front of everyone.

The queen was about to dismiss her council when a new guard entered, announcing another guest. Arsalan entered the room, and his presence stirred emotions among his friends.

Ali approached him and embraced him tightly, while Nisay joined in the heartfelt reunion.

Nora, with a smile adorning her face, remained in her place. The queen surprised everyone by walking towards Arsalan. He lowered his head respectfully and kissed her right hand.

"It's truly wonderful to see you, Lord Arsalan," the queen greeted him warmly.

Tears filled Arsalan's eyes as he looked at Ali and said, "I'm sorry for Sai. I heard about what happened."

Ali remained silent, and Arsalan inquired about Roulan's well-being.

The queen placed a gentle hand on Arsalan's shoulder and reassured him, "She will be fine, and so will her baby."

Arsalan nodded gratefully, and the queen advised him to rest. With a smile, Arsalan added, "But not before I share this with you. King Kemal is on the move."

The queen dismissed everyone, except Leah, who remained seated, still hoping that the queen would reconsider Sofia's fate. A few minutes later, Sofia arrived, bowing her head and greeting both Aznek and Leah.

Aznek's expression lacked warmth as she addressed Sofia with a firm tone, "Lady Sofia, I opened the gates of my castle for you and granted you a seat in my council. And what did you do in return? You disobeyed my orders, left the kingdom without my consent, and called me selfish in front of my generals and allies. Just one of these offenses could have cost you your life. But out of our friendship, I refrained from pursuing you. And now, you dare to show up in my castle."

Aznek paused for a few moments, then asked sternly, "Why?"

Sofia's gaze shifted towards Leah, who offered her a supportive smile and nodded. Sofia took a deep breath before responding to the queen.

"Your Grace, you honored me by accepting me into your council and granting me a seat among your trusted advisors. From the depths of my heart, I apologize for leaving your kingdom without permission and for the words I spoke in anger, calling you selfish. I didn't mean them. My emotions overwhelmed me. In my eyes, you are one of the greatest rulers in our history."

The queen, sensing what Sofia might say, chose to remain silent, refraining from uttering a single word.

"Lady Leah taught me many things, but the most valuable lesson I learned from her was to be sincere with the people I care about," Sofia said. She then turned to the queen and continued, "Your Grace, you were one of those people. And, in my opinion, accepting a truce from Ceres wasn't a wise decision."

Leah, alarmed by Sofia's boldness, exclaimed, "Sofia, is this how you ask for forgiveness?"

"Lady Leah, let her speak," the queen interjected, signalling her desire to hear Sofia's perspective. She then posed a question, "What if I were to make another decision that you do not agree with?"

"Your Grace, I have faith in you, just as I have faith in Ali and Leah. If you allow me back into your council, I will always speak my mind. However, this time, I promise not to disrespect you or abandon my duty," Sofia earnestly expressed her intentions.

The queen turned her gaze to Leah and offered a warm smile. "Lady Sofia, I appreciate your honesty. I am willing to give you a second chance to join my council."

Before Sofia could express her gratitude, Aznek couldn't contain her curiosity any longer. "And for God's sake, how did you acquire such formidable fighting skills?"

Sofia's eyes gleamed with determination as she replied, "Losing my friends and witnessing the strength of a queen like you inspired me to learn how to fight. Your Grace, I want you to consider me your sword."

The queen nodded, acknowledging Sofia's request, and dismissed the two guests. Sofia respectfully lowered her head and departed, while Leah lingered, waiting until the gate was closed before approaching the queen.

"I would never question your sense of justice, Your Grace, but why were you so severe with Sofia and not with Arsalan? After all, he also left the kingdom and vanished for over three years, yet you welcomed him back as if he were your prime advisor," Leah inquired.

The queen maintained her smile and responded, "My dear Leah, Arsalan did not leave the kingdom of his own accord. I sent him to Toprak to gather information for me."

Leah stood in stunned silence, her eyes wide with astonishment. The queen proceeded to reveal the truth. "Your father was not the only one working behind the scenes."

Leah, absorbed this revelation, realized that there was much more to the queen's strategies and alliances than what meets the eye. She nodded, her trust in the queen reaffirmed, and resolved to continue supporting her in any way she could.

CHAPTER 10

Roulan woke up in different clothes, and as she slowly opened her eyes, the surroundings became less blurry. The tent's roof displayed a combination of red and white, but Roulan didn't dwell on it. Her first instinct was to place her hand over her still-round belly, assuring herself that her baby was safe.

A male voice filled the room. "Your baby is doing fine,"

Wide-eyed, Roulan searched for the source of the voice. It was David, the man who had aided her in sneaking into Ramessess' residence and ultimately killing him. She offered him a smile and, before he could introduce the lady beside him, Roulan spoke in a soft voice. "You must be the healer who saved my baby."

David nodded with a smile. "And she's our chief, Lady Umali."

Attempting to sit up, Roulan was met with a gentle grasp of her hand by Umali, who hurried to her side. Roulan looked into Umali's eyes and said, "Forgive me, my lady. I wanted to greet you properly, not just for saving my baby's life, but also for standing with us."

Umali tenderly brushed her hand over Roulan's face and replied, "First of all, I'm deeply sorry for your loss. Though I never had the chance to meet Sai, his reputation extends far and wide, reaching even our enemies."

The last thing Roulan wanted to discuss was her loss, so she expressed her gratitude and swiftly changed the topic. She inquired about her due date.

"So soon? Why the hurry? Are you already bored of us?" Umali teased. Roulan gently clasped Umali's hand and replied, "No, please don't say that. I could never be more grateful."

"I know," Umali acknowledged, and Roulan couldn't hold back her tears. The chief lady glanced at David and commanded, "Leave us!"

Roulan sobbed, "I just want my unborn child to be safe! I don't think I can carry on without Sai."

Somehow, Umali understood her pain, for she had lost her husband when she was pregnant with her daughter. At that time, she had felt utterly alone and lacked the courage to raise two children on her own. Yet, she not only succeeded in doing so but also emerged as the leader of a tribe.

Umali was confident that when Roulan would hold her child in her arms for the first time, she would find a second reason to live. She will envision raising her baby, aspiring to shape him into someone as remarkable as his father, if not surpassing him.

They continued their conversation for a while, but eventually, Umali decided to let her patient rest. Roulan drifted back to sleep.

The next morning, Roulan's restlessness got the better of her. She rose from her slumber and dressed herself in robes thoughtfully provided by Umali.

As she stepped outside, Roulan noticed that the tents were made of various vibrant colors, and the ground appeared pristine, as if freshly swept. Walking alone, she exchanged smiles with everyone her eyes met. She continued her solitary stroll until a voice caught her attention from behind.

"Lady Roulan, Lady Roulan!"

She turned and found a young boy, no older than ten, standing with a sword in his hands.

"How can I help you, sir?" Roulan inquired.

"My name is not sir. It is Noah, my lady," the young boy replied.

Roulan chuckled and said, "Sir is a nickname given to brave knights like you. It's going to be Sir Noah."

Another boy of the same age joined them.

"What about boys who are good with tools?" a newcomer asked.

Roulan smiled and replied, "Mastermind."

"So I am Mastermind Adam!"

"No, you're just a coward!" Noah retorted, causing Adam to hold his ground and call Noah a murderer.

Roulan intervened, firmly holding their hands and stating, "If you continue this, I will never be your friend, and I will make sure that Ali will never accept you into his team."

The two boys apologized, and Roulan added, "Scientists need knights, and the other way around."

Noah and Adam both lowered their heads and left Roulan, who continued her walk, observing the village. One remarkable aspect of the Alinians was the diversity of its people. They hailed from seven different ethnicities, living together harmoniously.

Her smile grew when she spotted Umali approaching her.

"You look much better than yesterday," the Alinians' chief remarked.

Roulan returned the smile, "Thanks to you."

Umali inquired about Roulan's thoughts on the Alinians, and Roulan responded with excitement, "I'm delighted to see people from all over the world living as one nation. Especially the Grondies, after what Ceres did to them."

Umali invited Roulan to sit next to a tree and began sharing her wisdom. "I've lived for more than fifty years, witnessing a great deal. And if there's one thing I've learned, it's how weak humans can be. People like Ceres believe they can do whatever they want, but in reality, they always fail."

Roulan gazed at Umali with a smile, eager to hear more, and the Alinians' chief continued.

"Ceres and his father killed thousands of innocent people, corrupting six kingdoms and decimating Grond. But he couldn't keep his own daughters by his side. One left him for his number one enemy, and the other was killed."

Umali emphasized, "He thought he could erase the Grondies from the face of the earth, but here they are in my village, over two hundred men and women, training to restore their kingdom."

Since Sai's passing, Roulan's heart had yearned for solace, and now, as she listened to Umali's words, she felt a sense of healing.

"Why don't you join Queen Aznek and Ali?" Roulan suggested, "They could benefit from your wisdom and influence."

"I don't need to be by their side to help. I have my own agenda that serves two purposes."

Roulan smiled, answering in Umali's silence, "Taking down the empire and uniting the seven kingdoms under one ruler, yes?"

Umali winked and said, "You see? Despite the distance between us, we still think alike."

***

Kanoot donned his iron armor and sheathed his sword. He felt relieved when Ceres assigned him a new mission, though he had no idea what it entailed. Nevertheless, he placed his faith in his emperor and was prepared to give his life for him.

He entered the council room and saw all the generals seated, their eyes fixed on him as if they had been awaiting his arrival. Kanoot kept his head lowered as he walked toward Ceres, stopping a few feet away and kneeling before him.

"Lord Ben informed me that you have learned your lessons," Ceres said.

Kanoot remained kneeling and replied, "More than ever, Your Highness."

Ceres exchanged a knowing smile with his prime advisor and invited Kanoot to take his seat.

"The war has officially begun, and that is why I have gathered you all here: to devise a plan to eliminate Aznek and her rebels," Ceres announced.

The military chief was the first to react. "We have already taken Token from them. Why don't we assemble an army and breach the walls of Solum?"

Ceres responded impatiently, "The last time a general suggested that, I dismissed him from my council. So align yourself with our politics or make way for someone else with fresher ideas."

Without allowing the chief to apologize, Ceres turned his attention to the other generals, maintaining the same stern tone. "We control five kingdoms and possess immense wealth. All it takes is the elimination of one man, and everything will crumble."

Kanoot stood up, placing his hand over his chest. "Your Highness, grant me your blessing, and I shall bring you his head."

Ceres clenched his teeth. "He defeated you and your thirty soldiers. If you were to face him again, he would be the one to sever your head from your shoulders."

Prime advisor Ben, aware of Ceres' desire for an unconventional plan, spoke up, "Your Highness. Queen Aznek and Ali will not sit idly and wait for us. They will attempt to reclaim Token and take advantage of the turmoil in Turba."

Ceres turned to his general and remarked, "See, this is the kind of mindset I need," then he looked at Ben and said, "Please, continue."

"If I were Aznek, I would divert my attention to King Hosni. Taking control of Turba would facilitate their efforts to recapture Token," Ben suggested.

The military chief showed interest in the idea and tried to catch Ceres' attention. "Are you proposing that we send reinforcements to King Hosni?"

Ceres interrupted, acknowledging the potential of the plan. "This is where we require Kanoot's skills," he declared, then turned to Kanoot and said, "King Hosni faces problems with the surrounding tribes. They repeatedly ambush his merchants and soldiers."

Kanoot rose from his seat and knelt before Ceres. "Your Grace, what would you have me do?"

"You will lead a thousand skilled soldiers to King Hosni's aid and fight under his command. You will also deliver a letter to him."

Ceres turned to Ben and shared his idea, saying, "My plan is to join forces with Kanoot and eliminate the tribes that are rebelling against King Hosni."

Ben smiled and responded, "Not only will this stabilize the situation in Turba, but it will also send a strong message to anyone who dares to challenge us."

Kanoot eagerly embraced the new mission and left the council room, followed by the other generals.

Ceres made his way to his residence and found his daughter, Emily, waiting for him. His smile widened, and she approached him, giving him a warm hug.

"I consider myself fortunate," Ceres remarked.

Emily offered a shy smile and replied, "Father, one of the servants wishes to speak with you."

Ceres smiled and said, "I assume it's Mila?"

"How did you know?" asked Emily.

"A few days ago, while she was cleaning the room, she seemed uneasy... as if she wanted to say something but couldn't find the words."

"You're right, father," said Emily. Ceres asked his daughter to bring Mila in.

Mila entered the room, her head lowered. Before she knelt, Ceres addressed her directly, "What is it, Mila?"

"Your Highness, I didn't mean to eavesdrop, but during my cleaning, I overheard what the speakers said about your health," Mila confessed.

"Can you help me?" Ceres inquired, intrigued by her words.

"I cannot," Mila replied honestly, "but I know of a healer who might be able to."

Ceres glanced at his daughter and then back at Mila. "How is that possible? The speakers said that no one can cure me."

"My father used to say that when we're sick, it's better to seek someone who has experienced the same illness rather than relying solely on a healer," Mila explained. "This very healer I speak of had the power to cure my father from the same sickness that afflicts you, Your Highness."

"All right, Mila," Ceres responded, considering her words. "Bring her to my castle, and if she succeeds in curing me, I will make you one of the wealthiest individuals in this empire."

CHAPTER II

Another two miles remained before the rebels could reach Token. There was no army following them to protect them from the archers positioned on the city walls – they were alone, and the pressure weighed heavily on them.

Initially, Aznek had been hesitant about the plan proposed by Ali. Her instinct was to send her army, armed with a deadly weapon created by Sai, to annihilate the Usurper: Emil and his group. By doing so, her cousin and Nisay would assume the throne. However, Ali was a strategist who relished in surprising his enemies. He knew that both Emil and Ceres would anticipate such a move and likely prepare a trap for Aznek's army.

The queen came to realize that he was right. Instead of reclaiming Token, she would have risked losing her entire army and causing the downfall of her kingdom. Ali's plan seemed like a suicide mission, but he decided to bring along the best fighters who he trusted the most: Nisay, Nora, Leah, Arsalan, and Sofia.

"Arsalan! Have you briefed Sofia?" Ali asked.

Before Arsalan could respond, Sofia interjected, "Like it's something that needs teaching. Deception is my specialty. I've spent four years in the forbidden forest, hunting down the Unions."

Arsalan smiled. "Once our mission is complete, I would be grateful if you would be willing to impart your knowledge on me. Truly, I am in *awe* of your skills "

Sofia understood what Arsalan was doing—playfully embarrassing her with his humility—and it worked. They all smiled at her, and Nisay chimed in, "Never mess with the mind reader."

Sofia grinned and retorted, "Oh shut up, all of you."

"Everyone, let's maintain our focus on the mission," Ali urged. "One of our comrades is en route with a carriage and sizable barrels. Sofia will be at the reins, and the rest of us will conceal ourselves inside those barrels. Recall, our primary goal is to reach Emil."

The night passed, and the plan unfolded as Ali had envisioned. With Sofia as the carriage driver, everyone else concealed themselves inside the barrels, remaining hidden until nightfall. Sofia wore a black robe with a hat, stopping at the gate of Token and awaiting the guards' attention.

"What are you carrying?" one of the guards said.

"My lord, I am here to deliver the oil that Lord Emil requested," Sofia replied.

The guard stroked his beard and remarked, "I've never seen barrels of this size before."

"Neither have I, my lord. But I assure you, I personally inspected them. It's pure olive oil."

The guard exchanged glances with his comrades before stating, "We'll need to inspect them."

Sofia appeared surprised. "Is that really necessary?"

However, the guards ignored her and proceeded to open the barrels, only to find they did not have covers. Only wooden lids, and a tapered hole to let liquid out.

"How will you empty these bloody barrels?" one of the guards questioned.

Sofia offered a charming smile, stepped down from the carriage, and approached one of the barrels. Placing her hand on its side, she explained, "You see this bung hole? We just need to take off the cover..."

The guard interrupted her and attempted to remove the cover with his hand, but Sofia swiftly grabbed his wrist and squeezed it tightly until he released his grip.

"For a woman, you're very strong!" the guard remarked, nursing his sore wrist.

"If you remove the hatch, the oil will spill out, and we won't be able to close it again!"

The guard felt trapped, knowing he couldn't allow the guest to enter Token nor ask her to turn back. After a moment of silence, one of his companions came up with an idea. He retrieved his dagger and positioned its point on top of the barrel, using his palm to drive it into the wood. He created a square hole and turned to Sofia with a smile.

"That way, we can inspect the contents without losing a drop of oil."

He inserted the dagger into the barrel through the hole, then withdrew it, revealing the blade covered in yellow liquid. The guard brought it to his nose and caught a strong whiff of oil, causing him to pinch his nose shut.

"These barrels cost me ten silver coins each!" Sofia exclaimed in frustration.

Unfazed, the guard gestured to his comrade, instructing him to repeat the process for the other barrels. Upon finding nothing suspicious, he approached Sofia and said, "Then you've wasted fifty silver coins. And you know there's nothing you can do about it." Sofia remained silent, and he added, "Now get your stupid barrels inside and leave once you've made the delivery."

Sofia smiled. "As long as I receive my payment, I don't mind."

She then climbed back into her carriage and proceeded inward. She didn't halt until she reached the stable where Token stored their provisions.

A man with gray hair approached them and asked, "What do you folks have?"

"Just oil, my lord," replied Sofia.

The man with gray hair responded, "Before we bring it to our storage, we need to verify its authenticity. I don't mean to offend you my lady, but you know how people cheat these days to obtain gold."

Sofia maintained her smile and said, "No offense taken, my lord. You're simply doing your job."

He requested for her to wait while he summoned the expert, who arrived promptly—a thin man with gray hair and a beard.

"Call me when you're done," the bald man said before departing.

Sofia gazed at him for a moment and then declared, quietly, "She is a queen."

The oil expert's mouth formed a small smile. He replied, "And she's meant to be served."

Sofia breathed a sigh of relief. "Your queen is inside a barrel. Take us somewhere safe."

"Agron!" the oil expert called out to the bald man. "She's good to go. I'll personally take the oil to the storage."

The bald man, hearing this, didn't bother to come over and shouted, "Thank you, Shaaban!"

They proceeded to the storage area, where Shaaban examined one of the barrels and was taken aback by its contents.

"Even fish can't survive in oil," Shaaban remarked.

"Relax, Lord Shaaban. The barrels are only half full. The top half is well separated from the bottom one," Sofia explained.

"You mean they're at the bottom? How could they breathe?" Shaaban questioned.

A voice interrupted them, emanating from the depths of the barrel as if from a deep cave. "Are you going to let us out?"

Shaaban glanced at the side of one of the barrels and noticed the bung hole had been opened. Understanding the situation, he and Sofia carefully pulled the barrel to the side, disregarding the spilled oil on the ground. They opened the bottom hatch, allowing the rebels to exit.

Sofia intentionally saved Arsalan for last, purposefully approaching the barrel where he was confined. With unwavering determination, she let out a forceful scream, "You ridiculed me before, and now I demand that you retract your words."

Arsalan, taken aback, screamed back, "You must be joking!"

Sofia's gaze shifted to Nora, who was smiling. Meanwhile, Nisay, in the midst of stitching his own arms, interjected, "Sofia, the man is large and struggling to breathe!"

Nora turned to Nisay and retorted, "Mind your own business!"

Realizing that she had made her point, Sofia relented slightly.

At the moment, Arsalan squeaked. "Fine, you win."

However, Sofia, stubborn as ever, pressed for a more detailed response. "Tell me I am as skilled as any great knight."

After a moment of hesitation, Arsalan obliged. "You are as skilled – *more* skilled – than any great knight."

Sofia nodded to Shaaban, signalling him to open the barrel.

As Arsalan emerged, instead of launching into a tirade, he simply stretched his arms. Sofia offered a genuine smile and said, "Let's consider it settled."

Arsalan, still bristling with defiance, retorted, "Yeah, until I pay you back."

Ali addressed the group urgently, "Everyone, get on your feet quickly. We must reach Emil at the council." He then turned to Shaaban and inquired, "Shaaban, how much time do we have until they discover the missing barrels?"

Shaaban looked up. "We have until sunset, at most."

Arsalan rose to his feet, placing his right hand on his left shoulder and rotating his arm.

"Are you alright?" Ali asked, noticing Arsalan retrieving his axe from behind.

"Fine. I'll have enough time to stretch my arms by killing our enemies," Arsalan responded.

"No killing unless it's deserved!" Ali declared, surprising everyone with his statement. Then he continued. "There are two entrances, each guarded by at least ten soldiers. We'll split into two groups and meet in the council, Leah, Arsalan, and Nora will go from the south, while the rest of us will approach from the west."

Ali nodded in agreement and said, "Nisay, Sofia, let's go!"

Nora and the remaining rebels proceeded through the southern entrance, encountering a dozen soldiers, just as they had anticipated. Nora unsheathed her sword and approached them confidently.

"I am your queen. Drop your weapons," she commanded.

One of the soldiers spat and sneered, "You're just a whore who shamed her ancestors by bringing us a shepherd to... "

Before he could finish his sentence, a dagger pierced his throat, silencing him. Nora screamed at the others, "Drop your weapons or you will join him!"

However, the soldiers ignored her warning and charged toward her. Nora swiftly wielded her sword, dropping into a kneeling position as she killed the first attacker, then quickly pivoted to take down the second one.

Leah emerged from the left, brandishing her two daggers. With a precise motion, she sliced her first attacker's neck and used his momentum to push him into his comrade, impaling him on his own blade. Searching for another opponent, she realized there were none left. Arsalan and Nora had taken care of them all.

In the other group, the Token soldiers showed no loyalty to their king, Nisay, either and chose to attack. However, Nisay and Sofia fought like starved beasts, leaving none for Ali to engage. He stood back, observing as his two companions ruthlessly dispatched the traitorous soldiers.

With only five hundred feet remaining until they reached the council's door, Ali urged his comrades to press forward. But before they could advance, they spotted over twenty soldiers charging toward them, armed with spears.

"Drop your weapons, now!" One of the soldiers bellowed.

CHAPTER 12

Abla had to call her friend's name three times before she could get Izmir's attention. When Izmir finally turned to her with a smile on her face, she spoke softly. "You just interrupted the most beautiful thought."

Abla, who was the daughter of one of the wealthiest merchants in Toprak, grew increasingly concerned. She reached out and held Izmir's left hand gently, speaking softly. "Izmir, I know you've been through a lot. Your uncle was unjustly murdered. But now is not the time to be weak."

Izmir shifted her gaze to her friend. The smile vanished from her face as she spoke with determination. "I am not weak. Kemal and his traitors will pay for every life they've taken."

"That's my girl," Abla said, tapping twice on Izmir's knee.

Izmir returned to her initial state, smiling and fixating her attention on the piece of fabric stained with blood. "Did you see him?" she asked.

"Who?" Abla inquired.

"The way he stood in the execution yard, fighting to save my uncle despite the betrayal of his own soldiers. He didn't give up, fighting over a hundred soldiers."

"You mean the commander?"

"He's not just a commander. He's a rebel: one of Ali's friends," Izmir clarified.

Abla assumed that her friend might still be in shock and tried to bring her back to reality. "Izmir, now is not the right time to fall for a rebel."

Izmir sighed and embarked on a lengthy explanation. "What Kemal made me endure extinguished all sorts of emotions within me. Girls my age often dream of a brave and handsome man falling for them. I used to pity them for harboring such weak ambitions, as if tying their entire lives to a man was the ultimate goal."

Alba interrupted, "not all men are bad, and our purpose is not merely to tie our lives to them. Rather, it is to unite our souls with theirs, so that humanity can continue to exist."

Izmir snorted. "I have despised all the men in Toprak. Ceres was devouring our nation, and none of them stood up to defend their home. They either sat and cried or bent the knee, hoping to receive gold. But Arsalan proved me wrong. He stood alone in the execution yard and didn't give up. I wondered what kind of heart this man carries within his chest."

Izmir's words deeply moved Abla, "I suppose it's the same heart that Ali carries. Princess Leah left her home and title for him, after all."

"I exchanged a few words with Arsalan and realized that he is the kind of man who can free our world from Kemal and Ceres and help me reclaim my rightful throne."

"But women can't rule in Toprak," Abla replied

"Then It's time to change that."

Abla recognized the sheer audacity of her friend's ideas, but she also understood the unwavering determination within Izmir. Either she would achieve her goals or perish in the attempt.

Their discussion carried on for hours until Izmir's servant entered and informed her that Kemal wanted to see her in his council. Izmir asked the servant to leave and began to get dressed. Abla held her hand tightly and said, "Be careful," before giving her a warm hug.

Izmir had to climb eighteen stairs and walk nine hundred feet to reach the council. As she made her way there, the only thought that circled her mind was the memory of her mother's lifeless body. She recalled the day her stepfather had broken the news to her and then led her to her mother's corpse to bid her farewell.

At the tender age of fourteen, tears had streamed down Izmir's face uncontrollably. She had held her mother's cold hand and pressed it against her cheek. "Mother, how could you leave me alone in this world?"

Kemal placed his hands on her shoulders and leaned in to whisper, "Darling, you're not alone. You are my daughter." Izmir turned to him, and he gently wiped away her tears with the back of his index finger.

"Darling, give your mother a farewell kiss," he said softly. "Remember, the best thing we can do for the deceased is to give them a proper burial and offer a prayer."

Izmir nodded and followed her stepfather's request. As her lips were about to touch her mother's forehead, she noticed a small, bloody dot on her mother's neck. Hastily, she passed her thumb over the spot and realized it wasn't just a stain — it was a tiny hole.

She refrained from confronting her stepfather at that moment. Instead, she chose to confide in her uncle, seeking confirmation of her growing suspicions. It wasn't until she stumbled upon something she had never seen before—a two-inch needle in his desk's drawer, noticeably thicker than the regular ones—that her belief solidified.

She delved into days of research within the library, desperately seeking answers to how the needle might be used. Finally, she uncovered the truth: injection had always been a deadly method of assassinating high-profile individuals.

Fearing that she might be the next target, Izmir devised a plan to feign naivety. In front of everyone, she acted like an innocent young girl with dreams of marrying a charming prince. But behind that facade, she embodied the determination and strength of her father. The only thing she truly cared about was justice for her parents.

Finally, Izmir arrived at the council, and the guards opened the door for her. All the attendees, including the king, rose from their seats as she walked in gracefully: a match for her mother's elegance. The king invited Izmir and the others to take their seats, and turned his attention to his stepdaughter.

"Lady Izmir, do you recognize our guest?" he inquired, pointing to the seat on his left.

Izmir glanced at the man and shook her head. Before the king could respond, she chimed in, "He must be from Turang. I can tell by his narrow and small eyes."

King Kemal erupted in laughter, joined by his generals, while the guest grew visibly uncomfortable. To prevent the situation from escalating further, Kemal decided to intervene. "Lady Izmir, this is Choulou, the King of Turang."

"See, I told you he's from Turang," Izmir retorted, causing Kemal to struggle to contain his laughter. He nodded to the King of Turang, who approached Izmir.

"My lady, how would you like to become a queen?"

Izmir knew what was coming. It was her cunning nature that stopped her from panicking, and instead started to place. "I'm already a queen," she confidently replied. "My father is a king."

King Choulou, taken aback by Izmir's response, thought he could easily deceive her. "You will become the Queen of Turang."

"And if you die, will I inherit the rule?" the queen asked, stunning everyone present.

"No, Turang, like Toprak, does not allow women to rule," Choulou explained, smiling gently.

Izmir rubbed her chin with her finger, contemplating the situation. "Then why would I want to be a fake Queen of Turang? I'd rather stay here and live among people with regular eyes."

Choulou turned to Kemal, his face filled with anger. Kemal intervened, saying, "Darling, I am your father, but I won't be here forever for you. You need a husband."

Izmir looked at Choulou in confusion, then shifted her gaze to her stepfather, maintaining the same expression. "From his gray beard and hunched back, I'd say he's seventy. He will die before you."

"Did I come here to be insulted, Kemal?!" King Choulou shouted.

Kemal apologized to his guest and clapped his hands, summoning the guards. "Please escort King Choulou to his residence and ensure that he and his entourage are provided with whatever they desire." He then addressed his generals, "As for you, my lords, leave me alone with my stepdaughter."

Once the room was emptied, King Kemal unleashed his anger with a scream. "What the hell were you thinking?"

Izmir wished she could slit his throat, but she contained her rage and pretended to be frightened. "What?"

Kemal maintained his tone and responded, "This is the King of Turang, one of the wealthiest and most powerful men, coming here to propose to you. And you couldn't set aside your foolishness for once. Instead, you humiliated him."

"Father, do you want your one daughter to marry an old and ugly man?" Izmir retorted.

"Silence! I am not your father. If it weren't for your blood, I would have thrown you to the snakes!"

Izmir began to cry, and Kemal yelled, "The wedding will take place in two weeks. Now get out of my sight!"

Izmir turned and ran towards the exit, sobbing like a young child. As soon as she was out of sight, she wiped away her tears and muttered to herself, "You will pay for this."

The next morning, Abla was allowed into Izmir's room by the servants. She found Izmir sitting at the table, having her breakfast.

Abla hurried over to her and took hold of her hands. "I heard what happened in the council. I thought this news would crush you."

Izmir nodded and motioned for Abla to sit down. Abla pulled up a chair and fixed her gaze on Izmir. "Perhaps it's a good thing to accept this proposal and leave this doomed place! You will be safe as the king's wife."

"Safe, just like my mother was," Izmir sarcastically replied. "Let me ask you a question. How would you describe me to someone?" Abla looked at her friend with confusion, and Izmir pressed her, saying, "I'm waiting."

Abla coughed twice and began mumbling, "Hmm, I would say you're smart, determined, and strong." Izmir smiled, and before she could speak, Abla added, "And very beautiful."

"You're one hell of a friend," hummed Izmir. "You're not wrong, my dear. I'm like a stubborn baby. When I want something, I won't stop until I get it. And do you know what I want now?"

"Killing King Kemal!" guessed Abla.

But Izmir corrected her, "Reclaiming my throne."

Abla realized how insane her best friend's idea was, but she knew she had to support her. "How can I help you?"

"For now, I need to stop this marriage, and the only way to do that is by running away."

"Where?" questioned Abla, still confused.

"To the rightful queen and her loyal friends, Arsalan and Ali."

"You'll have to go at night. But the old secret hideout was sealed," replied Abla, concerned. "Where will you hide?"

"There's another one in the prime advisor's chamber," revealed Izmir. "Can you take me there? He's your uncle."

Abla felt uneasy about the situation, but she had no choice and agreed to help her friend.

The next day, Izmir donned a suit made of leather. She wore a belt around her waist with a sheathed sword hanging on the left side. Sneaking into the prime advisor's residence, located in the same building, Izmir managed to avoid the guards who were distracted by one of Abla's servants.

Izmir hid in a small provisions room, planning to wait until nightfall when Abla would take her to her uncle's room.

As planned, they arrived at the prime advisor's room, finding it empty.

Abla looked around, checking over her shoulder. "Where's the secret hideout?"

Instead of responding, Izmir took a bag filled with sand and poured it onto the fire, extinguishing the flames. She then repositioned the charred logs to unveil a concealed chain.

When Izmir pulled it, the back of the fireplace slid to the left. Izmir turned to Abla and said, "This is the secret passage. Once I'm gone, pull the chain to close the door and try to set a fire."

Abla was terrified and tried to dissuade her friend, but Izmir was resolute.

"You're the sister I never had. Farewell!" Izmir said, before stepping into the hidden passage. As she prepared to disappear, the cupboard's doors suddenly swung open, revealing four Topraki soldiers brandishing crossbows.

Izmir froze, contemplating her next move. The situation worsened when Kemal and his prime advisor entered the room.

"You think you're clever, but you're as foolish as your father!" Kemal taunted.

Izmir turned to her friend, anger in her eyes. "Did you betray me?"

"I would die before doing that!" Abla said.

"Next time you discuss a secret plan, make sure no one is listening," Kemal sneered, and another person entered the room.

"Damla!?" Izmir exclaimed in shock. "You are my most trusted servant!"

"Apologies, Your Grace, but my loyalty lies with King Kemal," Damla said, her voice tight.

Izmir scanned the room, searching for an escape route, but realizing there was none, she made a swift decision. She flung her dagger towards her unfaithful servant, and it struck Damla right in the forehead. Damla collapsed lifelessly to the ground.

Her step-father stood in shock as Izmir addressed him with defiance in her voice, "I did that to her for betraying me once. Just imagine what I'm capable of doing to the man who murdered my parents and stole my kingdom!" With those words, she let her other dagger slip from her hand, clattering onto the floor. She continued, undeterred, "If you would excuse me, I have a wedding to prepare for."

One of the soldiers moved forward, intending to arrest her, but Kemal raised his hand, halting their advance. "Leave her be. Allow her to retreat to her chamber, and seal this cursed passage."

Izmir turned to her loyal friend, Abla, and commanded, "Abla, come with me."

Abla, shaken by the recent events, nodded silently and stood by Izmir's side, ready to face whatever challenges awaited them.

CHAPTER 13

Emil shared the contents of Ceres' letter with his council members, which made everyone excited save for Emil himself. Despite having the support of the powerful Ceres, he knew that stabilizing Token would be an immense challenge. And it was on him.

It had been several weeks since Nora and her husband were expelled from the Kingdom, yet the people continued to revolt and demand the return of their queen and king. Seeking advice, Emil gathered his generals and asked for their input.

The military chief was the first to speak, suggesting, "Give the order, Your Grace, and I will unleash our soldiers upon them. They will come to their senses once they see the threat is real."

The financial chief addressed his partner, the military general, "I believe that's too extreme. Violence never solves anything."

The military chief glared angrily, but his partner quickly apologized, saying, "Forgive me, I didn't mean to mock your proposal. I simply think it's better to tighten our financial measures. When the commoners feel their gold and silver are at risk, they will do what they need in order to feed their families."

Emil stood up and sarcastically remarked, "So, one of you wants to kill the commoners while the other wants to starve them to death. Leaving the kingdom in your hands would spell its demise."

Both chiefs lowered their heads, and Emil sighed. "Here's the thing: if we want to rule over intelligent people like ours, the first thing we must avoid is making them angry. We can't tamper with their finances; they need to feel secure. Furthermore, we must never harm or insult Rajab's dynasty."

The agricultural chief spoke up. "You have lost me, Your Grace. What are the other solutions?"

Emil observed the curiosity on each face and continued his explanation. "Nora has to be eliminated, but the people need to believe that someone else did it, not us. Following that, we will organize a grand funeral for her and her husband." He then turned to the chief of law. "My lord, in the absence of a legitimate heir, how can we select another ruler?"

Proudly, the law chief responded, "The leaders of the houses will have to vote, and the individual with the majority will be chosen."

"With a little gold, we can influence people to select the candidate we desire," Emil added.

"Which will be you," said the military chief.

Emil smiled, about to elaborate, when a guard hurriedly entered and stood before the future King of Token.

"Lord Emil, our soldiers have captured Nisay, and it is believed that Nora is also in the kingdom."

Emil's face turned red with anger as he shouted, "And you came to inform me first? Bring him in, immediately!"

Without delay, the guard rushed to open the gate, and Nisay appeared, led by two soldiers, and his hands bound behind his back.

Emil remained in his place, relishing the moment and chuckling. "You amuse me, Nisay. You had a chance to survive, but instead of going where you belong and taking care of your flock, you dare to return to Token. Why?"

Nisay let out a loud laugh and retorted, "Because I'm not just here to make you laugh; I am here to take your head."

Emil rubbed his beard. "And how, exactly, do you plan to do that?"

This time, Nisay didn't respond with words. Instead, he swiftly pulled his right hand from behind his back and landed a powerful punch on Emil's face.

Four guards swiftly approached Nisay. As they moved closer, they removed their masks, revealing themselves as Sofia and Ali, the pair of ruthless rebels.

Sofia's eyes gleamed with a thirst for blood as she addressed Ali, saying, "May I?"

Ali's smile widened, "All yours, my lady!"

With deadly precision, Sofia drew two daggers and swiftly pierced the necks of two guards. She rolled over, her body covered in their blood, and prepared to face the remaining adversaries. But Nisay had already taken care of them. They laid slain on the floor.

"Those were mine!" Sofia exclaimed. "Honestly, can't I have fun anymore?"

The gate swung open, and a surge of over twenty soldiers poured in. Nisay turned to Sofia with a knowing smile and replied, "Here comes your fun."

Leah, Nora, and Arsalan emerged from the crowd, joining their friends. The six of them found themselves surrounded by over twenty soldiers and six council members, all drawing their blades and joining the fierce fight.

No one dared to make a move. Emil couldn't contain himself any longer and shouted, "What are you waiting for, soldiers? Kill them all!"

But still, none of the soldiers took a step, and even Nora and her companions remained still.

"Soldiers!" Emil screamed desperately, "You outnumber them. Take them down!"

Finally, one soldier hesitated and made a single step forward. At that moment, Nora screamed with authority, "As your queen, I command you to drop your weapons!"

Emil noticed the fear in the eyes of the Token soldiers, so he tried to rally them. "She's just a rebel! If you follow her, you will face the wrath of the empire."

Nora knew she and her companions had the advantage, but she didn't want to shed the blood of her own soldiers. She gritted her teeth as she continued, her voice firm, "Soldiers! Do as I ask if you want to live. We may be just six, but I wouldn't advise you to take another step. Look at Sofia here, on my left. See the fierceness in her eyes, like a lioness thirsting for blood. And behold your king, Nisay, a man capable of slaying beasts. Arsalan is no different; he once single handily took down a barrack of over a hundred soldiers." She paused, and added, "And I would rather face them all than Leah, the emperor's daughter."

Leah smiled. "Don't be deceived by your queen's sweet words. She once defeated nine commanders. Alone."

The military chief could no longer tolerate Nora's arrogance and lunged forward, moving with his sword towards her. But Nora reacted swiftly, dropping to her knees and stabbing him in the belly. He fell lifeless to the ground.

Nora's voice reverberated again, "Drop your weapons!"

Without hesitation, the twenty soldiers and the five council members dropped their weapons and bowed before Nora and her companions, acknowledging their new authority.

Nora approached Emil, who attempted to flee but found himself cornered. With no other option, he reached for his sword. Nora swiftly disarmed him after two strikes and placed her blade against his neck.

"Move!" she commanded.

"You're a fool to think you'll get away with this. The commoners and soldiers will listen to Ceres," Emil said.

"We shall see," Nora replied, "Now move!"

As they reached the balcony of the castle, a large crowd of commoners were gathered in the palace square. No doubt, they had heard the chaos coming from inside. Soldiers surrounded the commoners, awaiting orders from those in charge, while archers stood ready on the walls.

Nora appeared on the balcony, and cheers erupted from the crowd. The soldiers knelt, and the archers lowered their bows.

"People of Token," Nora began, "My ancestors painstakingly built this kingdom, brick by brick, and your ancestors aided them. Some even sacrificed their lives to uphold its greatness, which – until today – had nearly vanished. But with your support, Token, I will ascend as your queen, and together we will restore its glory." She paused, glancing to the door behind her, "Certain vermin, however, have chosen to aid our greatest enemy in our destruction. This cannot be tolerated."

Nora nodded to Nisay, who entered and brought forth Emil, forcing him to kneel.

The yard echoed with the shouts of the commoners. When Nora raised her hand, a hush fell over the crowd.

"This man usurped the rightful queen and sent her to be executed by our greatest enemy, Ceres. This traitor planned to hand over our gold and soldiers to the empire," Nora's voice grew louder, "People of Token, what does this man deserve?"

Everyone in the yard, including the soldiers, shouted a resounding word. "Death!"

The Queen of Token sensed the collective desperation of her people. They pleaded with her through tearful eyes, urging her to put an end to the tyranny that had plagued their land. Without a moment's hesitation, she knew what had to be done.

Summoning her unwavering resolve, the Queen retrieved her sword: a symbol of her authority and responsibility to protect her kingdom. With the swift grace that only a seasoned warrior could possess, she advanced towards Emil, the man who had brought so much suffering upon her realm.

Emil's cold, calculating gaze met hers, a final attempt to provoke fear in her heart. But the Queen remained steadfast, her mind focused on the greater good of her people and the peace they deserved. She would not let fear or doubt cloud her judgment now.

In one decisive stroke, she brought her blade down with unyielding force, severing Emil's head from his body. The once-feared tyrant fell, his reign of terror forever ended. The sound of steel against flesh echoed through the place, a resounding testament to the Queen's determination and the liberation she had achieved for her subjects.

Her people stood in awe and relief, witnessing the fall of their oppressor and the triumph of their beloved Queen.

The Queen of Token lowered her sword, her expression somber yet resolute. The price of peace had been high, and the memories of this moment would forever linger in her heart.

The cheering continued for a while, until Nora urged everyone to disperse.

***

The moment Nora's letter reached Solum, Aznek couldn't contain her happiness. Reclaiming Token from Ceres was a significant step in her agenda, and after a night of introspection, Aznek decided it was time to adopt a bolder approach. Unlike Ceres, though, she understood the importance of consulting her trusted allies before proceeding.

The next day, she set out for Token with a hundred soldiers, confident in the security of Solum, thanks to her prime advisor, Sam. Upon her arrival, she was astounded by the warm reception Nora extended to her. Multi-coloured flowers were strewn at the castle entrance, while soldiers dressed in golden suits, forming two ranks.

Aznek walked between the ranks, a wide smile on her face. The smile grew even broader when she saw her allies standing in front of her, smiling back at her. Nora delivered a formal speech, introducing Aznek as their ally, before escorting her and her companions to the council.

"Lady Queen, in your presence, the throne is yours," Nora declared. Seeing the surprise in everyone's eyes, Nora spoke again, "We all know that she deserves this title more than anyone. Not just due to her bloodline, but also because of her defiance against Ceres and his allies."

No one voiced disagreement, and Aznek took her seat on the throne. 'I'm not the sole one deserving of this title,' she remarked."

Once she was seated, Ali spoke up, "Your Grace, you could have asked us to join you in Solum instead of risking yourself by coming here alone."

"I wanted to share in your joy!" the queen replied with a smile, adding, "Truth be told, I came here to seek your counsel."

"Regarding what?"

"I believe it's unwise to remain solely defensive in our tactics. We need to switch to an offensive strategy," Aznek stated.

Leah didn't appear enthusiastic about the idea and responded, "It may be the right thing to do, Your Grace, but given our resources, we stand little chance against my father and his allies."

"I respectfully disagree, Lady Leah," Aznek asserted, "Just a few days ago, six of you managed to overthrow an entire kingdom. Imagine what we can accomplish with the combined armies of Solum and Token!"

Arsalan rubbed the bridge of his nose. "Reclaiming Token was a different scenario, Your Grace. We only needed to eliminate a few soldiers and council members because the commoners were loyal to Nora's dynasty. It is not the same for Ceres' followers."

"Every kingdom has its vulnerabilities," the queen explained, "Queen Nora, King Nisay. What are your thoughts?"

Nora exchanged a smile with her husband and replied, "Sitting in council chambers bores us. We feel more suited for the battlefield."

Aznek returned the smile and turned to Ali, asking for his opinion.

"When Nora beheaded Emil, that's exactly the thought that crossed my mind," Ali stated.

Aznek stood up and continued, "But Leah, Sofia, and Arsalan aren't on board."

Sofia couldn't contain herself and spoke up, "Your Grace, I've already unsheathed my sword, and it won't return until all seven kingdoms are under your command."

Leah smiled. "That's my girl!"

Before Arsalan could share his thoughts, Aznek eagerly interjected, "Lord Arsalan, what do you think about Toprak? I believe it's time to place Izmir as its queen, don't you?"

Arsalan stood up. "Your Grace, if you asked me to face that traitor and his army alone, I would do it. But unfortunately, Topraki law doesn't permit women to rule."

Aznek glared at him, "It's time to change this outdated law!"

As the discussion continued, a guard was granted entry into the council chamber. "Queen Nora, there's a wounded man outside who wishes to speak with you and Queen Aznek."

Nora exchanged a concerned glance with Aznek and said, "Let him in!"

A man with features reminiscent of the Turban tribes entered the council, holding his shoulder and moving slowly. Ali and Nisay didn't recognize him.

Nisay urged, "You need to see a healer!"

"The healer can wait, Your Grace," the wounded man replied, "Hosni has unleashed his armies, along with the Union's, on all the tribes revolting against the empire."

Nisay stood up, walking closer to the wounded man. "Tell us what happened!"

"They killed thousands of people, including children and elders," the man said.

"What about Okorom?"

"They suffered significant losses, but Lord Walid managed to escape for the time being."

Nora instructed the guard to escort the man to the healer, but the Turban-raised his hand, taking a deep breath before speaking, "I came all the way here not only to warn you but to deliver a message to Lord Ali." He turned to face Ali directly. "I assume you're him?"

Ali nodded silently, prompting the man to continue.

"When the soldiers shot two arrows into my shoulder, I could no longer wield my sword. I sought refuge under a wagon," Tears welled up in the man's eyes as he continued, "I wished I had died instead of witnessing what I saw." He paused, "A young boy took up his sword and stood before the leader of the Unionist army, a man named Kanoot. The little boy bravely attacked Kanoot with his tiny sword, but Kanoot disarmed him and struck him across the face."

Leah's voice was tight as she spoke. "Did he kill the boy?"

"Yes, he did. But do you know what the boy said before he died?"

A hushed stillness gripped the room, the air thick with anticipation, as everyone held their breath for what came next.

The Turban spoke next, his voice carrying the weight of his words, "He said, 'You can't kill me, Lord Ali will come and rescue me, as he always does.'"

Ali maintained his silence, gesturing for the wounded man to continue delivering his message.

"He called out your name in anguish four times before he drew his last breath."

Leah locked eyes with her husband, understanding the impact this tragedy would have on him. She knew the guilt he would carry in his heart for the death of the young boy.

"Lord Ali, let's take some time to rest. We can resume our discussion tomorrow," Nora suggested, seeing the blank look on Ali's face.

Everyone agreed to Nora's proposal, except for Ali, who stood with an emotionless expression. He walked towards the throne where Aznek and Nora sat side by side and addressed them both.

"My queens, my loyalty to you knows no bounds. I will serve you until my last breath, and I will ensure that my son, Noah, continues to serve your descendants. But today, I am asking for a favor."

Nora responded first, her voice filled with determination, "Anything, Lord Ali."

"Justice must prevail. Hosni and Kanoot must be held accountable," Ali stated.

Nora turned to Aznek, who appeared perplexed. Before Aznek could respond, she questioned, "What if I refuse, Lord Ali?"

Ali's expression remained unchanged as he replied firmly, "If you refuse, I will break my oath, for you would no longer be deserving of my loyalty. I will confront Hosni alone."

Aznek stood up, taking a few steps closer to Ali. She looked him in the eye. "That's not the Ali I know—the man who persuaded six homeless rebels to stand against the world, the man who convinced me to face the entire world for a righteous cause."

Ali continued to gaze at her, and Aznek added, "Take some time to clear your mind. When you are ready, we can work together to bring the right justice to the Turban tribes."

Ali nodded, his eyes reflecting a mix of emotions. He understood that hasty actions driven by anger and grief would not lead to the justice they sought. The burden on his shoulders remained, but for now, he would find solace in the unity of their purpose and the support of his queens.

CHAPTER 14

Ceres had been secluded in his room for hours, consumed by introspection and plagued by a mix of pride and despair. He couldn't help but feel a sense of accomplishment for what he had achieved. The Union's Speakers hailed him as a trailblazer, a ruler who had surpassed all others. From a small kingdom, he had built an empire, conquering and dominating every realm in his path.

As he turned his gaze to the left, he stared at the vast collection of codexes shelved in his personal library. Each book contained the summaries of his achievements, hundreds of parchments filled front and back. In an attempt to alleviate his sadness, Ceres randomly plucked a codex from the shelf, a habit he often indulged in during moments of melancholy.

The title on the first page read, "The Emperor and Kingdom of Turba." However, Ceres realized he couldn't delve into the contents. Instead of flipping the page, he impulsively discarded the codex and let out a scream that reverberated throughout the room.

"My life cannot end like this," Ceres seethed, his words echoing off the walls. No one was present to challenge or affirm his declaration.

Ceres found himself in the midst of a personal crisis, triggered by Leah's decision to abandon him, followed by the deaths of Helena, his prime advisor Ramesses, and even his own wife. Defeat. This is what it felt like.

"What good is gold and power if I am not in good health and my children are not by my side?" Ceres questioned himself, his voice filled with bitterness.

The sound of a knock on the door interrupted his thoughts, drawing his attention. "Come in."

A guard entered, bowing respectfully. "Your Highness, she is here!"

Ceres remained silent, his gaze fixed on the guard. After a momentary pause, he instructed the guard to allow her entry.

A woman in her fifties, tall with fair skin and brown eyes, entered the room. Her hair was covered by a black scarf, and she donned a white robe. She approached Ceres slowly, stopping a few feet away from him.

"Your Highness," she greeted respectfully.

"I presume you are Turban," Ceres guessed.

While the woman's features bore more resemblance to those of Toprak, inherited from her Topraki grandmother, but both her parents were Turbans, as was she.

"You are a perceptive man, Your Highness," she replied softly.

"Turbans are known for not bowing before humans. And it doesn't require a sharp mind to deduce that," Ceres remarked with a tinge of bitterness.

"Do you desire for me to kneel before you, Your Highness?" she asked.

Ceres raised his voice, frustration evident in his tone. "I have no interest in your loyalty. I brought you here to find me a cure. Can you do that?"

"I have successfully healed a man afflicted with boils in the past," she disclosed.

Ceres realized that the woman before him possessed intelligence. She made no promises, yet her words sparked a glimmer of hope within him.

"What is your name, woman?" he inquired with a hint of intrigue in his voice.

"Thaar, Your Highness," she replied, her smile radiant and unwavering.

"Thaar?" questioned Ceres, his curiosity piqued. "That's an uncommon name."

"We never choose our name, your highness!" the healer chuckled, a glimmer of determination in her eyes. "Can we begin?"

Ceres gazed at her intently. After a contemplative pause, he inhaled deeply and spoke with a mix of contemplation and resolve, "Usually, I reward individuals with gold, lands, and power. However, if you can find me a cure, I will offer you something far greater. I will grant you the gift of eternal life."

"That is exceedingly generous of you, Your Grace. But your blessing alone will suffice," Thaar said.

"You think I am delusional," Ceres chuckled. Before Thaar could reply, Ceres continued, a mischievous glint in his eyes. "Yes, you do. How can a dying man offer eternal life to a healthy woman?"

Thaar found herself at a loss for words, and Ceres pressed on.

"Everyone will eventually perish. Yet, some will be forgotten as they are buried. Others may be remembered by their fortunate children or grandchildren, but eventually, their names will fade from history," Ceres explained, his gaze fixed on Thaar. "The third category is the most fortunate. Their names will be inscribed in the Golden Book of the Highest Speaker, and people will always remember them."

Thaar offered a warm smile and replied, "You are a wise man, Your Grace."

"I rule over an empire and four kingdoms. I have to be!"

Thaar nodded, her smile widening. Ceres suddenly interjected, his tone light, "I bet you think I am a fool."

Thaar's eyes widened in surprise, her voice hesitant as she responded, "Did I say or do something wrong, Your Highness?"

Ceres chose not to reply and instead suggested they begin their work. He removed his robe and shirt, then positioned himself face down.

Thaar closely examined the lower left portion of his back and noticed three boils, each the size of an eye's iris. They were red with small black dots.

"I will apply pressure in various areas of your back. Please inform me if it causes any pain," Thaar instructed.

Ceres raised his hand, giving a thumbs-up as an agreement.

Thaar positioned her palm a few inches away from the boils on the right side and asked, "Does this hurt?"

"Not really!" Ceres replied. As she applied slight pressure, he said, "Now, I can feel the pain."

Thaar gradually moved her palm away from the boiled area, pressing lightly. As she expected, the further she moved, the less pain Ceres experienced. However, when she reached his right shoulder, Ceres winced in agony, mirroring the pain from the affected area.

Thaar apologized and requested that Ceres put on his clothes.

"How bad is it?" Ceres inquired while buttoning his shirt.

Thaar hesitated for a moment before responding, "These are not boils, Your Highness."

"From your tone, I can sense they are worse," Ceres remarked.

"No, Your Grace, they are neither worse nor better," Thaar clarified, recognizing the need for further explanation. "Ancient healers referred to them as the Black Spiders. Unlike boils, we can easily eliminate them with certain ointments."

It appeared to be good news, but Ceres knew there was another side to this discovery that had yet to be revealed. He braced himself for what Thaar was about to say.

"What's the bad news?" Ceres inquired.

"I'm afraid there is one thing, Your Highness," Thaar cautioned. She continued, "The danger lies in their reproduction. When you eliminate one, two others appear in different places."

"Does the pain in my right shoulder indicate that new Black Spiders will appear soon?" Ceres confirmed, his tone carrying a mix of curiosity and anticipation." When Thaar nodded, he licked his lips. "What if every time a new Black Spider appears, we use some sort of ointment to get rid of it?"

Thaar's smile turned melancholic as she replied, "In reality, it's not the ointment that kills the Black Spiders, but rather our own bodies. Every day, our bodies combat hundreds of diseases, including the Black Spiders, at an early stage. Unfortunately, there are times when our bodies forget how to fight these diseases for various reasons. The ointment simply serves as a reminder, helping our bodies regain their ability to fight."

Ceres focused intently, realizing that Thaar was indeed the exceptional healer his servant had described.

"What happens if we solely rely on the ointment?" Ceres inquired.

Thaar rubbed her chin in contemplation before responding, "Well, the Black Spiders will reproduce excessively. If I provide you with the standard cure, it will begin killing them. However, your body will become exhausted and lose the ability to defend against all diseases." Before Ceres could comment, she added, " There is a potential cure."

"Please, continue!" urged the emperor.

"There is a specific plant that works like magic. It brings all the Black Spiders to one location. Then we can use the standard cure to eliminate them once and for all."

"Let's proceed with that plan," Ceres urged, determination gleaming in his eyes.

Thaar smiled and replied, "I'm afraid it will take time. First, I will provide you with something for the pain, and a plant you need to consume regularly. The entire process will take around three months. I will make sure to visit every two weeks to monitor your progress."

The emperor locked eyes with her and asked, "Why do you insist on leaving the Union and returning? You could simply stay here."

"Forgive me, Your Grace, but I have a family to care for. Besides, any healer could provide you with the necessary medicine," Thaar explained.

Ceres smiled warmly and stated, "Well, I am entrusting my life to your hands."

He then clapped his hands, summoning a guard into the room. "Escort the healer to the residence of the financial chief and instruct him to provide her with ten gold coins."

Thaar's eyes widened in surprise as she protested, "That's far too generous, Your Highness!"

Ceres disregarded her objection and inquired if she required anything else. Thaar graciously declined, thanked him, and took her leave.

Immediately, Ceres called upon one of his trusted soldiers and issued a secret order, "Follow this woman discreetly and gather every detail about her, her family, and her village. Understood?"

The soldier lowered his head and replied, "Consider it done, Your Highness."

Ceres possessed a keen sense of discernment and could sense the genuineness in Thaar's demeanor. However, he had learned from past experiences, particularly with his daughter Leah, to never trust others blindly. That scepticism had remained ingrained within him ever since.

Taking a few drops of the medicine Thaar had provided, Ceres drifted into a deep slumber. Upon awakening, he was astonished to find that the pain had vanished entirely. He instinctively checked the afflicted area, only to discover that the buttons still lingered. Nevertheless, Ceres felt a surge of joy knowing that he had experienced an entire night of uninterrupted sleep, free from relentless pain.

CHAPTER 15

You can't kill me, Lord Ali will come and rescue me, as he always does.

That sentence kept haunting Ali throughout the night. He was overwhelmed by a profound sense of failure, knowing that he had not only let down the boy who had entrusted his fate to him, but also the entire village. Ali's absence during the enemy's devastating attack left him tormented with regret. He replayed the events over and over in his mind, searching for any possible way he could have prevented the tragedy.

Even Leah, his wife and the love of his life, couldn't calm his rage. But she knew Ali better than anyone, and she knew to give him the space and the time he needed to deal with the tragedy. As did the rest of his friends.

Queen Aznek held a council meeting, inviting all her trusted generals and allies – except for Nora, who had decided to keep a close eye on her Kingdom. Aznek initiated the meeting and asked who was in favor of declaring war against Turba.

Sam was the first to object. "Your Grace," Sam began, "It tore my heart apart when I heard what happened to the villagers there. But the attack was orchestrated by Ceres, King of Turba and King of Turang. If we attack one kingdom, we will have to deal with two others and Ceres. I don't think we're ready for that."

Three generals supported Sam's opinion. Aznek remained silent, staring at Ali's friends. The confusion in their eyes was evident, as Sam's words made sense, but they couldn't agree with him.

Aznek turned her gaze to Leah and asked, "Lady Leah, what do you think?"

Leah took a deep breath before replying, "The prime advisor isn't wrong. It's unwise to act impulsively against an empire and two kingdoms." Sam smiled and nodded as a thank you, but Leah dragged her gaze back to the Queen. "But it's not a good idea to stand down either."

The smile disappeared from Sam's face as he asked, "Then what do you suggest?"

Leah chuckled. "Lord Sam, the war has already started. If we sit and do nothing, do you think we'll survive?"

Before he could reply, she answered her own question, "We won't. The emperor and his allies won't stop until they get back Solum and Token."

"And kill Ali," added Arsalan.

Sam grimaced. "You're talking about Ali as if he's the lord king!"

Before the discussion escalated, the queen intervened. "Folks, let's stay focused on our main topic, please."

The room fell silent, and Aznek continued, "Lady Leah has a point. This world isn't big enough to hold both us and our enemies. I'm certain that Ceres and his allies think the same way. The question is, how do we handle this efficiently?"

Aznek scanned the room, looking at each individual, until her gaze settled on Sofia. "Lady Sofia, do you have something to say?"

Sofia glanced at her friend Leah, who smiled and nodded.

"Well, what if we repeat what we did in Token? We could take a few skilled fighters and sneak into King Hosni's room to slit his throat," Sofia suggested, "I don't see why not."

Aznek smiled and responded, "Lady Sofia, how many enemy throats do you plan to slit before you get bored?"

Everyone burst into laughter, except for the prime advisor, who interrupted their amusement and said, "The kingdom cannot afford to lose skilled fighters like you, my lady, nor your friends. You are the ones who have instilled hope in the Free People."

Sofia tapped the table with her fingertip, smiling. "A good plan always comes with risks, doesn't it?"

Before Sofia could continue, Nisay decided to speak up, saying, "Lady Sofia, the prime advisor is right. It's not worth the risk. Besides, there is a law in the universe: a good plan can only be executed once. If we try to repeat it, it is no longer good."

Silence fell upon the room, and Queen Aznek concluded, "So we bide our time, awaiting Ceres' next move before we respond?"

The prime advisor stroked his beard and reluctantly said, "I wish I could say no, but it's a lot better than losing our allies."

The queen immediately instructed the guard to summon Stephen, Sai's apprentice, who arrived promptly. Aznek introduced him to the group, explaining that he had taken over Sai's responsibilities. She then addressed Stephen, saying, "From now on, you answer to Arsalan. With your brilliant mind and his military skills, we can truly strengthen our kingdom."

Stephen enthusiastically embraced the order and dedicated three days to showcasing the array of inventions his team had created. Arsalan, captivated by the efficiency and diversity of the weapons, found himself thoroughly impressed.

After extensive discussions with Sam, Leah, and Nisay, Arsalan settled on a strategic plan that incorporated two specific types of weapons: twenty catapults and the Tears Dropper. The Tears Dropper was a colossal sphere that, upon detonation, released a potent substance capable of inducing temporary blindness in anyone exposed to its scent.

Arsalan's plan was to use the catapults to demolish Turba's walls, while the Tears Dropper would distract the enemy's soldiers. It would create an opening for the rebel's alliance.

Stephen spent two days trying to convince the queen of the efficiency of their new catapults, and she only agreed when she witnessed their destructive power first-hand. A single bucket launched by the catapult was able to destroy a twenty-foot-square wall.

The Solumy council finally reached a consensus to proceed with the attack, and they held their final council before the war. The atmosphere was filled with cheers as Ali and his wife entered the room.

Stephen, however, was the last to arrive, his face pale and speechless. The queen sensed that whatever he had to share was grave, so she stood and shouted, "What is it, Sir Stephen?

"Your Grace, our weapons storage!" He hesitated, shaking his head, "It's – it's –"

"Sir Stephen, look at me," Aznek said, placing her hand on his shoulder. "Whatever it is, speak!"

"It was destroyed, Your Grace!" Stephen shouted, his voice filled with despair. "Fire burnt everything—catapults, bombs, the Tears Dropper."

"Everything?" Aznek repeated, her voice barely a whisper. Tears welled up in Stephen's eyes as he nodded.

The queen sat in her chair, unable to utter a word. The room was filled with shock and disbelief, including Ali.

When Aznek finally regained her voice, she addressed everyone in the room. "I'm going to dismiss you now."

One by one, everyone nodded and rose to leave the council, their disappointment evident. But the queen had one more command. "No one can know about this," she declared. "Sir Stephen, ensure that all your men and women are briefed."

Disheartened, the members of the council departed, but none felt the weight of the news as heavily as the queen herself. She felt defeated and devoid of options.

The barrage of bad news didn't cease. The following morning, Aznek awoke to the sounds of screams emanating from the parlor of her residence. She recognized Leah's voice immediately.

Aznek hastily put on her robe and rushed to the living room, where she found her servant, Cara, attempting to calm Leah down.

"What's wrong, Cara?" the queen interrupted.

"Your Grace, you ordered that no one should be allowed in, and I was just explaining that to Lady Leah," Cara replied.

Leah approached the queen, her voice filled with tension. "Your Grace, I wouldn't bother you unless it was urgent."

Aznek glanced at Cara and commanded, "Leave us!"

As Cara exited the room, Leah broke the news. "Ali has disappeared."

Aznek gently took Leah's hand and motioned for her to sit. "Lady Leah, Ali is a grown man. I suspect he went to the woods, seeking some space."

"We both know Ali is not well. The young boy's words have affected him deeply. And let's not forget what happened with the weapons storage."

The Queen frowned. After a moment, she twisted towards the door. "Guard!" she shouted, "Summon all the gate guards. I want to see them immediately."

***

Leah's intuition about her husband was accurate. The moment the council had concluded, Ali sought out Stephen in secret and requested his assistance. Ali had anticipated that convincing the new mastermind would be challenging, but Stephen displayed no hesitation. In fact, he was eager.

They made their way to a small hut, where Sai used to conduct his experiments. Ali placed a parchment on the table, displaying the blueprint of Turba's castle. Pointing to the southern side, he explained, "This is the only part of the wall that is usually unguarded because it's impossible to climb. The wall is smooth and over thirty feet high."

"We can simply use a rope," suggested Stephen.

Ali took a deep breath and said, "The top of the wall is very wide, over ten feet. That means we can't attach any hooks there."

Stephen remained silent, and Ali stared at him, waiting for a response. But the new mastermind didn't speak.

"Stephen, this is where you tell me there's nothing impossible," Ali said, "If you want to be our new mastermind, this is your chance."

Stephen bowed his head for a moment. "I believe I can come up with something."

"Good. You have until dawn to figure it out. I'll see you then."

Ali knew Stephen would be under immense pressure, but he trusted his abilities and knew he would deliver.

After a few hours, Ali returned to find Stephen sitting idle. Before Ali could say anything, Stephen stood up and offered a smile.

Ali returned the smile and said, "Fill me in."

Stephen led Ali to the corner of the room and uncovered a small device.

"A catapult?" Ali asked, perplexed.

"I wouldn't call it that," Stephen replied, "It's similar to a catapult, but smaller. Instead of throwing balls, it releases a rope."

Stephen removed the top cover, revealing a rolled-up rope inside. Then he uncovered the front, surprising Ali with a large iron object resembling an arrow, but much larger.

"So, this device releases the rope and the arrow pierces the wall?" Ali inquired.

"Exactly, my lord!" Stephen said, "The rope will be securely fastened to the wall, and with your formidable strength, I am confident that you will be able to ascend to the top."

Stephen's smile widened, and Ali asked, "How can I use this little device?"

"I will come with you, my lord," Stephen responded.

Initially, Ali objected, not wanting to put anyone's life at risk. However, Stephen explained that the device was more complicated than it seemed. Ali understood that Stephen was eager to be part of the adventure, so he decided to grant him the opportunity, even if it was dangerous.

***

Three days had passed since Ali's disappearance, and Aznek had found no clues except for the fact that Stephen had vanished at the same time. It could only mean one thing—they were up to something.

Aznek was infuriated by Ali's behavior. Not only did he disobey her and disrupt the council, but he had taken away the one person who could help the kingdom recover from the loss of the weapons in the storage.

Some suggested gathering a team to search for them, while others believed Ali would succeed in whatever he had in mind, and urged the queen to focus on solving the weapons problem. The debate continued, and suddenly, a guard interrupted the queen in the council, his face pale and his hands trembling. He struggled to speak a single word.

The queen's impatience grew, and she yelled, "Did I employ you as my guard to bring me nothing but bad news? Speak!"

"Your Grace," the guard stammered, his face pale, "the guards on the wall have informed me that there is a massive army gathering in front of the castle."

"What army?" the queen demanded.

"Union, Turang, and Turba, Your Grace. There are over thirty thousand soldiers," the guard replied, handing a letter to the queen, "They shot an arrow into the castle with this letter."

Aznek unfolded the parchment and began reading it aloud, her voice filled with anger, "From Ceres to the bastard. Your castle is under siege, and your armory has been destroyed. Surrender yourself, and your people shall be spared. Otherwise, you will all starve to death."

The queen's eyes blazed with fury as she crumpled the letter in her hand. It was clear that war had come to their doorstep, and she would not bow down to such threats.

CHAPTER 16

Izmir sat alone in her new room, contemplating her future in Turang. All she could envision was a future cloaked in darkness. *How can I live with a man older than my father? A man with no principles and no affection!*

Standing up, she stalked towards the mirror, which reflected a beautiful girl with royal blood. The flowing white dress she wore made her appear angelic. The door to her room creaked open, and Izmir heard the sound, assuming it was one of the servants. But when she heard a dry, male cough, her heart sank. It was the last person she wanted to see - King Choulou.

"You look astonishing, my queen," the old king said.

Izmir forced a smile but remained silent.

"Did you enjoy your wedding?" Choulou inquired.

Izmir replied hesitantly, "Very much, Your Grace."

The king approached her and took hold of her right hand. "We are husband and wife now. There is no need to be shy."

Izmir wished she could take a knife and slit his throat, but she knew it wasn't the right time. Instead, she asked, "Your Grace, why did you marry me?"

Choulou released her hand and moved to sit on his bed. He tapped the spot next to him with his right hand, as if inviting her to join him. Izmir hesitated, but she realized she had no choice.

As she sat next to him, Choulou began to explain, "Fools get married for an illusion called love. They are so naive, thinking that souls can truly connect, when in reality, they are merely drawn to each other physically. Unfortunately, a few months after they consummate their marriage, they grow bored and ultimately leave each other disappointed, not just in their marriage, but in life itself."

"And what about wise people like you?" questioned Izmir.

Choulou offered a smile. "Wise people seek mutual interests. For them, marriage is a deal that benefits both parties."

Izmir gazed at him, perplexed, and he continued, "Take our marriage, for instance. You are the daughter of the previous King of Toprak, and I am the King of Turang. If we have a son, he will be the heir to both kingdoms."

"So, we both win?" asked Izmir. "But why do you seek to gain control over two kingdoms?"

Choulou smiled. "Why stop at just two kingdoms? I have a plan to conquer Dharatee as well. And, of course, I won't be satisfied until all the kingdoms are under my rule."

The king stood and removed his robe, then looked at Izmir with excitement in his eyes.

Izmir lowered her head and softly said, "Your Grace, I don't feel ready. Can we please just talk tonight?"

The smile vanished from Choulou's face. He seized Izmir's arm and squeezed it tightly. "I don't have time for the games of spoiled girls. Take off your clothes."

"Please!" Izmir begged, but her words fell on deaf ears. He raised his hand and struck her across the face.

Pain broke across her skin. As she held her cheek, the world spun, but her anger rose with it. The knife at her side itched.

"Do as I say, wife."

And that made Izmir reach her limit. A small knife swiftly emerged from her sleeve, and with lightning speed, she directed it toward his throat.

Choulou felt the blade in his throat before he even registered what had happened. A wide gash opened up, and Izmir took pleasure in the sight of his blood flowing. Holding his arm, she uttered, "You should have listened to me!"

Releasing his grip on her arm, he collapsed to the ground, lifeless.

Izmir was left unsure of what to do next. Leaving Turang without being caught seemed impossible, but staying there would lead her straight to the executioner's block. Though her hands trembled, she knew it was not the time to panic. She wiped the blood off her hands and grabbed a dish.

As she approached the exit, two guards stood in her way. She greeted them with a smile, and one of them asked, "Your Grace, do you need anything?"

Izmir maintained her smile as she replied, "His grace desires to be served by his new queen."

The guards exchanged surprised glances, and one of them said, "A new bride cannot cook for the first three days."

"I will go and check with his grace," said the other guard.

Izmir used the dish to strike one of the guards in the neck. The second guard reached for his sword, but Izmir was quicker. Dodging his blade, she swiftly knelt and plunged a dagger into his belly. She intended to finish off the first guard, but before she could turn, he had crawled back into the room and pulled a rope connected to a bell.

It sounded throughout the halls.

Within a few steps, two soldiers appeared before her. She hurled a dagger, hitting one of them with precision, while the second soldier charged toward her. Though she had no weapon in hand, she assumed a fighting stance. However, before the soldier reached her, he fell to the ground with an arrow lodged in his back.

No one else emerged. Izmir wondered if the arrow came from a friend or if it was a missed shot from a Turangy soldier. Scanning her surroundings frantically, she found no answers.

Just as she was about to make her escape, a faint whisper reached her ears.

"Lady Izmir, over here."

She grabbed a sword from the fallen soldier and turned her gaze toward the window where a light beckoned. Gathering her courage, she approached the window. To her surprise, the adjacent door was open.

As she drew nearer, the picture became clearer. It was a tall man with a head of black curly hair, his brown skin indicating his origins from Dharaatee.

"Who are you?" Izmir questioned.

The man, clearly in a hurry, had no time for explanations. "No time to explain. Follow me if you want to survive."

She pressed her sword against his neck, but he made no attempt to resist her. "Stay here, and you will die. Follow me, and you have a chance to avenge Lord Murat."

Uncertain of her next move, Izmir kept her blade at the Dharatian's neck. The sound of the bell persisted, and the approaching footsteps of soldiers grew nearer. With no other viable options, she reluctantly chose to trust the man and entered the room.

He closed the door behind them and proceeded forward.

"Where are we going?" Izmir asked. Her savior simply motioned for her to follow.

He opened a hatch, revealing a set of stairs beneath the floor. Before descending, he turned to Izmir and stated, "If you wish to escape this doomed kingdom, it's best if you follow me."

This time, she did not object. They walked for several miles, and Izmir could hardly believe it when she found herself in the safety of the woods, successfully evading capture for committing the highest crime in Turang.

Curious, she inquired, "Who are you?" as the Dharatian began setting a fire.

"My name is Suresh. Her grace, Queen Aznek, asked me to save you," the man responded.

***

The baby was coming.

Roulan had to endure the pains of labor once again – the intense pain, the squeezing, the feeling that she was being ripped inside out. She had assumed it would be easier, considering she had already given birth eight years prior. But this time proved to be much more challenging. It couldn't be due to her age, as she was still in her twenties, nor could it be attributed to Kanoot's kicking, since Umali had assured her it would not impact the baby.

The midwife held a hypothesis, but she kept it to herself. With her experience in assisting women during childbirth, she knew how difficult and frightening it could be for a single mother to bring a child into the world.

"Lady Roulan, you are a remarkably strong woman. Push as hard as you can," the midwife encouraged.

Roulan clutched the ends of two ropes tightly, the cords tied to a wedge embedded in the wall. With all her strength, she squeezed the ropes and exerted herself to push, but the nurse declared, "Not good enough."

The midwife continued to offer words of encouragement, urging Roulan to push harder, but there seemed to be no progress. Frustration mounted within the room.

"Look at me! Look at me!" the midwife screamed, locking eyes with Roulan. "The moment this child emerges, you will be blessed with two lives—yours and your baby's. They will become your primary focus, and all you will care about is their happiness and success."

Roulan remained silent, focusing on her breaths.

"Take a deep breath and push. If you don't want to do it for yourself, do it for Sai," the midwife said.

Roulan followed the midwife's instructions precisely, filling the room with her cries and pushing with all her might.

"I can see the head. Give me one more push!" the midwife encouraged her.

Roulan obeyed. Each time she paused, the midwife pleaded for another push, promising it would be the last. But it wasn't until the fifth one that the baby finally emerged.

The midwife swiftly pulled the new-born out completely and covered him with a sheet. A nurse whispered to the midwife, "Why isn't the baby crying?"

The midwife hushed her, but Roulan overheard and anxiously asked, "Why is my baby silent?"

The midwife disregarded Roulan's question and continued rubbing the baby's back until his cry filled the room. Joy returned to the atmosphere, and Roulan erupted with tears mixed with laughter. The nurse approached her with a cloth, wiping Roulan's face and smiling at her. Then, the midwife handed the new-born to Roulan.

"He's a boy!" the midwife announced.

Roulan held her son in her arms, unable to stop her tears. She hadn't felt a hint of joy since Sai's death, but in that moment, it felt as though all her beloved ones—Sai, Li, and her little boy—had come back to life. The feeling of loneliness dissipated, and her sole attachment to life now revolved around this little boy.

"What's his name, my lady?" the nurse inquired.

"Sai!" Roulan declared with a smile, "Sai, of course. But please, where is Lady Umali?"

The midwife grasped Roulan's hand and replied, "She had an urgent matter, but she will be here today or tomorrow morning."

Umali arrived the following day and was overjoyed to see the baby breathing. She spent the entire night beside Roulan, discussing the future. Umali was certain that the little Sai would play a significant role in the destiny of the Free People.

After a week of recovering from childbirth and gaining her strength back, Roulan decided it was time to dress up and pay a visit to the tribe's leader, Lady Umali. As she made her way, she discovered Umali sitting by the river, accompanied by Zaya and Ashil.

"Lady Roulan, I was just about to visit you," Umali said.

Roulan greeted them and remained standing. "I grew bored in my tent, so I came here hoping to find someone I could practice with," she explained, then turned her gaze to Zaya. "What do you think, Lady Zaya?"

Surprise flickered across Zaya's face. "No, who would dare stand against the Beast-Slayer?"

"The Beast-Slayer?" Roulan laughed.

"It's the nickname we've given you here. I hope you don't mind," Umali replied, inviting Roulan to sit beside them.

Roulan settled next to Zaya and replied, "Why would I mind? I'm not the only one who was able to slay a beast, though. Nisay defeated three in one week."

Zaya's lips curved into a smile, her tone light as she clarified, "But he didn't kill Ramessess."

Roulan couldn't help but chuckle at the jest, but Umali interjected, her voice carrying a sense of urgency, "We have more pressing matters to address than nicknames," Umali smiled, "We need your advice."

"My advice?" Roulan said, adding, "My sword has never been sharper, and its blade will find its sheath in the enemy's chest."

Umali exchanged a knowing smile with her daughter before addressing Roulan. "We could truly benefit from your assistance, but you must also take good care of your baby."

A tear rolled down Roulan's cheek as she responded, "There is nothing I desire more. But if our cause were to falter, he might be enslaved by the enemy."

Umali didn't argue. Instead, she stood up and began explaining the pressing matters at hand.

"You're not wrong – the threat to us has never been greater. We've never been weaker. Solum is under siege, Token is unstable, and Ali has disappeared," Umali sighed.

The three pieces of news hit Roulan like a shock, leaving her rooted to the spot, petrified.

Umali approached Roulan, speaking softly. "The Seven of you ignited hope in our hearts. Three gave their lives, and three others are currently fighting for survival," Umali paused for a moment before continuing, " You are the only one capable of leading us out of this crisis."

"How?" Roulan asked, her voice hushed.

"Take Zaya and Ashil, and find a way to save us," Umali replied.

***

"Why don't I feel homesick here? I don't miss Roulan?" Sai questioned.

"That's because your role there has come to an end. Remember, we were all created to live eternal lives. The life you lived before was just a test, and you passed," Keita explained.

"Where are we going?" Sai asked as they walked amidst the colorful trees.

"You seem afraid, Sai," Alighieri observed, "But there's nothing to worry about for a man like you."

They continued walking and conversing until they arrived at a place that seemed familiar to Sai. He recognized it from his previous life.

"The Blessing-Tree?" Sai said, and both his companions nodded.

"Can we go in?" Sai inquired, taking steps forward, but Alighieri and Keita hesitated, refusing to follow.

"I'm afraid we're not allowed to enter there," Alighieri admitted.

Sai halted, confusion etched on his face. "But you both are decent and good people, I'd say you're better than me."

Keita smiled and responded, "It's not for you to judge who is better."

Sai nodded, pressing on. As soon as he placed his hand on the trunk of the Blessing-Tree, everything transformed around him. He found himself surrounded by three circles of light.

A booming voice reverberated through the space. "Welcome to the heart of the universe, Sai, son of Jaya!"

Sai felt no fear. Instead, he experienced a sense of peace in his heart, reminiscent of the moments he had shared with Roulan.

Sai's curiosity grew, and he asked, "And why am I here?"

"To be given the purest purpose: to guide people to do good deeds for as long as your lineage lasts," they replied.

Sai's gaze scanned the three circles around him, attempting to comprehend their words. The female voice then provided clarity, "You are on the verge of joining the Thinkers and becoming one of them."

Sai recalled Ali mentioning the Thinkers, individuals who were granted a resurrection beyond life and tasked with guiding the living to preserve a benevolent world. "I have heard about the Thinkers, but I bear no resemblance to them."

The female voice responded, "That is because you have yet to become one. To achieve that, you have a mission to fulfill."

Sai's confusion deepened, and he inquired, "What mission?"

The three voices spoke in unison, "Help the Free People find the One Ruler."

"You mean a Lord King?" Sai asked.

"Or a Lady Queen!" the voices echoed.

CHAPTER 17

Only ten miles to go, and Izmir would be out of Turang's territory, accompanied by her savior, Suresh. Their journey had been filled with fear and uncertainty. The once pampered princess now found herself transformed into a fugitive.

Lost in her thoughts, Izmir was brought back to reality by Suresh's suggestion. "The night is falling, Your Grace. It would be wise to set up camp and get some rest," he said.

She nodded in agreement. "Yes, that's a good idea. Let's start a fire while I go look for something to eat."

Suresh retrieved his bag from his back. "Don't worry about that. We have enough food for three days."

Izmir couldn't refuse the offer, considering her physical exhaustion and hunger. They shared bread and apples, and once they had finished, Izmir couldn't hold back her curiosity any longer. "What is a Dharatian doing in Turang? How did you end up in the royal residence?" She paused, "And don't tell me you're a slave."

Surprised, Suresh asked, "Why not?"

"The two kingdoms agreed not to enslave each other. I've read about the history of the seven kingdoms."

Suresh nodded. "History is knowledge, and knowledge is key to survival."

"And besides, I've never met a slave who possessed such ancient wisdom," Izmir added with a wink.

Suresh tossed the remains of the apple on the ground and replied, "Choulou kidnapped me and imprisoned me in his castle for five years. Recently, he wanted to use me as a weapon against the Dharatians and gain control over our kingdom."

Izmir's face reflected a mix of confusion and surprise as she processed the information. But before she could respond, Suresh added with conviction, "I am Suresh, the son of Ghandy, the rightful king of Dharatee."

Silence enveloped them momentarily, until Suresh finally spoke again. "Do you realize that we are now fleeing from three kingdoms?"

Izmir smiled and replied, "Yes. We'd better rest and make our way to Solum."

They agreed to take turns sleeping while the other kept watch. Suresh took the first shift, and before dawn, he fell asleep and awoke to a blade pressed against his neck. He glanced to his left and saw several soldiers in Turangy uniforms. One of them had a sword at Izmir's throat.

"Get up, filthy traitors," the soldier barked. "I wish I could cut your head off, but Prince Bao wants both of you alive."

There were around twenty soldiers, and Suresh found himself unarmed. He knew he had no choice but to comply with the Turangy soldiers.

Izmir looked at him with a smile. "Get up, Lord Suresh. You have served your queen honorably. Even if we fail, the queen and the rebels will not."

The leader of the soldiers approached Izmir and struck her in the face, causing her nose to bleed.

"Oh, you haven't heard," the soldiers' leader taunted her with a smile. "Let me enlighten you. Ali drowned in his sorrows and has abandoned the cause. And your queen, along with the rebels, is now under siege." Izmir spat on the leader's face, and he responded with another punch. Gripping her by the neck, he said, "All the rebels are gone"

"Not the Beast-Slayer," a voice called out from behind. The soldiers' leader turned just in time to meet an arrow that pierced his left eye.

Emerging from the trees, three fighters sprinted toward the soldiers, swiftly taking them down one by one. Izmir and Suresh stood in awe of their saviors, particularly a tall girl with short hair who displayed exceptional skill. She wielded a sword in her right hand to parry her opponents' attacks and used a dagger in her other hand to swiftly dispatch them.

Though Izmir didn't know their identities, she was in awe of witnessing them effortlessly kill the soldiers. One of the saviors approached Izmir and Suresh.

"I assume you are Izmir and Suresh?" their savior asked.

Suresh exchanged a surprised glance with Izmir before responding, "We are deeply grateful. May we know who you are?"

"I am Roulan, and these are Zaya and Ashil."

A tear trickled down Izmir's cheek as she spoke, "Roulan, as in the rebel?"

Roulan chuckled in response. "If that's what you want to call me."

Zaya approached Izmir with a piece of cloth, intending to tend to her wounds, but Izmir stopped her. "There's no time for that. Solum is under attack."

She proceeded to explain what the soldiers' leader had told them. Roulan initially dismissed it as a bluff, but Suresh confirmed its truth. "Ceres, Choulou, and Hosni were planning to strike Aznek, but I didn't expect it to be a siege."

Zaya couldn't help but speak up. "What about Ali?"

"The soldiers informed us that he left the cause," Izmir replied, her voice filled with sorrow.

Roulan almost laughed. "Ali would never abandon the cause. He is the cause."

Silence fell upon them, and Roulan continued, "Zaya, you take Izmir and Suresh to Token." She then turned to Ashil and said, "Come with me."

Zaya expressed her surprise, questioning the need to split up. Roulan understood that she didn't want to be separated from her husband. She approached Ashil and whispered, "Go and say something to your wife."

Roulan then asked Izmir and Suresh to give Zaya and her husband some space.

Tears welled up in Zaya's eyes as she placed her hand on Ashil's face. "This is the first time we will be apart," she lamented.

"It's a good thing, don't you think?" Ashil attempted to tease her. "I'll stop annoying you, and you'll miss me."

But Zaya didn't smile in return. "You're like the air I breathe. I can't bear to be away from you."

"Don't worry," Ashil assured her. "Roulan and I will save the queen, and you will be proud of me."

"I'm already proud of you. You're the man I choose to spend the rest of my life with. Of course, I'm proud of you."

***

Ali and Stephen were just a mile away from the Turban castle, and surprisingly, the road remained unguarded. For a while, they progressed without encountering any soldiers. Ali couldn't help but feel that luck was once again on his side, even if it hadn't been for so long.

As the sun began to set, they moved cautiously towards the west. True to Ali's expectations, the castle walls appeared vacant, devoid of any archers. Stephen unveiled the small catapult and adjusted its aim towards the wall.

"Whenever you're ready, my lord," Stephen said.

Without a moment's hesitation, Ali gave the order, "Now!"

Stephen triggered the small device, and a rope shot out with the speed of an arrow, embedding its pointed tip into the wall. Ali tugged on the rope, and it seemed stuck. Turning to his companion with a smile, he remarked, "Sai would have been proud of you. Return to Solum!"

Ali tightly coiled the rope around his fingers and dashed towards the wall. As he approached it, he vaulted into the air, pressing his right foot firmly against the wall's surface, immediately followed by his left. With unwavering determination, he ascended, unfazed by the daunting height and the peril of the rope possibly snapping. His singular objective was to conquer the summit of the wall.

But just a few feet in the air, the rope made a splitting sound. Just quiet at first, then louder. When it snapped, Ali went tumbling to the floor.

He cursed. Stephen was no longer around.

Getting back on his feet, Ali searched for an alternative solution. Before he could find one, an arrow whizzed by, landing just inches away from his feet. Ali turned his head, hand on the pommel of his sword, and found himself surrounded by over fifty Turban soldiers.

"Drop your weapon!" shouted one of the soldiers, whose face was familiar to Ali's.

"Kanoot!" Ali exclaimed, drawing his sword. "Come and claim it if you dare call yourself a man."

"Take one step, and you will be obliterated!".

Half of the soldiers raised their bows, poised to shoot. Ali had no choice but to surrender. He dropped his sword and raised his hands in defeat.

Kanoot ordered two soldiers to chain and escort Ali to a cell, and Ali offered no resistance. As the soldiers locked the cell door behind him, Ali finally realized the gravity of his mistake. He berated himself for acting without consulting his friends, not even his wife, Leah.

Ali had no idea about the situation unfolding in Solum, but he was aware that his impulsive decision would come at a heavy cost. Sleep eluded him, and when he finally drifted off, he was awakened by a splash of water hitting his face. Startled, he sat up, only to be struck by sticks from all directions.

Kanoot reveled in watching Ali cover his face with his hands, desperately trying to shield himself from the soldiers' blows. Commanding the soldiers to restrain Ali, Kanoot watched as they spread his arms apart, chaining his hands.

Approaching Ali with a mocking laughter, Kanoot taunted him. "Ali, the rebel! I've heard so much about you, so much that I started to believe you were a hero. But it seems you're nothing more than a puppy with a loud bark."

"Do you think you're the first one to capture me?" Ali asked, inhaling deeply. "Many have succeeded in sneaking up on me like cowards and throwing me into their cells. But you know what? It only made me stronger."

"I've caught countless rebels with big mouths like yours," Kanoot boasted, "And I always silence them by cutting their tongues before slitting their throats."

Ali, despite his weakened state, smiled. "You talk as if you act on your own, when we both know that's far from the truth. You're nothing but a dog who can't even bark without the approval of his owner."

Kanoot's face went red with anger. "The last time I caught your wife, I hit her hard in her belly and face. And you couldn't do a thing about it. Yet, you claim to be the protector of the Free People, unable to even protect the love of your life."

Ali leaped up with both feet and delivered a powerful kick to Kanoot's chest, sending him sprawling to the ground. "Consider that a small down payment on the debt I owe you," Ali remarked.

Kanoot got up, dusting off his clothes and sporting a sinister smile. He advanced towards Ali, stopped, and then punched him in the face. "And what will you do about this?" Kanoot taunted, continuing to rain blows upon him. With each strike, Kanoot screamed, "How about this?"

Ali's face became covered with blood to the point where he could no longer lift his head.

"Awaken him!" Kanoot commanded. Another splash of water jolted Ali back to awareness, pain coursing through his entire body. He could barely move his lips to muster a warning. "You will fall, I promise."

Kanoot burst into laughter and ordered the soldiers to escort Ali to the council of Turba, where Hosni sat upon his throne, eagerly awaiting their meeting.

Ali entered the room, his anger burning within him, but directed not at Kanoot or Hosni, nor even Ceres. His rage was aimed at himself. He knew that Hosni and Ceres wouldn't stop at killing him; they would attempt to use his capture to trap the two queens.

"Finally, I have the pleasure of meeting you, Ali," King Hosni began, "I wish the circumstances were different."

Ali spat on the ground and remained silent.

"It's a shame to kill someone like you. We could be friends and leave the past behind," Hosni said.

"Do you think killing me will bring an end to our cause?" Ali retorted.

"You're a fool! Queen Aznek was a stranger in Solum with just one ally, and she conquered it. King Nisay walked alone through the streets of Token, facing eight thousand soldiers. Arsalan and Roulan infiltrated the empire and assassinated a prime advisor., Ali paused to catch his breath before adding, "Imagine what they can accomplish with two armies."

"Winning a few battles doesn't make you winners; it merely makes you rebels who caught us off guard. And I assure you, it's over," King Hosni declared, a smile playing on his lips. "Solum is currently besieged by three armies, and all communications between Aznek and Nora in Token have been cut. It seems the situation is dire and your options are limited."

Ali chuckled confidently, his voice laced with determination. "Unlike you, we have harnessed the power of science to fortify our kingdoms. We possess the means to endure a siege lasting even two years. Not only that, but rest assured, Queen Nora will soon be made aware of your tyrannical ways."

Hosni's confidence wavered as he responded, "I always thought you were a smart man, but now I have my doubts. How do you think we managed to capture you?"

Ali remained silent, allowing Hosni to answer his own question.

"Our whisperers are like shadows to you and your queen. Just as we brought you here, we will bring the widow Roulan to us, as soon as she dares to make a move."

CHAPTER 18

Aznek and her allies deliberated over various strategies to confront the ongoing siege, ultimately agreeing to await the enemy's next move. Bao, the newly crowned king of Turang and the leader of the attacking forces, requested a meeting with Queen Aznek, who invited him to the council chamber alongside her trusted companions.

King Bao was renowned throughout Turang for his exceptional swordsmanship, having even emerged victorious in the Union tournament. He stood tall and possessed a well-built physique. His long, soft black hair cascaded down to his waist, while his eyes, like those of all Turangies, were narrow and dark. Notably, he sported a peculiar moustache—a full horseshoe-shaped moustache with vertical extensions extending from the corners of his lips to his jawline.

Entering the council chamber, Bao exuded an air of arrogance. Nisay and Leah stood by Aznek's throne, their presence indicating their role as protectors. However, Bao chose to provoke the queen by disregarding the designated spot and continuing forward.

As Bao drew closer, Nisay raised his hand, signaling for him to halt. But instead, Bao seized Nisay's hand and swiftly revealed a dagger concealed behind his back, aiming it towards Nisay's wrist.

Anticipating the attack, Nisay released his wrist and delivered a powerful punch to Bao's face. Without hesitating, Nisay seized Bao's wrist, exerting pressure until he relinquished his blade, which clattered to the ground.

Nisay's retaliation did not end there; he drew his own dagger and slashed Bao's cheek.

Clutching his injured cheek, Bao attempted to stem the flow of blood. "How dare you, you son of a whore? I am a king!" he shouted indignantly.

"Consider this your first and final warning!" Queen Aznek asserted firmly. "Should you disrespect my council again, I will sever your head and cast it out of these chambers."

Bao tore a strip of fabric from his shirt and applied it to his wound, attempting to stanch the bleeding. "You will pay for this!" he threatened.

"Hurry along then, so you can tend to your wounds and return to your army. It appears you've suffered quite a deep cut," Leah taunted, her words laced with sarcasm.

Bao seethed with anger. "Surrender Solum and Token, and no harm will befall you. These are the terms set forth by myself and His Highness," he stated.

"Go and relay the following to Ceres: if he wishes to retain his empire, he had better return back my kingdoms, namely Toprak, Turba, Dharatee, and Turang. Failure to comply will result in his destruction, and I will reclaim my realm by force," Aznek said smoothly.

Bao laughed mockingly before asking, "And how do you intend to accomplish that, Lady Queen?" Before Aznek could respond, he interjected, "Your leader is under our custody, and we both know that you are powerless without him."

Leah swiftly unsheathed her dagger, but Aznek restrained her by grasping her wrist. Nisay, unable to contain his anger, shook his head, "You're bluffing!"

"We spared the life of your mastermind solely to confirm my claims. We shall allow him to come to you and dictate the terms on behalf of His Highness," Bao declared, before turning on his heel and making his way toward the exit.

"I will kill you and your masters!" Leah screamed in fury.

Bao paused at the door and turned, his expression revealing nothing. "You have three days to surrender Solum and Token; otherwise, we will send you Ali's head and we will still get our two kingdoms back," Bao declared.

Ever since Leah learned of Ali's intention to join the Thinkers, she had been mentally preparing herself for the possibility of losing him. She believed she was ready for it, especially after giving birth to their son, Noah. She had hoped that their child would fill the void that Ali's absence would create, but now she realized she was mistaken. Unable to steady her trembling foot, she found herself unable to utter a single word, and neither Nisay, Arsalan, nor the queen spoke.

After a prolonged silence, Aznek shouted, "Guards! Bring me Sir Stephen immediately!"

No one uttered a word as they awaited Stephen's arrival. When he appeared, his face covered in bruises and limping, Sofia approached him and seized him by the neck.

"I have a strong suspicion that you are the traitor responsible for Ali's capture by the enemy," Sofia asserted.

Lowering his head, Stephen whimpered, "I am more than just a traitor."

His five words captured everyone's attention. Arsalan demanded, "Say that again!"

"Ali devised an elaborate plan to overthrow Turba, and he relied on me to execute it. But I fell short of Sai's abilities. And for that, I deserve to die," Stephen confessed, kneeling before them.

Sofia, unconvinced by his words, yanked his hair. "Death would be a mercy compared to what awaits you," she hissed. She then turned to the queen and spoke through gritted teeth, "Your Grace, grant me your blessing, and I will make him talk."

"Lady Sofia, the accused is presumed innocent until proven guilty. And Sir Stephen has not even been formally accused," the queen responded.

Sofia disliked the queen's words but dared not voice her objection.

"Sir Stephen, tell us what transpired," the queen commanded.

Stephen proceeded to recount the entire story, which resonated with Ali's methods. However, the queen sought further assurance.

"Sir Stephen, is Ali your king?" Aznek inquired.

Stephen shook his head.

"Ali acted without my knowledge, embarking on a mission without my blessing. And you aided him without returning to me or consulting Arsalan, your direct superior. This constitutes treason against your queen. Why did you accompany Ali without consent?" Aznek questioned.

"Your Grace, I made an error in not seeking your approval. But I have no regrets. I am akin to the commoners; I believe in this man, and I held hope that we could conquer Turba, without shedding blood," Stephen explained, "This time, he failed, and I am prepared to face the consequences for my part in it."

"Guards!" the queen bellowed, "Escort this man to the healer and ensure his wounds are tended to."

The discussion carried on for hours, and no one in the council proposed surrendering Solum.

Sofia remained silent throughout the proceedings, and Aznek sensed her feelings of exclusion from the council, despite her skills and intelligence.

"Lady Sofia, you were raised in a royal household, and your father is both a politician and a military man. Do you have any suggestions?" the queen inquired.

Sofia felt a surge of delight upon hearing this compliment, but she composed herself before responding.

"Ali has taught us many valuable lessons over the years, but do you know what has inspired me most about him? The pursuit of excellence. We have two options: either surrender Solum and Token to secure Ali's release, or sacrifice Ali's life and find a way to break the siege," Sofia proposed.

Silence hung in the air, prompting Sofia to continue, undeterred.

"I suggest a third solution: summon Nora's army to aid us, rescue Ali, and reclaim Turba. With three united forces, we can overwhelm the enemy at our doorstep."

"Lady Sofia, that is a desire shared by all of us, but we are currently under siege and outnumbered," Sam objected.

Turning to Sofia, the queen asked, "Do you have any further suggestions, Lady Sofia?"

"Leah, Nisay, Arsalan, and I will carry out Ali's original plan: infiltrating Turba to rescue Ali," Sofia explained.

Sam couldn't contain himself any longer. "This is madness, Lady Sofia!"

The queen interjected, "Do you have a better suggestion?"

It left Sam speechless. She then turned to the rest of the group, seeking their opinions.

Leah rubbed her hands together. "I had intended to go alone, but with Sofia by my side, our mission will be considerably easier,"

Arsalan added, "I would willingly give my life a thousand times for a man like Ali. I will come."

Sofia met Nisay's smile and he affirmed, "Gladly!"

The queen then posed a question, "What about Sir Stephen? He could prove to be very valuable."

"I don't believe he is a traitor," Arsalan voiced his opinion, with Nisay concurring.

Leah spoke softly, "I agree Arsalan. But do we truly need to include him?"

The queen explained, "We are confined within our castle, and the only way out is through the underground tunnels. Stephen possesses extensive knowledge of those passages. And you may require a mind like his to breach Turba."

Sofia, who harbored reservations about Stephen, expressed her concerns, but ultimately agreed to abide by the majority's decision.

With little time for extensive planning, the next day, the five of them commenced their journey to Turba via the concealed tunnel to avoid detection by the enemy forces stationed outside Solum. Luckily, their route remained uneventful, and within just two days, they arrived at the outskirts of Turban Castle.

Setting up camp a mile away, the group engaged in a lengthy discussion. Despite Stephen's insistence and reassurances, they did not allow him to conduct solo reconnaissance. Ultimately, they decided to take the risk and infiltrate the castle, disguised in soldiers' uniforms. It was a perilous undertaking, but time was of the essence. If they did not act swiftly, Ali would face execution the following day.

As night fell, they all retired to sleep, except for Leah – her thoughts remained consumed by Ali.

The next morning, donning the uniforms of Turban soldiers that they had brought with them from Solum, they approached the castle, bracing themselves for the dangerous mission that lay ahead.

A carriage pulled by a horse departed from the castle, driven by two soldiers.

"This is how we will gain entry," Arsalan said, "We will follow the carriage and seize it from the soldiers."

Everyone agreed, relying on their disguises and the presence of the carriage to assist them in infiltrating the castle. As soon as the carriage disappeared from the archers' view, the four rebels sprinted towards it, swords clenched tightly in their hands.

However, before they could reach the carriage, Turban soldiers emerged from the surrounding trees.

Leah and her companions halted, their bodies tense as they spotted the soldiers. The enemy forces numbered more than a hundred, encircling them with bows and spears at the ready.

There was no way out.

"Leah," a man's voice came, and he stepped forward from the crowd. "We have unfinished business."

"Kanoot," Leah uttered through gritted teeth. His previous blows were still visible on Leah's body.

"I expected you to be smarter, but you have truly disappointed me," Kanoot said.

Stephen advanced towards Kanoot, sword poised in his right hand.

"Stephen, don't!" Arsalan screamed.

As Stephen drew nearer to Kanoot, he sheathed his sword and turned his attention to his friends, spitting on the ground.

"You should have heeded the words of this deranged girl," Stephen mocked, his gaze fixed on Sofia. "She's got good instincts, if not intelligence, it seems."

Sofia yearned to say *I told you* to her friend, but she bit her lip. Instead, she growled his name. "Stephen!"

"Save your breath, whore!" Stephen said, "Your time is up, along with your idiotic friends. Soon, your queens will follow."

Stephen's words struck a chord with Sofia. Ali was imprisoned, Aznek was under siege, and Nora's forces were miles away. It seemed like the end for Sofia.

"Drop your weapons!" Kanoot commanded.

Everyone obediently complied, except for Sofia. She couldn't bring herself to release her sword, her gaze fixated on Stephen.

"Sofia, do as he says! *Please*!" Leah implored.

Reluctantly, Sofia dropped her sword and unsheathed her dagger. Before she released it to the ground, she fixed one last angry glare at Stephen – and then launched it at him with all her might. It struck Stephen squarely in the forehead, and he fell lifeless to the ground.

Kanoot screamed, "What have you done!?"

Sofia raised her hand and smiled. "Now, I surrender."

CHAPTER 19

Three agonizing days had passed since Ali's arrest. He endured meager rations of mouldy bread and a few drops of water to sustain his life. The pain from the beating inflicted by Kanoot and the Turban soldiers seared through his body. A constant, unwelcome friend.

On the fourth day, ten guards arrived at Ali's cell, chaining him and forcefully pulling him by his arms to meet King Hosni in the council chamber.

Hosni remained seated on his throne, resting his hands on the armrests. "Ali, I trust that your sojourn within my castle has been a delightful experience!"

Ali remained silent, prompting Hosni to continue.

"When I look at you and witness your courage and intelligence, it reminds me that life is unjust. If only you would think wisely and join us, the world could be a better place."

"King Hosni, the one thing I know about you is that you are my enemy. Let's get to the point, shall we?" Ali asserted firmly.

"That was in the past, Lord Ali. Enemies can become friends," Hosni replied with a smile.

"What do you want from me?"

Hosni smiled wider, rising from his throne. Approaching Ali, he gestured to one of his generals, who held a quill and parchment in his hand.

Taking the writing tools from his general, Hosni stepped closer to Ali, stopping ten feet away.

"There is a way out for you, Lord Ali," Hosni proposed. "Write a letter to the queen, informing her that you have escaped and wish to meet her in secret."

Ali smirked and replied, "You want me to hand over the Lady Queen?"

"If that is how you choose to address her," Hosni sneered.

"Nisay was right about you," Ali retorted with a smile, "You are foolish."

"Is that a refusal?" questioned the King of Turba, to which Ali nodded.

Hosni clapped his hands, and the gate swung open. Ali, weakened and struggling to stand, watched as his wife Leah, Sofia, Nisay, and Arsalan were dragged in by their chains. Turban soldiers armed with spears surrounded the council chamber.

"I will ask you once more: surrender the queen, and you and your friends will be granted freedom," Hosni demanded. "You have one day to respond."

Ali and his companions remained silent, refusing to entertain the king's demands.

Hosni shifted his gaze to one of the soldiers. "Prepare the execution grounds."

The Turban soldiers led Ali to an isolated cell, warning him. "Tomorrow will be a momentous day for you and your companions. Until then, you will be beaten like a stubborn mule."

The soldier had not been bluffing. The moment they tied Ali, the torture began. Each of the five soldiers took turns striking him, relishing the sight of his anguished expression. Ali refused to scream, though his eyes watered, and he had to squeeze them shut.

It was the fourth soldier's turn, and he displayed the most enthusiasm, aiming a forceful punch at Ali's belly. One of his comrades intervened, pulling his arm back.

"Are you trying to get him killed?" the fourth soldier exclaimed.

The other soldier glared at him and retorted, "Is he your friend?"

"No. But King Hosni would have us executed if we lose him. Remember, his grace needs him to trap the Lady Queen," the fourth soldier explained.

The soldier took two steps closer, his voice filled with suspicion. "The Lady Queen you're talking about is already under siege. And *Lady Queen*?" He barked a laugh, "That's treacherous talk. Who are you?"

"What?"

"You heard me," said the soldier, his tone firm, "Take off your mask."

The fourth soldier hesitated, objecting that the other soldier lacked the authority to issue such a command.

"Either you take off your mask, or I will kill you and take it myself," the soldier declared, reaching for his sword.

Left with no choice, the fourth soldier reluctantly obeyed, slowly removing his mask to reveal a white man in his twenties with blue eyes. It was evident that he did not belong to the Turban faction.

Before the interrogator could process this revelation, the blond man struck him with his own mask, catching him off guard. Swiftly, the blond man drew a dagger and slashed his belly.

Turning his attention to the scene before him, he saw two soldiers lying lifeless in their own blood. He didn't bother engaging the remaining soldiers because his companion had already dispatched them.

Despite Ali's weakened state, a smile crossed his face. "Roulan, Ashil. Your timing couldn't be better."

Roulan took the keys from one of the fallen soldiers and swiftly unchained Ali. "We need to get out of here," she urged.

"Not before we rescue our friends," Ali replied, rubbing his wrists. "They have Leah, Sofia, Nisay, and Arsalan. Let's go!"

Not far from Ali's cell, Hosni sat in his council chamber, unaware that Ali had been freed from his shackles. He held a mug in his hand, addressing his council members with a boisterous voice.

"My generals, today is no ordinary day. Drink with me!" he exclaimed.

The room filled with cheers, and joyous smiles adorned the faces of the council members until they heard a commotion at the door.

"Guard!" Hosni screamed, expecting the door to open and reveal his loyal guard. To his surprise, it swung open, revealing a Roulan, who forcefully kicked the door and strode toward the throne.

Four soldiers rushed toward her, but Roulan dispatched them, her skill evident.

Ali and Ashil followed Roulan into the chamber and locked the door behind them.

King Hosni stood, his voice filled with alarm. "This is madness! Do I have to remind you that I have your wife?"

"And my three friends," replied Ali firmly. "And you're going to ask your soldiers to bring them here."

Hosni chuckled dismissively. "And why would I do that? I have an army at my disposal. You think you can beat them all?"

Ali calmly drew a dagger from one of the soldiers he'd cut down. "All I need to do is hurl this blade to finish you. Not even Ceres' army could stop it. And trust me, I never miss."

Realizing that Ali was not to be underestimated, Hosni's demeanor shifted.

"Roulan!" Ali called out, and the Beast-Slayer understood the unspoken command. She moved toward Hosni, who drew his sword and aimed for her neck. However, Roulan effortlessly evaded his attack and delivered a powerful punch to his face, then swiftly restrained him with her forearm around his neck.

"Who is the military chief here?" Ali demanded.

A man wearing a red robe stood and replied, "I am!"

"If you care about your king, ask your soldiers to bring my friends," Ali ordered.

The military chief turned his gaze toward his captive king and realized the severity of the situation. "I'm not going to do that," he warned.

The next thing he saw was a dagger flying from Ali's hand, piercing his chest. He fell to the ground.

Ali turned his attention to another general, asking him the same question. Hoping the general had learned from his fallen comrade, he went towards the door and unlocked it. Outside, over forty soldiers stood ready to attack, but the general restrained them.

"The military chief is dead, and our king will follow if we don't bring the prisoners," the Turban general declared, raising his voice. "Go and fetch them."

More soldiers flooded into the council chamber, and the sound of bells filled the air. Ashil grew anxious and approached Ali to whisper, "How are we getting away from here?"

Ali placed his hand on Ashil's shoulder reassuringly. "Don't worry, my brave friend. We are not going to die today."

The soldiers brought the captive rebels, who, despite their battered state, were overjoyed to see Ali alive and their friend Roulan.

"Ask your soldiers to move away," Ali commanded the general.

The general resisted, stating, "Not until you free our king."

"There are still four generals who would be happy to carry on after you!" Ali warned, glancing at Roulan.

Recognizing that Ali was not bluffing, the chief reluctantly obeyed and ordered his soldiers to step aside. Ali walked toward the balcony and saw hundreds of soldiers and commoners gathered in the palace courtyard.

His plan was to take King Hosni with him until they were out of sight, and then release him. He knew such a request would not be accepted, but he had no choice. Placing his faith in Hosni's word was out of the question. While considering the various scenarios, his ears caught the sound of a horn. He turned his gaze to Nisay, whose face lit up with a wide smile.

"Nora!" he exclaimed.

It was Token's horn, and the sight of soldiers rushing to the top of the wall indicated one thing: Nora had brought an army to Turba. Everything had changed for Ali. He now had the leverage, with King Hosni at his mercy and the Token army under his command. He couldn't determine their exact numbers, but he knew that the Turban soldiers were significantly depleted, as many had been dispatched to Solum.

Ali took two steps forward and addressed the prime advisor, "Summon all the leaders of the houses to the palace square"

"How dare you command me!" The prime advisor sneered, spitting on the ground, "You're just a shepherd!"

Before Ali could react, a commander interjected. "Lord Ali, what is your purpose in summoning the leaders of the houses?"

Ali stared at the commander for a moment and then pointed at King Hosni. "Turba has suffered greatly because of this man, and it is time for his trial."

The commander challenged him, asking, "And who are you to judge him?"

"I am not the judge," Ali replied firmly. "It is you, the Turbans, who will pass judgement. Now go and bring me the leaders of the houses!"

Without uttering another word, the commander swiftly disappeared from sight.

Leah approached Ali and whispered, "Let's get out of here."

"Where?" Ali asked. "The queen is surrounded by twenty thousand soldiers. This is our chance to strike the enemy and save Solum."

Before Leah could respond, Ali spotted the commander returning on horseback, accompanied by hundreds of men.

"Lord Ali!" the commander called out. "I have brought the men you requested."

Ali raised his hand in gratitude and addressed the people of Turba gathered in the square. "I am certain that many of you have had the opportunity to read about Turba's history. Some of you are old enough to remember how this kingdom used to be before the empire took it from us, the Turbans."

He paused briefly and continued, "But look at us now. Half of us are living in ignorance. Poverty is ravaging our lives, and instead of worrying about how to take care of our loved ones, our minds are consumed with paying taxes to the emperor! Is this fair?"

Ali allowed his words to sink in before proceeding. "No, it is not! I want us to reflect on how we ended up in this dire situation. This man, who claims to be a king, conspired with the emperor to usurp the dynasty of Tamim."

A voice emerged from behind, questioning, "How do you know this?" It was the prime advisor.

Ali turned to him. "Prime advisor, perhaps you can enlighten us on how this man ascended to the throne?"

The prime advisor rubbed his forehead in frustration. "This is beyond the understanding of a shepherd like you."

"Most of the Turban people are shepherds. Are you suggesting they should be excluded?" Ali countered without waiting for a response. "According to Turban law, when the dynasty of a Turban king is extinguished, a new king must be elected by the leaders of the houses."

"Now I ask you, the people of Turba, to raise your hands if you voted for this man."

No one in the crowd raised their hand.

"This man was placed here by a stranger to rule over you. But he didn't even do that. He took your children and your gold and handed them over to his own kind," Ali declared.

King Hosni chuckled lightly. "And you are the king who will restore their glory, aren't you?"

Roulan tightened her grip on his neck with her forearm, but Ali raised his hand to halt her. "Let him speak, Lady Roulan."

She released her hold, allowing King Hosni to continue. "I have kept this kingdom safe for over a decade. If it weren't for me, you would have suffered the same fate as Solum."

Ali turned his attention to the people gathered in the palace square. "If my intention was to rule, I could signal the Token army to tear down these walls and conquer this kingdom. But I would never do that," He paused, "Here is what I propose: option one, myself and my friends walk away from Turba with the Token army, leaving you to live under this dictator's rule. Option two, we adhere to our law and choose a king from among the leaders of the houses. We would then join forces with Token and Solum in their quest to restore the peace that once existed."

Ali fell silent, observing the faces in the crowd. Many appeared perplexed by the choices presented to them. Suddenly, a man emerged from the masses. Ali recognized him as Othman, the commander who had gathered the leaders of the houses earlier.

"People of Turba, most of you are likely leaning toward the first option, choosing to maintain our current way of life and remain safe from the empire's wrath. But what kind of life is this?" Othman proclaimed, raising his voice.

"I am a commander, a seventh-ranked soldier, and I cannot even afford to get married. Why? Because our wealth is handed over to the empire, and what do we receive in return? Safety," he scoffed, "The only danger we face is the empire itself."

The prime advisor interjected sharply, "Beware, ignorant traitor! The true peril lies with the rebels who hold a blade to the neck of your king."

"Silence!" Othman yelled, "The rebels have reclaimed Token and Solum and restored them to their rightful queens. The leader of the rebels is married to Ceres' daughter. He could have ruled the entire world if he wished. Instead, he chose to stand next to us, the Free People. I want to live a decent life. I want to be able to marry, raise my children, have access to education, and afford a healer when I am sick. These are not unreasonable requests; they are my rights as a Turban," Othman passionately shouted, "So think about it. Do you have these things? If you do, go back to your lives. If not, follow Ali's counsel."

The commander raised his hand high in the air and proclaimed, "From this moment forward, I will follow Ali until a worthy king is elected."

The commander's words resonated deeply with the Turbans, and even the soldiers in the square raised their hands in agreement.

The commander's voice boomed, "Turba is free, and it shall always be!"

CHAPTER 20

It was the fifth day of the siege, and Aznek's frustration continued to grow as no news came from Leah and the others. Communication had been cut off between her and Token, and her army of eight thousand soldiers stood little chance against the three opposing armies. Sam, her trusted advisor, suggested for her to use the tunnel to escape and save herself and her son. However, Aznek refused, determined to stay and fight.

"Your Grace, we are outnumbered, and our allies are not with us. I do not believe it is wise to engage in the battle," warned Sam.

"You are my prime advisor, for God's sake! Open your mind!" Aznek shouted, "Battle does not always have to be fought with swords and catapults."

Sam looked at her in confusion. "Let us go to Stephen's team," she suggested.

Though the prime advisor did not understand her reasoning, he dared not question her command. They made their way to the laboratory, only to find everyone sitting idle, not doing anything. All the scientists got to their feet and knelt when they saw their queen.

Aznek's expression revealed her dissatisfaction, but instead of expressing her disappointment, she posed a question, "Why do you believe we need scientists?" she inquired.

Silence filled the room, and the queen's gaze fell upon one of them.

"You there, what is your name?" she asked.

"Carl, Your Grace," the man replied.

"Why do you believe the council employs you and provides you with a wage every week?"

Carl spoke softly, "To serve you, Your Grace!"

The response was not what she had hoped for, but she could not fault him. She proceeded to ask each scientist in turn, and their answers all proved to be disappointments, until she reached the last one—a short man in his twenties with long black hair cascading to his shoulders.

"Scientists are meant to make the impossible possible," the young man stated.

The queen's interest was piqued, though she revealed no emotion.

"And what is your name?" she inquired.

The young man lowered his head as he replied, "Albert, Your Grace."

"Raise your head when speaking to your queen," the queen commanded. "Do you truly believe we can make the impossible possible?"

Albert raised his head but found it difficult to meet the queen's gaze.

"Your Grace, before the invention of ships, if you were to tell anyone that humans could cross vast distances of hundreds of miles without drowning, they would say it was impossible."

The queen made no immediate comment on Albert's words. Instead, she addressed the entire group. "Who agrees with Albert?"

Every scientist in the room raised their hand. The queen spoke once more, "Surviving this siege may seem impossible, but who can make it possible?"

Albert raised his hand once again, prompting the queen to take two steps closer to him.

"How?" she asked.

"I do not know how, Your Grace," Albert replied honestly.

Laughter erupted throughout the room, filling the air, until the queen's piercing scream cut through it all, demanding, "Silence!" She said, and then dragged her eyes back to Albert. "You volunteered to save us from the enemy, and you don't even know how?"

Albert locked eyes with the queen as he spoke, his voice steady and determined. "Your Grace, I must confess that I do not possess a ready-made solution. However, I firmly believe that for every problem, there exists a solution. We may not know it immediately, but if we take action and work towards finding it, we will have a shot."

Aznek remained silent for a while, contemplating his words. Finally, she made her decision.

"Sir Albert, you are in charge now. Get us out of this siege!" she declared firmly.

The queen retired to her chamber, feeling a sense of desperation. Her weapon storage had been destroyed, her castle was under siege, and the man who could have aided her was captured by the enemy. Yet, she knew she couldn't give up. She had faced worse challenges in the past and emerged victorious.

The following morning, she instructed her prime advisor to gather the people of Solum in the palace square and the surrounding alleys. Standing on the balcony, she appeared in a war suit rather than her usual regal attire. thousands men and women gazed up at her, their eyes filled with hope. It pleased her to know that even in such dire circumstances, her people still placed their faith in her, from the elders to the children.

"When faced with a crisis, people can be divided into two groups: those who think about how to solve it, and those whose minds and hearts can only see failure," she began, drawing her sword.

"The first thing we do when we come into this world is cry. As we grow, we learn how to laugh and how to cheer. That is the way of life. We encounter crises and learn how to confront them because it is in our nature. Sadly, many lose this attitude and prefer to do nothing, hoping that the crisis will resolve itself. But it never does!"

She paused, collecting her thoughts before continuing.

"Today, the enemy is at our doorstep, demanding that we give up our kingdom. Some might think that surrendering will spare our lives. Perhaps it will, but it will only return us to the state we were in five years ago—starvation, ignorance, and oppression. But what kind of life is that?"

Raising her sword high, she screamed, "We will not surrender this great kingdom! We would rather fight and die!"

A soldier from the crowd spoke up, "How can we fight without catapults and explosives?"

"Our victory does not depend on our weapons, but on our will to defend our home and our loved ones," the queen proclaimed.

"Are you asking us to die?" Another question arose from the crowd.

"No!" the queen shouted, her voice emotional. "I am asking you to be prepared to kill the enemy and keep your families safe."

No one else uttered a word as the queen concluded her address.

"Prepare yourselves to win, and if you have even an ounce of doubt, s tay in your houses and wait for the enemy to rape your wives and enslave y our children."

The next day, Aznek sought out Albert, the new scientist, hoping he would surprise her. When she entered his presence, he bowed and rose when the queen requested him to do so.

His face was pale, and he could hardly mumble a word.

"Speak, Sir Albert. I'm not going to hang you if you don't find us a solution," said the queen, but before he could reply, she added, "However, the enemy will!"

Albert lowered his head and spoke in a soft tone, "Your Grace, it's not the real enemy I'm concerned about."

"If you're implying that there's a traitor among us, then you've wasted my time. I am already aware." the queen said.

"Can I show you something?" Albert asked, and when she nodded, he led her to a nearby room.

Removing a carpet, Albert revealed a hatch, and upon opening it revealed several black balls surrounded by a thick red line. They were about the size of a human head. The queen suspected they were some form of explosives and asked her new scientist to confirm it.

"Your Grace, I have examined the contents of these balls. They are a powder known as Blinding Powder," Albert explained.

"Blinding powder?" the queen echoed.

"I have read about it. When thrown in someone's face, it blinds their eyes for hours," Albert clarified.

Curious, the queen picked up one of the balls and inquired, "Who made these, and why weren't they in the unit storage?"

"Sir Stephen," Albert revealed. "I just discovered this now."

He handed her a parchment, and as she read it, she realized that Stephen had been making these balls for the enemy, not for her.

She gritted her teeth in frustration. "*Stephen!*"

Albert said nothing, patiently waiting for her to compose herself.

"Sir Albert, can we use them against the enemy?" the queen asked.

"With a few catapults and skilled shooters, they could help us destroy the enemy," Albert replied confidently.

"You have two days to prepare this," the queen commanded.

Albert smiled proudly and responded, "I have already begun working on it with my team. The catapults will be ready tomorrow! All we need are skilled shooters."

The queen returned his smile and praised him, "Good job, Sir Albert!"

***

Meanwhile, the three armies were positioned just a few hundred feet away from Solum's castle. King Bao of Turang was furious at what Nisay had done to him, and he urged Kanoot and the Turban leader to tear down Solum's walls.

"Why the rush, King Bao?" Kanoot questioned, with a cunning smile. "We shall wait patiently until they willingly open the gate for us."

Kanoot's plan hinged on Stephen, his trusted spy, who was tasked with creating a diversion and securing the opening of the gate. Unbeknownst to them, however, tragedy had struck. Their spy had been killed.

Filled with anxiety, Kanoot and Bao eagerly awaited Stephen's arrival, anticipating his support in their mission. Yet, instead of Stephen's presence, a Turban commander rode forward alone, clutching a parchment bearing King Hosni's seal.

The Turban leader read the parchment and solemnly declared to his companions, "Lord Kanoot, Lord Bao, I'm afraid I must withdraw."

Anger burned in the eyes of both Kanoot and Bao, and the Turban leader added, "Forgive me, but these are the orders of the king."

Kanoot walked toward the Turban leader, his voice filled with fury, "Go to hell, you and your king. Tell him that he's going to be next!"

The army's leader remained silent, but he commanded his army to withdraw.

Bao, nervous, turned to his companion Kanoot. "What are we going to do?"

"Stephen should be here any minute, and we will still destroy this whore who calls herself a queen," Kanoot replied, his determination unwavering.

However, instead of Stephen's arrival, a vast army approached them. Kanoot initially believed it was from King Hosni, who had perhaps changed his mind. But his fear intensified when he saw the leaders at the front—Ali and his friends.

The army halted a few hundred feet away, but Ali continued to advance towards the middle of Kanoot's men, accompanied by Nora, Nisay, and the Turban commander, Othman.

Kanoot and Bao mirrored their movements, stepping forward to meet them.

As Nisay approached, he placed his hand on his cheek, a reminder of the wound he had inflicted to the Turangy king.

Bao remained passive, while Ali spoke first, his voice filled with authority, "Kanoot, Bao, take your army and walk away."

Kanoot laughed defiantly. "Not before I claim Solum."

Nisay turned to Ali, remarking, "I told you he's insane."

Ali smiled at Nisay before redirecting his attention to Kanoot, stating firmly, "You have no leverage. You are outnumbered, and your spy is dead."

Kanoot's disappointment was palpable, but before he could react, Ali escalated the pressure. He reached into a bag and produced a severed head, unmistakably that of Hosni. With a swift motion, he tossed it near Kanoot's horse, leaving both Kanoot and Bao visibly shocked.

"Present this to your emperor," Ali proclaimed triumphantly. "You ventured here with the intent to claim a kingdom, yet, you have lost another."

Kanoot, a seasoned military man, realized the futility of his position. He had no choice but to accept Ali's terms and reluctantly leave Solum, defeated.

CHAPTER 21

It was Thaar's third visit to the empire, and this time it was markedly different. She was welcomed as if she were a council member, offered a whole residence with servants.

Ceres had been sick for over a year, and no healer had been able to provide relief except Thaar. While she hadn't cured him completely, he had experienced zero pain since she had touched him. Despite Kanoot's failure and the loss of Turba, Ceres didn't care as much, because he had started regaining his strength. Perhaps there was hope for a complete recovery, after all.

The guard allowed Thaar into Ceres' residence. It was the first time she had seen Ceres in such a joyous state, and she was pleased.

"Your Highness, you look well today," Thaar began.

Ceres stood up, placing both hands behind his back. "Thanks to you!" he said. "Is this a good sign?"

Thaar nodded, and Ceres asked further, "Why couldn't I simply take the medicine you gave me and live with my illness?"

"If only it were that simple, Your Highness," Thaar responded.

Ceres' smile vanished, and Thaar noticed the change. She decided to shed some light on the matter.

"Think of it as facing a dangerous enemy. Winning a single battle against them doesn't make you victorious. To win the war, you must defeat them completely. In other words, the first time I gave you the medicine, it surprised the Black Spiders and weakened them. However, they will soon recognize the medicine's effect and fight back."

"So you're saying the pain will return?" Ceres asked.

"If we do nothing, Your Highness," Thaar affirmed with a smile. "The good news is that your body has responded to the treatment I provided, and I can assure you that the chances of curing them are higher now."

Ceres removed his robe and top, then laid down on his belly, allowing his healer to do her work. Thaar massaged his back with an ointment and handed him a small jar containing liquid. She instructed him to drink two drops before going to sleep.

"When shall I see you again?" Ceres inquired while buttoning his shirt.

Thaar understood his implication and smiled as she replied, "You don't need me here every day. Besides, I have a family to take care of."

Ceres had never felt as dependent on anyone as he did in front of this woman. He wished she could stay in the castle, where he could simply command her to do whatever he desired. However, he needed her mind, and that could never be forced, especially when it belonged to an intelligent woman like Thaar.

"As you wish. I entrust my life to your hands!" Ceres declared with a smile.

Thaar excused herself and left. The guard entered and asked Ceres, "Do you want our men to follow her?"

Ceres remained silent for a while, inhaling deeply, before replying, "There's no need. She is trustworthy. However, you can summon my generals to join me in the council."

Soon, all the generals arrived at the council chamber to find Ceres seated on his throne. Kanoot was among them, feeling fearful and doubting that he would leave the council alive. After kneeling before their emperor, Ceres invited them to sit, and asked Kanoot for a briefing.

"We had Solum under siege, and the queen's army was outnumbered with no one to lead them. Sadly, things fell apart in Turba, and Ali appeared with an army," Kanoot explained, pausing to observe Ceres, who remained silent. "Suddenly, the balance shifted. We were about to face the armies of Token, Turba, and Solum. When Ali suggested sparing bloodshed and proposing an alternative..."

Kanoot struggled to find the words but was interrupted by Ceres, who yelled, "Carry on!"

"I believed it would be better for us to walk away, as we stood no chance against them. It was my decision, your highness, and I take full responsibility," Kanoot confessed.

Ceres turned to the generals and asked, "What do you think?"

Ben, the prime advisor, smiled and responded, "The odds were in Ali's favor. I believe it was the right decision."

The other generals concurred with Ben, and Ceres offered a smile to Kanoot before asking, "Since we all support your decision, how do you suggest we retaliate?"

Kanoot requested permission to stand, and Ceres granted it. "The queen and her rebels have taken Solum, Token, and Turba. I don't think launching a direct attack would be wise. Even if we muster a formidable army, the possibility of losing the battle cannot be ignored. And it is imperative that we prevent such an outcome from occurring, do you know why?"

The financial chief chimed in, "We would lose our men."

Kanoot nodded and continued, "For sure, but that's not what I fear the most. What I fear is that our enemy will grow in the eyes of the commoners. Not only their own kingdoms but even within our own empire. They will view Aznek and Ali as heroes who can offer them the luxurious life they have always dreamed of—gold, no taxes, and freedom of speech."

Ceres felt a figurative slap to his face. He had contemplated this scenario before, reassuring himself that it was merely a hypothetical situation. But now, as Kanoot brought it to his attention, it felt frighteningly real.

Ben spoke up, voicing his concern, "I hope you're not just trying to scare us, Lord Kanoot."

"No, my lord. But what if we reverse the situation? Instead of launching a direct attack, we could send well-trained soldiers disguised as bandits to the outskirts of each kingdom. They will spread terror, stealing from merchants, kidnapping children, and assaulting commoners. That way, the lands will lose the one essential thing that people desire even more than gold and land—safety."

Ceres had always relied on the wisdom of his council to rule the empire. Typically, he would not approve a proposal until he had examined every angle of it. However, what Kanoot suggested was a game-changer, and the emperor immediately agreed.

"Kanoot, assemble the soldiers you need and instill fear in the Turbans," Ceres commanded, then turned to his prime advisor. "Summon King Kemal and King Bao."

***

Nora was in the guest room, preparing to leave for her kingdom, when a servant entered and told her that Leah wanted to see her.

"Bring her in," Nora commanded, her voice firm and authoritative.

Leah entered the room, her presence drawing Nora's attention. Nora couldn't help but notice the distress etched on Leah's face. "Lady Leah, you don't look well. What is troubling you?"

Leah blushed. "The queen has exiled Ali!"

The five words Leah uttered left Nora speechless for a moment before. "Say that again?" she said.

Leah knew she had been heard, so she remained silent. Nora, sensing her distress, reached out and held both of Leah's hands.

"Don't worry, Leah. Ali is off-limits," Nora reassured her. "Despite the allegiance I swore to the queen, Ali takes precedence."

Leah let out a sob. "Ali made a mistake, Nora!" Tears streamed down her cheeks. "He went to Turba without informing his queen and the council."

"A mistake that brought Turba back," Nora replied, her smile filled with reassurance. "Go to Noah. I will speak with the queen."

Nora wasted no time and headed straight to the council chamber, where the queen was having a private meeting with her prime advisor. The guard tried to stop Nora, but she swiftly placed a blade against his neck, threatening him. The guard, showing no resistance, allowed Nora to pass through the gate.

Four guards came rushing behind her, but upon the queen's signal, they were dismissed. Nora locked eyes with the prime advisor and said, "Leave us."

Sam, the prime advisor, was about to exit the room, but Aznek intervened, saying, "Sam is my prime advisor, and whatever you have to say, you can say it in his presence."

"Very well, Your Grace," Nora replied, her tone tinged with sarcasm. "Why have you exiled Lord Ali?"

"That's none of your business, Queen Nora!" the queen retorted in a similar tone. "However, I will extend you the courtesy of an explanation. Ali made a mistake, and as his queen, I have punished him."

"A mistake that freed Turba!" Nora exclaimed, her voice rising in frustration.

Nora was about to continue, but Aznek interrupted, "You swore an allegiance, and yet here you are, disrespecting my council and contemplating breaking your oath. I will tolerate no more of this."

Nora took a few steps forward, her teeth clenched tightly. "You are only my Lady Queen until you mess up. Banning Ali will bring us destruction!"

"Is this a threat, Queen Nora?" the queen questioned.

Nora smiled, her tone unwavering. "Yes, it is! But not from me. It is a threat from Ceres and his allies. Without Ali, the world will remain in the hands of the empire."

When Aznek said nothing, Nora lowered her head slightly. "If you will excuse me, my lady, I am returning to my kingdom. I hope you will reconsider your decision."

The queen smiled, raising her hand dismissively as a signal for Nora to leave. Sam noticed the sadness in the queen's eyes and attempted to comfort her, but she dismissed him as well.

The queen retreated to her residence and invited Leah to join her for dinner. Surprised by the invitation, Leah arrived to find the table filled with a lavish feast. The queen, dressed in a red gown without her crown, appeared as if she was waiting for a relative.

"How do I look?" the queen asked, a smile gracing her face.

Leah controlled her anger and responded with a forced smile, "You look astonishing, Your Grace."

The queen extended an invitation for Leah to sit beside her and said, "You can call me Aznek, by the way."

Leah's eyebrows rose. "Aznek, as a friend?"

"No, as a sister," replied the queen.

Leah had reached her limit. The queen had banned her husband and now she was pretending to care about her like a sister. *Does she take me for a fool?*

"You're a woman who I respect, and I wouldn't mind serving you for the rest of my life. But I am human, and you just exiled my husband from your kingdom. Instead of giving me an explanation, you're..." Leah struggled to find words to express her frustration with the queen's actions. "Doing *this*."

The queen fell into a thoughtful silence, her gaze fixed on Leah, before she eventually broke it. "When I first met Nora and observed her interactions with Ali, I thought that she was in love with him," the queen confessed. "The strong friendship I witnessed between you and her further piqued my curiosity. But upon learning about Nora's feelings towards Nisay, I realized that what she had for Ali was not romantic love, but rather deep respect."

"In fact," the queen continued, "it wasn't just Nora who displayed such devotion. Roulan, the niece of the King of Turang, Commander Arsalan, and all those who stood by Ali's side exhibited unwavering loyalty. Witnessing their profound admiration left me utterly bewildered. Despite lacking royal lineage or any inherent claim to the throne, Ali emerged as the most respected and beloved individual I had ever encountered."

Leah was left momentarily speechless, a mix of pleasure and confusion swirling within her upon hearing the queen's words. She couldn't find the words to respond, so Aznek smiled and carried on, "I ventured to the Blessing Tree myself, delving deep into the story of Ali. It became clear to me just how remarkable your husband is—a courageous man, with a kind heart and the humility to decline the position of the new King of Turba."

Leah remained silent, her gaze fixed on the queen, her mind still perplexed by this unexpected revelation.

Aznek poured strawberry juice into both their mugs and took a few sips from her own before continuing. "Lady Leah, why do you think I exiled Ali?"

Leah hesitated, not reaching for her mug. "Because he went behind your back to Turba?"

Aznek chuckled before responding, "He liberated another kingdom for us, and as a result, I punished him. What kind of queen do you think I am?"

A queen with a massive ego, Leah thought to herself.

"There's a way out, Leah," the queen said, her tone shifting.

"What do you mean?"

"Ali doesn't have to die after the war. He can grow old with you," Aznek explained.

Leah's eyes filled with tears as she asked, "You know?"

"Yes, the Thinkers informed me," the queen revealed. "They also informed me that there is a way for Ali to break his oath. When I offered him this option, he refused. That's why I banned him. I gave him two choices: either renounce the Thinker's path or leave my kingdom."

CHAPTER 22

*A*znek found herself running through the woods, the barking of dogs growing nearer. She desperately called for help, but there was no one to answer her pleas. As she ran, her right foot was trapped in a branch protruding from the ground, causing her to fall. When she managed to stand up, she saw three men and four dogs surrounding her. She realized one of the men was Ceres when he spoke.

"And now, queen bastard, where is your Ali?" Ceres taunted.

Aznek grabbed a stick from the ground and spoke with resolve, "He's coming for you, and soon you will be defeated."

"Yet, you won't live to see that day," Ceres retorted, and then turned to his companions. "King Anand, King Kemal, release the dogs."

Ceres' allies obeyed his command, freeing the dogs from their restraints. The four dogs charged toward Aznek, barking ferociously. She knew she had no blade to defend herself. As they closed in, ready to devour her, Aznek refused to close her eyes, and prepared to face her fate and die as King Rajab had.

But just as the dogs reached her, a brilliant light enveloped the area, causing everything around her to disappear. When the light dissipated, Aznek found herself in the Toprak council. She had never been there before, but she recognized it from the crescent moons drawn on the walls.

"Oh no," she murmured, anticipating King Kemal's arrival. However, instead of him, a man she recognized appeared before her. He was dear to her.

"Sai?" she said, a tear sliding down her cheek.

"Hello, Queen Aznek," Sai greeted her with a smile.

Upon hearing his voice, Aznek broke down, crying and whimpering, "I'm so sorry you had to die because of me."

Sai approached her, offering comfort. "Everyone, except the Creator, dies. Thanks to you, I had the best death a rebel could wish for."

He thought his words would bring solace, but Aznek's tears continued to flow.

"Your son will grow up without a father. And not just any father, but a loving husband and a brilliant scientist," she lamented.

"Ali grew up without a father. Look at how he turned out."

Aznek finally managed to calm herself and, wiping away her tears, asked, "Why are you here?"

"To guide you on your quest," Sai replied, smiling.

"My sole purpose in this life is to restore the peace that once existed," Aznek expressed. Sai gazed at her, and she continued, "But I feel powerless without my allies. Nora, Nisay, Leah—they are all angry because of what I did."

"Do you regret exiling Ali?" Sai inquired.

Aznek couldn't find the words to respond, but Sai spoke on her behalf, "You banned Ali because he refused to assist you. And you made a wise choice."

"We both know what he has done for us," Aznek replied.

"So you need him to make the world a better place," Sai stated. "There's no shame in that. Great rulers become great through their allies."

Aznek took a deep breath, "In order for Ali to break his oath, two conditions must be met. Firstly, he would need to become a king in his own right. Secondly, he would require the blessing of his blood relatives to justify this act of oath-breaking."

Sai stared at her and asked, "And what are you waiting for?"

Aznek paused, considering the situation. "Ali doesn't want to be king, and all of his relatives are dead."

"It's still possible. I wouldn't have come to you if it wasn't," Sai assured her.

Aznek woke up from her dream, her body covered in sweat as if she had just run for miles. She sat up, reached for her jar of water, and took a drink. A smile crossed her lips.

She dressed quickly and made her way to the council chamber. Things were in disarray. She hadn't heard from Nora for over a week, and their last conversation had left them on bad terms. On top of that, she had banned Ali from her kingdom, which had angered her most trusted allies—Arsalan, Leah, and Sofia. But somehow, the conversation with Sai had stirred hope in her heart.

Entering the council room, Aznek immediately sensed that something was amiss. Sam, her prime advisor, could barely meet her gaze. Her patience wore thin.

"What is it, Lord Sam?" she demanded.

Sam spoke hesitantly, "A man arrived from Turba this morning. Kanoot and King Bao have launched an attack on many Turban tribes. They slaughtered thousands of people, including children and elders."

Aznek was rendered speechless for a moment, trying to comprehend the devastating news.

Sam continued, "Lord Othman dispatched a thousand men to pursue those responsible for our fallen comrades. Shall we provide him with additional reinforcements?"

The queen regained her voice and shifted her gaze to the left side. "Arsalan, Roulan, Sofia," she said, her tone resolute, "Assemble a thousand of our most skilled warriors and bring me Kanoot's head on a spike. Do not return without it." Suddenly, her voice turned into a scream, filled with concern. "Where is Leah?"

No one in the council room replied, and Aznek turned to Sam, urgency in her voice, "Find her, now!"

Leah, however, was not in the castle. She had gone to meet her husband in a secluded spot they had agreed upon in the nearby woods. She tied her horse to an isolated tree and before long, Ali appeared, riding towards her.

Memories of their early days together flooded Leah's mind. This place had been their sanctuary, where they could speak freely and find solace.

"I feel young again," Ali initiated as he dismounted his horse and embraced his wife.

Leah's heart raced as if she were meeting him for the first time. "After all," she responded, "the queen did the right thing by exiling you. Meeting you in secret makes me feel young again too."

After a long and romantic conversation, Leah mustered the courage to address the matter that consumed her from within.

"The queen told me there's a way out for you. Is it true?" she asked.

"It's impossible, Leah. Besides, I am not an oath breaker," Ali replied firmly. He took hold of her right hand. "Remember, we agreed on that."

Leah withdrew her hand abruptly and screamed, "You think this is a business deal we're conducting? No, for god's sake! This is your life we're talking about. You're breaking my heart, and you're jeopardizing Noah's future. Don't you want to be with your wife and son?"

Ali stood there, frozen, unable to utter a word, while Leah collapsed into tears.

"If there's a way out, that means there's no oath to break. And I know you want that too," Leah asserted.

Ali took a deep breath, contemplating the situation before responding. "If I were to accept that proposition and if the Turbans were to accept me as their king, there is a challenge we would face. I have no blood relatives who could bestow their blessings upon such a decision."

"You don't know that!" Leah screamed, her voice filled with frustration.

Ali matched her tone, saying, "Yes, I do. I've spent my whole life searching for one, and I've never succeeded."

Leah mounted her horse, her determination unwavering. She spoke firmly, "It's not your death I'm against. After all, we're all going to die. It's your *willingness* to die that makes me doubt if you even want to live. If Noah and I just mean nothing to you."

Without waiting for a response, she galloped away, feeling a mixture of anger toward Ali and frustration within herself. She knew how difficult the situation was for him, but it seemed worse for her. She would have to live with his death.

As Leah entered the castle, a guard informed her that the queen was looking for her. Instead of heading to the guest room, Leah made her way to the council chamber where Aznek was conducting her meeting.

"How is Ali, Lady Leah?" the queen inquired as Leah entered the room.

"Stubborn!" Leah yelled. Her gaze then fell upon three empty seats. "Where are Arsalan, Roulan and Sofia?"

The queen briefed Leah on the situation, and Leah immediately suggested joining her companions. The queen neither approved nor denied the idea, instead dismissing everyone else from the room, leaving Leah alone with her. Leah understood that the queen wanted to discuss Ali.

Once they were alone, the queen asked, "How is Ali?"

Leah's brow furrowed as she responded, "I don't know, Your Grace. On one hand, I've never seen a man so devoted to his family and cause like Ali, but on the other, he's unwilling to renounce the Thinker's ideals for us."

The queen contemplated sharing her dream with Leah but hesitated, fearing that Leah might consider her insane. "Don't worry about Ali," she said, "We'll find a way to change his mind. His heart hasn't healed from what happened to the Turban child who cried out his name before dying," the queen explained. "It will take some time."

Leah nodded, and the queen continued, "Our priority is to punish that bastard, Kanoot, who is killing innocents. Trust me, when Ali beheads him, we'll have the rebellious Ali back."

Leah rubbed her lips together, "What about the bloodline relative?"

The queen walked closer to Leah as she spoke, "Let me worry about that. As for you, go and bring me Ali."

***

The pain had completely dissipated, and Ceres felt reborn, filled with renewed motivation to conquer the world. Although he had lost control over Solum, Token, and Turba, as well as suffering the loss of two of his daughters, none of it mattered compared to the news he had received yesterday.

Thaar informed Ceres that his body was responding well to the treatment she had administered. She explained that he would fully recover within the next two months, as long as he remained under her constant care. Ceres had no objection to that.

The healer arrived early in the morning, carrying a small glass jar filled with a purple ointment that caught Ceres' curiosity. He asked, "What is this?"

"It's an ointment, Your Highness," Thaar replied, removing the jar's cover. "The cure I administered yesterday helped gather the Black-Spider in one place, but it had a side effect—a terrible pain throughout your body."

Ceres arched an eyebrow. "And this ointment is meant to alleviate that pain?"

"You are a very astute man, Your Highness."

"I should be, shouldn't I?" Ceres laughed. He continued, "Thank you for agreeing to relocate here to the Union."

Thaar smiled and said, "Shall we get to work, Your Highness?"

Ceres removed his robe and shirt, then laid down on his belly. Thaar began massaging him with the purple ointment, and Ceres felt an immediate sense of comfort.

"Lady Thaar, do you believe I am a good man?"

Thaar stopped massaging, taken aback by the question. "Your Highness, I do not believe I am qualified to answer that question."

Ceres maintained his gaze on the table as he responded, "I rule over two hundred thousand men and women. If I were to pose this question to any of them, they would claim that I am superior to the five gods." He heard Thaar giggle and then adopted a more serious tone. "I have a keen sense of judgment, and I wager that you possess the wisdom even the Speakers lack."

"I am greatly flattered, Your Highness," Thaar replied. "And I will provide you with an honest answer."

Ceres remained silent, allowing Thaar to continue.

"Good and bad can be deceptive," Thaar began. "In the past, giving birth to only girls was considered shameful. Many men and women took their own lives because of it. Yet now, people regard women who have only daughters as having angelic blood."

"People were foolish in the past," Ceres muttered.

"I agree," Thaar concurred. "But perhaps if we had lived in that era, we might have held the opposite opinion. Our perspectives are largely shaped by societal pressure."

Ceres turned his gaze toward Thaar. "But there is common sense."

"Exactly, Your Highness," Thaar responded. "Only you can determine whether you are good or not. Just be sure to answer honestly."

Ceres struggled to answer the question honestly, especially when the memory of murdering his wife, the love of his life, resurfaced. It was a painful reminder that hindered his self-reflection.

After Thaar finished her treatment and left, Ceres dressed himself and made his way to the council chamber. As he entered, he noticed the delight on everyone's faces, and it pleased him to see their happiness. Ben, his prime advisor, was the first to speak, waiting until Ceres had taken his seat.

"We have news from Kanoot, Your Highness," Ben announced, a smile evident on his face.

"Please proceed, Lord Ben," urged Ceres.

"Over two thousand Turbans were killed, and King Bao is pursuing Walid, Nisay's father." Ben reported.

Ceres's smile broadened at the positive development. "And how did Aznek react?"

"That's the best part, Your Highness," replied Ben. "She has dispatched an army of her finest soldiers."

Ceres remained silent, absorbing the information. Ben continued, "One of the leaders is the Turangy, the one who killed Ramessess."

Ceres gripped the armrests of his chair, his voice laced with determination, "I hope Kanoot does not disappoint me, and brings her back alive!"

With a renewed sense of purpose, Ceres knew that this was the opportunity to exact his revenge and achieve his ultimate goal. The anticipation of the impending confrontation fueled his resolve, and he eagerly awaited updates on the unfolding events.

CHAPTER 23

Walid and the surviving members of his tribe had been on the run for five days. They had been constantly searching for hiding spots, only to be discovered by their pursuers each time, to the extent that he suspected the presence of a traitor among them. There was no time to investigate, though. With only a hundred people left, they desperately aimed to reach Token for safety.

On the sixth night, they set up camp near a cave, and Walid decided it was time to change their strategy. Gathering all his people together, he addressed them with a determined tone.

"We can't keep running like this, especially with children among us," Walid declared.

Dirgham, one of his most trusted men, responded, "My lord, we seem to have no other choice."

Taking a deep breath, Walid continued, "We are the last remaining leaders of Okorom. If we fail to reach Token and reunite with the rest of our tribe, our twelve-hundred-year history will be lost."

His followers stared at him, unsure of his intentions. Walid pressed on. "We will split up. Twenty of us will head east toward Solum, while the rest will continue toward Token. Since Bao is after me specifically, the majority of you will have a higher chance of making it to Token alive."

Dirgham and the other house leaders expressed their concerns, believing it to be a suicide mission. Walid listened to each of their arguments, appreciating their worries.

"I understand your concerns, but consider this: do we risk the lives of over a hundred lions, including innocent children, or do we risk only twenty? It's critical, the majority have a higher chance of stealthily maneuvering and reaching Solum undetected."

With resolve, Walid nominated nineteen men to accompany him. Not one of them questioned the command, fully aware of the sacrifice it entailed—a certain death, but for a noble cause.

The following morning, the plan was set into motion. Walid and his companions took the eastern road, weaving through the trees. After half a day of riding, they were confronted by Bao. It didn't come as a surprise.

"Lord Walid, what took you so long?" Boa said smugly.

"I don't get the opportunity to kill someone like you every day. I was preparing a proper ceremony for the occasion!" retorted Walid.

Bao rubbed his chin, feigning contemplation. "Let me understand this correctly. You have twenty men, and we are five hundred well trained soldiers. By my calculations, each of you is planning to take down twenty-five of us." He covered his face with both hands and added, "I must admit, I am truly intimidated."

Laughter erupted among Bao's forces, filling the air with a boisterous energy. Bao, amused by the reaction, couldn't help but smile. "Very well, I shall put your mettle to the test. You will be given the challenge of proving yourself with a mere sixty soldiers. How does that sound?"

Without waiting for a response, Bao commanded the first rank of his army to attack.

Walid and his nineteen men drew their swords and charged toward their adversaries. Among them was Az, a seemingly unremarkable man—skinny and short – but in battle, only a few of the most skilled knights could survive his deadly blade.

Az galloped toward four Turangy soldiers. One of them threw a dagger at him, but Az effortlessly dodged it, maintaining his momentum as he rode towards them. He leaned low on his saddle, making it difficult for his opponents to target him accurately. Blades whirled above his head.

Two of the Turangy soldiers swung their swords at Az, but their attacks fell short. As they attempted to turn back, two daggers found their way into their chests, piercing their hearts.

The third Turangy, fueled by rage, charged towards Az, aiming for his chest. However, he proved to be unpredictable. In a swift move, Az leaped off his horse and thrust his blade into the Turangy's neck, ending his life.

Bao watched in astonishment at the skill and ferocity displayed by these warriors. He realized that even with a hundred men, victory was far from certain. In a fit of desperation, he bellowed, "Shoot them all, except the old man. I want him alive!"

Arrows rained down upon the Lions, none of whom could evade the onslaught. All were struck down, falling one by one like cut crops, except for Walid. He watched with defiant screams, shouting to challenge Bao to face him directly.

Bao remained silent, but he raised his bow and notched an arrow, taking aim at Walid's foot. However, Walid skillfully deflected the arrow with his sword.

Undeterred, Bao continued to shoot arrows, four finding their mark. One pierced Walid's shoulder, followed by another in his opposite shoulder, and two more in his legs.

The leader of the Lions could no longer stand, and Bao commanded his men to chain him and transport him to Turang.

***

Arsalan dismounted his horse upon entering one of the Turban tribal settlements and surveyed two lifeless bodies on the ground, their blood long since dried. He turned to address Sofia, his voice firm.

"Lady Sofia, we shall divide our forces. Take fifty soldiers with you to the eastern side of the village, and I will lead the remaining half to the west."

One of the soldiers' leaders voiced his concern, "My lord, what about our men stationed outside?"

Arsalan placed a reassuring hand on the leader's shoulder. "You will remain there and await my signal."

The leader placed his hand over his chest and replied, "Loaded and clear, my lord!"

Arsalan added a word of caution, "Lord Johnathan, be vigilant. The enemy may attempt to surprise you."

Sofia and her team meticulously inspected more than eighty-two tents, discovering no signs of life. Arsalan's experience mirrored the same grim outcome.

In his search for any survivors, Arsalan's heart sank when he encountered a gruesome sight—a puppy impaled by a spear through its belly. A young boy clung to its left leg, drenched in blood.

A voice interrupted Arsalan's grief from behind. "They were protecting each other!"

He wiped his tear-streaked eyes and turned to find Lady Izmir standing there, sheathing her sword. Surprised, he took a step towards her, "Lady Izmir, what are you doing here? I specifically instructed you to stay with the army."

Izmir smiled and replied, "Even a great swordsman like you may need assistance, Lord Arsalan."

"I've heard that your skills are on par with Roulan's, but it would have been safer for you to remain with the army outside," Arsalan remarked.

"A woman does not appreciate being compared to another woman. We are all great." Izmir playfully retorted.

Another tear slipped down Arsalan's cheek, which he discreetly wiped away with the back of his thumb.

Izmir looked at him, her eyes filled with intrigue, and remarked, "All these lives we lose every day, and a puppy makes you shed tears?"

"These tears I shed are filled with shame and regret," Arsalan explained, his voice heavy. "They were both so small and vulnerable. And yet, in their powerlessness, I could sense their unwavering dedication to protect one another."

Izmir, deeply moved by Arsalan's words and the poignant scene he described, felt a tear well up in her eyes.

Arsalan noticed Izmir's tears and recognized the need to share his own thoughts on the matter of innocents being harmed. But before he could delve into that discussion, he posed a question to her. "Lady Izmir, do you find pleasure in reading?"

She nodded, her gaze still full of surprise. Arsalan continued, sharing his thoughts. "Once, I read a parchment that spoke of the intricate structure of a puppy's body. It amazed me how this small creature was formed. Hundreds of interconnected bones covered by delicate flesh, with blood coursing through, giving life to its tiny frame. No man could create such a wondrous being, nor could those who would come thousands of years later. Yet, an ignorant person blinded by greed snuffed out its existence with a single blade."

Izmir stared at him, unable to conceal her admiration.

Arsalan added, "The little boy, recognizing the worth of this puppy, protected it with his life. Don't you believe that shedding tears is the least we can do for both of them?"

A smile played on Izmir's lips as she replied, "This little boy and his puppy are fortunate to have a man like you shed tears for them."

"They would have been even luckier if they had been rescued and lived in a home with a mother and father," Arsalan lamented.

Izmir fell silent momentarily, then walked toward a small structure made of bricks. Returning with two shovels in her hands, she handed one to Arsalan.

"My uncle once told me that when someone dear to us dies unjustly, we owe them four things," she shared.

"Bury them, pray for them, and bring justice," Arsalan anticipated, before adding, "I've never heard of a fourth, though!"

"Perhaps someone knows five," Izmir replied with a smile. "The fourth is to ensure that what happened to them does not befall other innocent lives."

A smile spread across Arsalan's face. She was clever – perhaps more clever than Arsalan himself, though he had not admitted it to himself for a long time.

Together, they dug two graves and laid the boy and his puppy to rest. They offered prayers and then made their way to the exit, where they encountered Sofia and her men.

With the sun on the edge of setting, Arsalan suggested camping in the nearby woods and waiting for Roulan and her team. The smell of blood lingered in his senses all night.

The following morning, the Beast-Slayer arrived with three hundred Solumy soldiers, accompanied by Ashil and Zaya. The leaders were all confused; they didn't know what their next move should be, as the enemy always seemed one step ahead.

Zaya proposed splitting up, arguing that continuously chasing the enemy hadn't yielded fruitful results.

But Sofia disagreed. "We might be able to intercept the enemy, but we have no knowledge of the size of Kanoot's forces."

"Then we are faced with a decision," Ashil interjected. His wife smiled at him, encouraging him to continue. "Either we stay together and continue pursuing Kanoot; it may be safer, but we may never find him. Alternatively, we split into two teams, which will increase our chances of finding the enemy, but it's riskier."

Arsalan couldn't disagree, but he decided to do what Ali would have done in such a situation: consult his friends.

The way Ashil presented the two scenarios persuaded everyone to vote in favor of splitting the armies. Arsalan led the first army, while Roulan took command of the second one, heading south.

For three days, Roulan, accompanied by Ashil and Zaya, rode without any sign of the enemy. On the fourth day, they even contemplated joining Arsalan in the east, but a soldier approached them with news that lifted their spirits.

"Lady Roulan, we have just spotted soldiers not far from here. They are wearing Union suits," the soldier reported.

Roulan stood up and grasped his arm. "How many of them?"

"Approximately one hundred," the soldier replied.

Roulan wasted no time, instructing him to prepare all her men. Then, she turned to Zaya and Ashil. "Select twenty skilled soldiers and follow me."

Roulan had learned through experience that deception was often the key to winning battles.

. She suspected that the one hundred soldiers spotted by her informant were merely a ploy by the enemy to mislead her. Her plan was to sneak around and investigate the area. Climbing tall trees, they extended their vision, but nothing peculiar caught their eyes. Roulan sent one of her men to fetch the rest of her army. Upon the soldier's return, the Beast-Slayer gave the signal to launch an attack on the Unionists.

Two hundred men advanced slowly toward Kanoot's soldiers, who remained in their position. Some were gathered around a fire, while others sat atop their horses or lay on the ground. A roar erupted from the two hundred men as they charged toward the enemy, brandishing their swords.

To their astonishment, none of Kanoot's soldiers made a move, yet they began to collapse the moment they were touched.

One of the Solumy soldiers turned over a fallen enemy and instantly regretted it. The dead man had been gruesomely mutilated, with his eyes gouged out and his forehead tattooed with the words, "You have been fooled."

"Lady Roulan!" the Solumy soldier cried out. "It's a trap! Run!"

Before he could finish his sentence, arrows rained down from all directions, decimating the entire group of two hundred men that Roulan had sent forward.

"Form ranks and use your shields!" Roulan screamed.

However, none of Kanoot's men appeared. But Roulan knew he wouldn't delay in making his presence known. True to her intuition, the ground started vibrating beneath their feet. Roulan extended her vision and saw a massive dust cloud behind a hill, with a well-armed force riding towards Roulan's people.

"I didn't realize you missed your husband so much, Lady Roulan. I will ensure that my sword will take you to him," Kanoot said.

"Shields!" Roulan commanded, and everyone swiftly positioned their shields in front of them.

Kanoot bellowed, "Archers!"

More than two hundred Unionist soldiers prepared their arrows, and upon Kanoot's signal, they let them fly. However, most of the arrows failed to find their mark among Roulan's men.

"We can't hold them much longer, Lady Roulan. We need to take action," Zaya yelled from behind her shield.

The Beast-Slayer felt trapped and devoid of options.

"Lady Roulan, surrender yourself, and none of your soldiers shall be harmed," Kanoot proposed, tauntingly.

Roulan shifted her gaze from Zaya to Ashil on her right, considering their words carefully.

"He kills children. There's no honor in his blood. Whether we surrender or not, he will still attack us," Ashil said. "Do not believe him."

Roulan then turned her attention to the other soldiers, seeking their thoughts on the matter. One of them raised his voice and declared, "We would rather die ten times over than surrender our leader."

A mixture of sadness and pride welled up within Roulan. She was saddened by the encroaching defeat, yet uplifted by the unwavering faith her comrades had placed in her.

"We have lived with honor, my friends, and so shall our deaths be!" Roulan screamed. "On my command, we shall launch our attack. Do not look back, and focus solely on the enemy. Let us teach them the lesson of honor and dignity before we depart this world!"

The cheers of her soldiers resounded, fueling their determination. Kanoot, on the other hand, grew ecstatic, eagerly anticipating the moment he could capture Roulan and bring her back to Ceres, where she would face the consequences of her actions.

CHAPTER 24

Walid struggled to maintain his balance; the pain from the arrows consumed his every movement. With great effort, he managed to stay on his feet as four guards approached him, forcefully dragging him towards the arena. Waiting for him there was a tall man, his towering figure holding a colossal sword in his hand. As the man removed his mask, Walid's heart sank with recognition. It was none other than King Bao, the very same man who had slaughtered his Lions and captured him.

"Lord Walid, what happens to a lion when we strip away its claws and canines?" said Bao.

Walid defiantly spat on the ground before replying, "A lion remains a lion, even without its roar. The same goes for a hyena like you."

Bao erupted into laughter, his amusement mingling with contempt. "I am glad to be seen as a hyena, that means I'll have the pleasure of severing the head of an old shepherd like you."

"The shepherd's son, Nisay, will avenge me. He will tear down these very walls and claim your throne," Walid retorted, a glimmer of satisfaction in his eyes. "And I see that he has already made his mark on you."

Walid smiled, his hand itching to rub his right cheek.

Without further hesitation, Bao commanded, "Bring him to the chopping block!"

Summoning the last remnants of his strength, Walid launched a surprise attack. With a kick, he shattered the leg of one of the Turangy soldiers, relishing the satisfying snap of bone. In one fluid motion, he followed with a powerful punch to the face of another soldier. However, his rebellion was swiftly quelled as a soldier pressed a sword against his throat.

Forcing Walid forward, the four soldiers guided him up the stairs, his head held high, his eyes filled with defiance as he locked gazes with Bao. When they reached the top of the stairs, the soldiers forcefully pushed his head down, seizing him for the execution that awaited.

Bao approached, raising his sword high above his head, poised for the final strike. With a chilling calmness, he inquired, "Any last words?"

In a voice filled with unwavering determination, Walid bellowed, "Bao, my son Nisay will bring these walls crashing down upon you, and he will sever your head from your shoulders!"

Without a moment's hesitation, Bao swung his sword, slicing through the back of Walid's neck. The leader of Okorom's head tumbled to the ground, rolling over the crimson-stained execution yard.

But the satisfaction Bao sought from murdering Nisay's father eluded him. Every time he caught sight of his scar in the mirror or felt its presence beneath his touch, it only served as a haunting reminder of Nisay's audacity. Bao, known as one of the world's most formidable swordsmen, had been humiliated by Nisay, his face marked with a scar that would forever tarnish his reputation.

Yet, there was one thing that could momentarily ease his torment—the Arena of Turang. The thrill of slaying gladiators ignited a twisted ecstasy within Bao, and despite the objections of his generals, he resolved to indulge in this bloodlust in the days to come. Donning his signature red and black leader's attire, Bao concealed his face behind a mask.

***

Roulan signaled her men and women, fully aware that her chances of survival were minimal. She had no choice but to either fight and die with honor or surrender and still meet her demise. Despite her love for Sai, the prospect of joining him in the afterlife did not excite her. It wasn't because she doubted the existence of a second life, but rather because she cherished her current life—the presence of her beloved son, her friends, and her burning desire to witness the day the empire would fall. After all this, she wanted to see victory.

Unfortunately, life doesn't always conform to the wishes of good people, and Roulan had a duty to fulfil—fighting for what was right. Positioned at the front line, a sword in her right hand and a dagger in her left, she joined the clash between her army and the enemy forces.

Amidst the chaos, she quickly identified her first opponent—a tall man donning a gray suit and wielding a massive sword. The Turangy warrior gracefully assumed a kneeling position to evade his strikes. Seizing the opportunity, she cut off his right foot, causing the towering man to collapse. Before he could emit his first scream, a dagger found its mark in his chest.

Retrieving the dagger, Roulan dispatched another assailant approaching her from behind. Once he was cut down, she hurled another dagger at an enemy riding a horse. Her primary objective, however, was to find her husband's killer—Kanoot. Her desire for vengeance was not solely driven by the need to avenge her spouse but also to tip the scales of the battle. Eliminating the leader was critical to winning the battle – it would demoralise the men and make them weaker.

Kanoot was not far from Roulan, ruthlessly taking the lives of her Solumy soldiers. He proved to be a formidable and merciless fighter, having slain over twenty soldiers, including two high-ranking individuals. Ashil and Zaya fought alongside Roulan, displaying the same determination and skill, cutting down anyone who stood in their path.

"Kill them all and bring me the Beast-Slayer!" Kanoot's voice boomed across the battlefield.

Roulan and her remaining twenty-five soldiers stood shoulder to shoulder, ready to face a force of over two hundred men. Even if they were all as skilled as Ali or Leah, the odds were stacked against them. However, Roulan conceived an idea and wasted no time in shouting Kanoot's name.

"You proclaim yourself the king of the Arena, yet you hide behind your soldiers!" Roulan accused Kanoot, her voice filled with conviction. "If you truly consider yourself a man, let us settle this in single combat."

Laughter erupted from the Unionist ranks. "Who would accept such a challenge?" echoed amongst them.

However, Kanoot had other intentions. Beating the Beast-Slayer would not only satiate his ego but also serve as a significant blow to Ali and Aznek. Roulan was one of their pillars, a hero in the eyes of the common people.

"Halt," Kanoot shouted, his voice cutting through the clash of arms. His soldiers and those of Roulan paused in their combat, frozen by his command. "Very well, Lady Roulan," he continued, his tone measured. "I shall honor your request and dispatch you to reunite with your beloved."

"My lord, this is madness!" one of the Unionist leaders screamed. "They call her the Beast-Slayer. She is highly skilled."

Kanoot turned, his face contorted with anger. Without uttering a word, he flung his dagger, striking a soldier and causing him to fall to the ground, gasping for breath. He then strode toward Roulan.

"Men, if she wins, you walk away!" Kanoot's voice thundered across the battlefield. He then addressed Roulan directly, his words laced with malice. "That was merely to give you false hope, so you could fight with everything you have. But make no mistake, you cannot emerge victorious."

Roulan recalled their previous encounter, where Kanoot had proven himself to be a merciless and swift combatant. He had effortlessly defeated her, but she was not in her prime during that encounter. She had been heavily pregnant and mourning the loss of her beloved Sai. He did not know her fighting skill – not truly.

Raising her sword, Roulan sprinted towards Kanoot. As she closed in, he attempted to kick her, but she anticipated the move and evaded to the left. Undeterred, she turned and swung her sword towards his neck, only to have it parried by his dagger. In response, Kanoot struck her belly with a powerful punch. He then tried to grab her arm, but Roulan's agility allowed her to evade his grasp, causing her to fall to the ground and roll back up.

Without delay, Roulan hurled a dagger at Kanoot, who effortlessly evaded it and charged towards her. Their swords clashed, each strike resonating with equal strength. Roulan recognized that Kanoot held the advantage of sheer muscle, making it impossible for her to sustain his forceful blows indefinitely. Recalling a strategy Leah had taught her, Roulan transitioned to a defensive stance, misleading Kanoot and preparing to surprise him.

She focused on blocking Kanoot's attacks rather than initiating her own. His strikes were so potent that she was forced to gradually retreat. Just as she was about to catch him off guard, her sword failed her and slipped from her grasp. Before she could retrieve her dagger, Kanoot positioned his blade against her neck.

Zaya, overcome with concern, attempted to move forward, but her husband restrained her.

"Consider yourself fortunate, as his highness wants you alive," Kanoot taunted, striking Roulan on the head with the pommel of his sword. She crumpled to the ground, and Kanoot bellowed, "Kill the rest!"

"Ashil, you were the greatest blessing in my life," Zaya whispered tearfully, her eyes brimming with sorrow.

"If I had known you would say that, I would have willingly walked into a trap long ago," Ashil replied, smiling sadly. He added, "You are the love of my life. I will find you in the next world."

Ashil and Zaya, like everyone else, were supposed to meet their end that day. However, fate had other plans. A horn reverberated through the air, originating from a Turban—a sight that seemed unbelievable to Zaya and Ashil. Initially, they assumed it was a reinforcement sent to aid Kanoot, but they soon realized their mistake when they recognized the leaders at the forefront: Ali and Leah, the beacons of hope for the Free People.

They were accompanied by their new ally, Commander Othman, along with an army of over two thousand soldiers. The tides shifted as they overwhelmed Kanoot's forces. When Ali spotted Roulan lying on the ground, he hurried to her side, hoping she was still alive. A smile played across his lips as he felt her breath against his fingertips.

Leah joined Ali, and gently touched Roulan's face, attempting to wake her up. Roulan opened her eyes, expecting to see her husband's face, but instead, she found her friend's concerned expression, realizing that she had not died.

Without uttering a word of gratitude, Roulan stood up and surveyed the battlefield. She was relieved to witness the enemy's army vanishing, but her attention quickly turned to the two missing individuals. She hurriedly approached a Solumy soldier and demanded, "Where are Zaya and Ashil?"

"Kanoot managed to escape. They went after him," replied the soldier.

Roulan turned to Ali, her voice filled with urgency. "Ali, please go after them. They don't stand a chance against him. Only you can stop him."

Ali didn't require the compliment to spur him into action; his seething anger alone was enough motivation. Gritting his teeth, he declared, "I'm not returning without Kanoot's head."

With determination burning in his eyes, Ali galloped into the woods, and Leah quickly followed suit, hoping to save Ashil and Zaya.

The couple pursued Kanoot relentlessly until they cornered him. He stood alone, unscathed, with his sword still firmly gripped in his hand.

"You two are the most foolish couple I've ever encountered. Instead of celebrating your fleeting victory, you came here to meet your death," Kanoot taunted, unsheathing his sword.

Ashil began counting, "One, two, three." Then he bellowed, "Now!"

The couple raised their swords and charged at Kanoot simultaneously. However, their strikes failed to find their mark; Kanoot was astonishingly quick, skillfully parrying their attacks as though he wielded two swords.

In a moment of opportunity, Zaya spotted a weak spot and instead of trying to strike Kanoot's sword, she knelt to avoid his attack. From her boot, she retrieved a dagger, aiming to pierce his belly. But Kanoot reacted, seizing her wrist and forcing her blade to drop. Ashil, unable to come to her aid, found his sword blocked by their opponent's defense.

Kanoot delivered a powerful kick to Ashil's abdomen and landed a punch on Zaya's face. Wielding his sword menacingly, he aimed for Zaya's neck, but her quick reflexes saved her from the lethal blow. It slashed instead across her thigh.

Ashil rose to his feet, lunging at Kanoot's vulnerable back with his sword. However, Kanoot seemed like a monstrous creature with eyes on the back of his head, blocking Ashil's blade with his dagger.

As he twisted, Kanoot's sword found its mark – piercing Ashil's chest and emerging from his back.

"Ashil!" Zaya screamed, standing defenseless and weaponless. She rushed towards Kanoot, but he seized her by the neck, retrieving his second dagger and redirecting it towards her throat. It was his favorite method of dispatching opponents, reveling in their agonizing demise.

Yet, as Zaya prepared to meet her end, an arrow suddenly struck Kanoot's blade. He turned his gaze to behold the last two individuals he wished to confront—Leah, who had nearly defeated him in their previous encounter, and Ali, the nightmare of every gladiator who believed himself to be the true King of the Arena.

Realizing that escape was his only option, Kanoot made his way to his mount and galloped away

Leah dismounted from her horse and rushed to check on Zaya. However, despite her own injuries, Umali's daughter disregarded her wounds and crawled toward her dying husband, Ashil, who struggled to cling to his last breaths.

"Ashil, stay with me. We'll take you to my mother, and she will heal you," Zaya pleaded, her voice filled with desperation. "Stay with me, I need you!"

Leah tore a piece of her shirt and used it to cover Ashil's wound, but the sight of the profuse bleeding left her with little hope. She knew that he was fading away.

Ali gripped Ashil's other hand, his own tears streaming down his face. "We'll need a brave man like you in the coming battles," he whispered.

Ashil spoke weakly, blood trickling from his mouth. "Zaya, I'm grateful to die in your arms," he managed to say before turning his gaze towards Ali. "Take care of this woman as if she were your own blood."

Ali, unable to contain his emotions, sobbed uncontrollably.

Ashil added, "It was an honor to fight alongside you, Lord Ali."

Ashil then turned his attention back to his wife, offering her one final smile before his eyes fluttered closed. His last breath came out weakly, and he relaxed in Zaya's arms, going limp.

Zaya collapsed onto his chest, consumed by grief, her cries echoing through the air.

"Roulan will be here any minute. You take Ashil and Zaya to Umali," Ali instructed Leah, his voice filled with determination.

Leah stood, her confusion evident. "And what about you?"

"Shame on me if Kanoot lives to see another day," Ali declared resolutely.

Leah couldn't help but scream before he took off, "At least take a horse!"

"It will only slow me down," Ali replied.

Who would agree to such a thing? On average, a horse was six times faster than a running man. While Ali possessed extraordinary abilities, he was still a human and could never match the speed of a horse.

It wasn't a matter of insanity, but rather a strategic plan that didn't accommodate the use of a horse. Ali knew exactly where Kanoot was heading. A defeated and solitary man had only one place to seek solace — home.

Ali understood that there was only one route to the Union, and instead of taking the conventional path on horseback, he opted for a shortcut through the dense forest and treacherous hills.

He didn't know how many miles he had run, whether it was one or five, but he didn't care. Ali just kept running, consumed by thoughts of Sai—the mastermind Kanoot had taken away from Roulan and their son. He couldn't help but think of Ahmed, the little boy who had called out for him, and how Ali wasn't there for him. The rage inside him grew, urging him to push even harder, disregarding the challenges of the treacherous road.

Ali reminisced about the first time he met Ashil—a young man brimming with life and love, who tragically died before witnessing the joy of raising a child.

"Kanoot!" Ali's voice reverberated through the air.

After covering a mile, Ali's vantage point atop the hill revealed Kanoot mounted on his horse, approximately six hundred feet away. Rather than heading directly towards Kanoot, Ali turned and sprinted in the opposite direction, following a shortcut that would lead him to a location where he anticipated Kanoot would be after galloping three miles.

Impatience consumed Ali, so he removed his armor and the belt holding his sword and dagger, hoping to increase his speed. Finally, he reached the road, positioning himself at a point where Kanoot had yet to arrive. He stood unwavering, waiting for his enemy to appear—and appear he did.

Kanoot galloped relentlessly, showing no intention of stopping. He aimed to trample Ali with his horse, striking from behind with a determination to overwhelm his opponent.

Ali remained rooted to the spot, as if ready to face the charging steed alone. As the horse drew nearer, Ali snatched a hefty rock from the ground and took aim at Kanoot. He hurled it, and the rock struck Kanoot's chest with a forceful impact. The shock was so severe that Kanoot lost control of the reins, tumbling to the ground.

Rolling over, he regained his footing, only to witness Ali still standing—unarmed and seething with anger.

"Ali in the flesh!" Kanoot exclaimed, unsheathing his sword. "You want to join little Ahmed?"

Ali clenched his fist and gritted his teeth. Patience was key.

"I will kill you, and soon, you will join little Noah," Kanoot retorted, lunging towards Ali with his sword, intent on severing his enemy's neck. However, the rebel leader was resolute and swift. Taking a knee, he spun, striking Kanoot's belly with his elbow. The blow was so powerful that Ali wasted no time, rising like a force of nature and delivering two fierce punches to Kanoot's face.

Kanoot staggered backward, yet he did not fall, nor did he relinquish his sword. Taking a few steps back, he wiped the blood from his nose using the back of his forearm. His anger surged upon seeing the crimson stain, and he launched another attack. This time, Ali seized his opponent's wrist, exerting pressure until the sword slipped from Kanoot's grasp and into Ali's hand. He then delivered a swift kick to Kanoot's chest.

This time, Kanoot fell before even considering his next move. Ali positioned his blade at his adversary's neck. A droplet of blood formed under the blade.

Kanoot realized his time had come. "You may kill me, but little Ahmed will remain dead."

Pressing the sword harder against Kanoot's neck, Ali commanded him to stand—and Kanoot obeyed.

"What do you think will happen when your head is separated from your body?" Ali questioned.

"I'll burn in hell, probably!" Kanoot laughed, "Hell, heaven, the gods – they are mere illusions created by kings to control fools like you. After death, there is nothing but ashes."

Ali maintained his sword against Kanoot's neck and calmly responded, "You seem quite certain. Have you ever experienced death?"

"That applies to you as well, believer of heaven," Kanoot retorted.

A smile crossed Ali's face as he replied, "Indeed, neither of us can claim absolute certainty. However, as a believer in the Creator, I am choosing the safest path. If I am wrong, I have nothing to lose. But you, on the other hand, have much to lose. If the Creator exists, you will suffer in the depths of hell."

Confusion and anger flickered in Kanoot's eyes. "Is this some sort of redemption, an attempt to recruit me to your cause?"

Ali released his grip on the sword, "No, it is simply to ensure you know where your ultimate destination lies."

Without allowing Kanoot to utter another word, Ali summoned all his strength and swung his sword towards his opponent's neck. The blade was razor-sharp, and as Ali struck, he felt as if he were cutting through air. The next sight that greeted him was Kanoot's severed head rolling to a halt at his feet. Blood pooled on the dirt beneath him.

It was over.

CHAPTER 25

While the war still raged on, Aznek felt compelled to host a celebration to commemorate her and her allies' triumph in bringing another kingdom under her rule. It was also a moment to seek justice for her mastermind, Sai, whose life had been taken before her eyes. Nora, burdened by the affairs of Token, could not join the festivities and remained behind to safeguard her own kingdom. On the other hand, Nisay eagerly attended, his heart filled with delight at the prospect of reuniting with his friends.

Throughout the night, the kingdom buzzed with energy, as its inhabitants indulged in merriment. The streets were alive with music, and feasts adorned every corner of the city. Sleep eluded the people, consumed by the joyous atmosphere.

The following morning, Aznek summoned Ali to a council meeting, where they found themselves alone. Ali understood the purpose of this meeting, and the weight of the impending conversation settled upon him.

After the customary discussions, the queen broached the main topic. "Why do you believe I should be the Lady-Queen?"

Ali, aware of the direction this conversation was taking, chose his words carefully before responding, "Your Grace, you possess a remarkable blend of intelligence and courage. You hold a deep sense of care for every innocent person, treating them as if they were your own. These qualities are unique, and I cannot think of anyone else who embodies them as you do."

The queen's gaze remained fixed on Ali as she posed another question, "And what about my four royal bloodlines?"

Ali hesitated briefly, contemplating his answer. "While it may serve as a compelling argument to sway the commoners, it alone does not define one's ability to rule with excellence."

Aznek rose from her seat and made her way toward the windows on the left side of her council room. Placing her hand behind her back, she gazed out at the sprawling palace square as she began to speak.

"We have liberated three kingdoms and vanquished many powerful adversaries, and none of this would have been possible without you," Aznek declared, her voice carrying a sense of gratitude. She turned to face Ali, her eyes fixed upon him. "Tell me, Ali, do you know of anyone more capable than yourself to rule Turba?"

Ali attempted to respond, "Your Grace..." he began, but Aznek was insistent.

"Answer the question, Ali!"

"I am deeply honored by your words, Your Grace," Ali replied, choosing his words with care. "But it is not for me to decide who is best suited to rule Turba." He met the queen's gaze, his voice unwavering. "And it is not for you either."

A smile graced Aznek's lips, a flicker of amusement in her eyes. "I couldn't agree more. It is up to the Turbans, isn't it?"

Ali nodded, acknowledging the truth in her words. In response, the queen called out, summoning a guard into the room.

"Bring them in," she commanded, and as the guard complied, the council members and Commander Othman entered, accompanied by four unfamiliar Turban men.

Aznek motioned for everyone to take their seats, and then she turned her attention to one of the Turbans, urging him to speak. The man, Omar, appeared to be in his sixties, with a white beard and piercing black eyes. He wore an orange robe and a white turban, a mark of his authority.

"Your Grace, my lords," Omar began respectfully, addressing the room, "My name is Omar, and I am one of the house leaders in Turba. Despite possessing the wealth and influence to easily claim the title of King of Turba, I choose not to do so."

Roulan stroked her chin thoughtfully before posing a question. "Are you suggesting that there are individuals who reject the allure of power?"

Leah, seated beside Roulan, was quick to respond. "I know of one such man!" she exclaimed, the implication clear to everyone present.

The queen interjected, "Perhaps we should allow Lord Omar to continue," Aznek suggested, a smile playing on her lips.

Omar cleared his throat, coughing twice before resuming his speech. "Lady Roulan is not mistaken. Power is inherent in our nature, much like the need for sustenance and other desires. In fact, that is precisely what led us astray when King Yusuf passed away. We were consumed by our yearning for the throne, rather than seeking the rightful ruler. One of our own ascended to power, selling his soul to the empire, and as a result, our kingdom experienced its darkest days."

Pausing to catch his breath, Omar continued, "I refuse to allow history to repeat itself. I do not trust myself upon the throne."

Arsalan couldn't help but interject, seeking further clarity. "So, you do not believe in your own ability to rule?"

A knowing smile graced Omar's lips. "As a matter of fact, I don't, Lord Arsalan," Omar replied with conviction. "While my intentions may be noble, I do not feel that I am the right person for the role, and the same sentiment is shared by others in Turba."

Leah's head tilted to the side. "Then, who do you believe should rule Turba, Lord Omar?"

Omar smiled warmly before responding, "A good ruler, Lady Leah! Unfortunately, none of us can see into the future to determine whether a candidate will make a good king or queen. Based on my experience and the wisdom of many people before me, good rulers can fall into one of two categories. The first consists of individuals with royal blood, who have been raised and groomed to assume the role of king or queen – such as her Grace or Queen Nora."

Nisay and Sofia interjected simultaneously, stating, "There are no legitimate heirs left in Turba."

"Well, as I mentioned, good rulers can fall into the second category as well. These are individuals who are extraordinary, unlike anyone we have ever encountered. Fortunately for us, we have Lord Ali. And all agreed that he's the right ruler for Turba."

Ali turned his gaze to observe the expressions of delight on the faces of those present. Othman and the other Turban men stood up, showing their support for Omar's suggestion.

Ali spoke again, addressing the room, "Your Grace, my lords, you have honored me with such a request, but if you truly place your trust in me to the extent of offering me your kingdom, then please hear this from me."

The queen's smile vanished, aware of the direction Ali was taking. Still, she refrained from interrupting him.

"I suggest that Lord Othman be appointed as the protector of Turba," Ali proposed. "He will represent the Lady-Queen in Turba until the war is over. Then, if the leaders of the Turban houses vote for me, I will accept the crown."

Aznek, Omar, and Othman made efforts to sway Ali's decision, but ultimately, they came to agree with his suggestion. It was a wise choice, as Ali could not remain in one place while fighting against Ceres.

Before they could raise their glasses to seal the agreement, their gathering was interrupted by an unexpected guest: Nora. Accompanying her was a soldier from Solum.

The sudden appearance of Nora was cause for concern, as she would not leave Token without a pressing matter at hand. Additionally, her pale face hinted at unsettling news.

Nisay immediately stood up and rushed towards Nora, grasping her hand tightly. "What's wrong?" he asked, his voice filled with concern. "You are not supposed to be here."

Nora's tear-filled eyes couldn't hold back any longer, and she spoke through her sobs. "Lord Walid is dead."

Nisay released Nora's hands and his head sank down for a moment. Then, he looked at his wife with determination and asked firmly, "How did it happen?"

Nora turned to the man who had accompanied her and implored him to provide Nisay with the details. The man took a deep breath and began to explain, "King Bao pursued your father relentlessly and slaughtered all of his men. He then took Lord Walid to Turang and executed him."

Nisay's initial anger dissipated, replaced by a profound sense of grief and sadness. At that moment, all Nora could do was hold her husband in a tight embrace.

Everyone, including the queen, approached Nisay and Nora, offering their condolences and support. Amidst the grief-stricken atmosphere, the man who had brought the news spoke again.

"King Nisay," he addressed him, "I didn't witness the execution of King Rajab, your father-in-law. Yet, I could not fathom the level of courage a man could possess until I saw your father display the same unwavering bravery. Despite his injuries and the arrows piercing his flesh, it took four soldiers to bring him to the execution yard, and another four to force his head down. Do you know what his final words were?"

Nisay stared intently at the man, tears streaming down his cheeks, as if urging him to reveal his father's last words.

The Solumy man bowed his head, 'Bao, my son Nisay will bring these walls crashing down upon you, and he will sever your head from your shoulders!'

CHAPTER 26

In the tense waiting room of the Arena in Turang, Boa's kingdom, five gladiators awaited their chance for freedom, their collective focus honed on a single task: disarming Bao, the key to their liberation. Their very lives hung precariously in the balance, fully aware that failure would bring about a gruesome death at the merciless hands of their king.

The King had called for a competition in light of the death of Lord Walid. The potential reward made the risk worthwhile. Aside from gaining their freedom, each gladiator stood to receive a thousand gold coins—enough to secure a life of wealth and independence.

One of the gladiators broke the silence, posing a question to his comrades. "What will you do once you've earned your freedom?"

A dismissive response came from one of his companions. "You speak as if we're facing a mere kitten in the arena."

"It never hurts to enter with the intention to win!" said the gladiator, his determination unwavering. The shared ambition among all five was to join the Union's army.

Turning to the gladiator who had asked the question, another comrade inquired, "And you, my skinny friend?" Without waiting for a reply, he continued, "Even if we survive his grace's blade, I will personally present your head to him."

Laughter erupted in the room, mocking the supposedly slender gladiator. Unbeknownst to them, his physique did not reflect his true abilities. A young man in his twenties, Nisay, was unparalleled in skill. He had already been hailed as the king of the arena and now ruled a kingdom alongside his wife, Nora. This was just another thing to conquer for him.

Nisay had used the connections of a Solumy spy to infiltrate Turang and become one of the candidates to face Bao, seeking vengeance for his father's death. None of his comrades could dissuade him from this suicidal mission, and now he found himself mere feet away from his father's killer.

Aware that killing the King of Turang would unleash the wrath of an entire kingdom upon him, Nisay had a plan of escape. But first, he had to face Bao and fulfill his quest for justice.

A voice reverberated through the arena, calling out, "Let the gladiators enter the arena!"

Whistles and cheers filled the air as anticipation grew.

In the center of the arena stood a man, his voice booming as he raised his right hand. "Behold! His Grace, King Bao, son of King Choulou — the man with a heart that combines the tenderness of a king with the bravery of a knight."

The king himself stepped forward, clad in a black leather suit adorned with red stripes, his head concealed by a black mask. Without waiting for the man's cue, Bao took a few steps back and bellowed, "Let the battle begin!"

The king stood in anticipation, waiting for the gladiators to make their move. To his surprise, one of the gladiators in the middle retrieved two daggers and swiftly struck two of his comrades in the neck. Then he rolled to the left, stabbing one gladiator with his dagger, and with a quick turn, he hurled his other blade directly into the heart of the last standing opponent.

A moment of silence fell upon the arena, soon replaced by thunderous cheering from the Turangies, celebrating Nisay's triumph.

"You want their rewards," the king exclaimed as he sprinted forward, "Too bad, you won't get a single coin!"

Nisay flung his daggers and awaited his opponent. The king swung his sword towards Nisay's neck, but the nimble gladiator easily evaded the attack, seizing the king's wrist and forcing him to drop his sword. Bao stared at his adversary, contemplating the kind of man he was facing.

Nisay delivered a powerful kick to Bao's belly, causing him to stagger, and then removed his mask. Confusion filled the king's eyes as he asked, "Who are you?"

Nisay discarded his mask and retrieved his sword, aiming it at Bao's neck as he bellowed, "The man who kills you!"

With a swift strike, Bao's head rolled across the ground, leaving the arena momentarily stunned before erupting into a frenzy of screams and shouts.

Nisay ran back to the waiting room, where the Solumy spy awaited him, ready to guide him through a secret tunnel. However, as Nisay attempted to open the door, he discovered it was locked. He hurried to the small window and began calling for the Solumy spy, Damien, desperately seeking an escape.

Damien appeared, wearing a sinister smile, and Nisay pleaded, "Hurry, unlock the door!"

Damien's smile widened as he replied, "Welcome to your grave, shepherd's son."

He spat on the ground. He had deceived the queen and everyone in her three kingdoms, and now Nisay was trapped.

Nisay turned, expecting to see an army of soldiers surrounding him, but to his surprise, only the bald man stood there, shouting, "His grace, King of Turang, Bao, son of Choulou."

Confusion clouded Nisay's face as he said aloud, "What is happening?"

Shock washed over him as Bao emerged from the crowd and took his seat between two beautiful and young ladies, applauding mockingly. Nisay finally realized that Damien and Bao had orchestrated an elaborate deception, and the masked man he had killed was merely a regular gladiator.

"Nisay, son of Walid!" Bao screamed, "You've made things easier for me, willingly leading yourself to your grave."

Nisay was stunned, desperately searching for an escape route. But before he could devise a plan, six enormous gladiators stormed into the arena, charging towards him, brandishing swords and axes.

Nisay wielded a sword in his right hand and a dagger in his left. Two adversaries attacked simultaneously, but he evaded their strikes. With precision, he plunged his dagger into one opponent's chest and sliced open the other's belly.

His assault didn't cease there as he dispatched the remaining four opponents unscathed.

The king, however, had anticipated Nisay's prowess. Although he could have ordered the archers to eliminate the intruder, Bao craved a more thrilling spectacle and thus chose to reveal his second card.

"Unleash the beasts!" he bellowed.

Nisay stood in the center of the arena, his body drenched in the blood of the eleven men he had already slain. The bald man exited the arena, leaving Nisay alone to face his next opponent. A door swung open, and five lionesses entered the arena, their presence hushing the entire place and freezing Nisay in his tracks.

The lionesses remained stationary, observing him. With their powerful paws and menacing jaws, they wielded one of nature's most fearsome weapons. Nisay felt a surge of fear, realizing that facing one or two of them was feasible, but taking on all five was insurmountable. Nevertheless, he assumed a fighting stance, prepared to confront his attackers. Fortunately, only one lioness made a move, rapidly closing the distance and leaping toward Nisay's chest. With lightning reflexes, he rolled away and stood ready with his blade as the beast soared above him. He held his dagger upwards.

Nisay was quickly adorned with the gore and entrails of his first adversary. He wiped his face with his hand and braced himself for the other beasts. His luck ran out as the remaining four lionesses simultaneously charged toward him, sprinting with lethal intent.

The crowd displayed a mix of shock and awe, marveling at the sight of this man standing against four ruthless lionesses. Just as the predators closed in on Nisay, two spears emerged from the audience and impaled two of the lionesses. Nisay never had a chance to identify his saviors, as the remaining lionesses disregarded their fallen companions and lunged at him. Before they could reach him, two more spears dispatched them.

The stage remained empty, a realm untouched by other performers. Nisay's gaze swept across the expanse, his curiosity piqued as he sought to unravel the enigma of his unexpected saviors. In a swift turn of events, five figures emerged from the thronged audience, springing onto the stage. As they removed their masks, a shock of realization coursed through Nisay's veins – for standing before him were none other than his friends.

Ali, Leah, Sofia, Arsalan, and Nisay's wife stood together, ready to confront an entire kingdom for the sake of their comrade. Despite the thirty soldiers surrounding them, spears pointed menacingly, Ali tapped Nisay's shoulder and spoke, "Take Sofia with you and bring justice to your father!"

Nisay shook his head, "Let Sofia and me help you handle these bastards."

"No time, Nisay," Ali replied firmly. "The four of us can handle them."

Nora winked at Nisay as she joined the fray alongside her companions.

Nisay and Sofia ran towards the grandstand of the arena, where Bao sat surrounded by ten colossal guards atop a platform accessed by more than fifty stairs. Nisay's gaze remained fixed on his father's killer, contemplating a way to reach him. Suddenly, a forceful kick struck him from behind, causing him to lose his balance and fall to the ground. He spun around, ready to strike with his sword, only to halt when he realized it was Sofia who had kicked him to save him evading a spear.

"Did you just save my life?" he said, disbelief etched across his face.

Sofia hurled a dagger that found its mark on another Turangy soldier who had attempted to ambush Nisay from behind. She grinned and replied, "Twice!"

Startled by his friend's actions, Nisay stared at her before she exclaimed, "Gather yourself and bring us the usurper's head!"

"Eagerly listening, my lady!" declared Nisay, seizing a spear from one of the fallen soldiers. With a few quick strides, he leaped high into the air, drawing his arm back to its fullest extent before releasing the spear forwards. It streaked toward the King with such speed that no guard could intercept it, coming within a few feet of piercing Bao's chest.

But the king's reflexes were quick. He seized one of his servants by the hand and used her as a shield, causing the spear to impale her chest instead.

Bao discarded the lifeless woman, escaping through a nearby door. Frustration surged within Nisay and he shouted, "Damn it!"

"Nisay, go after him. I will handle the guards," Sofia urged.

Nisay couldn't allow Sofia to face the approaching ten guards alone. "There are too many for one knight to defeat, even one as skilled as you, Sofia."

A voice emerged from behind them, "She won't be alone,"

Nisay would have typically hesitated, but upon seeing who had come to join Sofia, he made an exception. It was Leah, one of the swiftest and most ruthless fighters he had ever encountered. Covered in blood, her armor and face obscured, she exuded a hunger for vengeance.

Leah positioned herself beside Sofia and remarked, "Do you realize this is the first time we'll fight side by side?"

Sofia smiled and responded, "Scribes will need countless jars of ink to record this battle."

Indeed, the spectacle created by the two women would become a legendary tale recounted by Turangies for generations to come. With synchronised movements, they advanced directly towards the ten soldiers, anticipating their every move with uncanny precision.

Sofia assumed a kneeling stance, her hands grasping a blade each, severing a soldiers' abdomen. Rolling across the floor, she flung a blade at a third opponent. Glancing back, Sofia witnessed Leah dispatching six adversaries and preparing to confront the last, who was hurtling towards her on horseback. Sensing Sofia's desire to face him herself, Leah obliged without hesitation.

Leah watched her best friend soar into the air. Sofia's abdomen dove above the soldier's head, and then she tilted her head toward the ground as though diving into a river. As she touched the ground, she extended her arms, using her feet to ensnare the soldier by the neck. With her palms pressing against the ground, she twisted to the right, brutally snapping the Turangy's neck.

"Poor soldier!" Leah laughed, offering a macabre compliment.

Meanwhile, Nisay shattered the door that Bao had used to flee, revealing a dimly lit corridor. It provided enough illumination for the Turban to navigate his path as he sprinted for half a mile, yet he found no trace of his elusive enemy.

He reached the end of the corridor, only to be confronted by a locked iron door. *Go back to the arena and find a way to breach that door*, Nisay thought, but the idea of missing this crucial opportunity was unbearable. In a desperate act, he attempted to use his dagger as a makeshift key, realizing the futility of such a notion as the blade failed to fit into the keyhole. Frustration surged through him, and he smashed the dagger against the ground, letting out a scream of frustration. As he raised his head, his gaze fell upon Bao, who had become trapped in the rafters above.

"Trying to hide?" Nisay said dryly.

The Turangy King managed to free himself, plummeting from above with his sword aimed directly at Nisay. In a desperate attempt to evade the strike, Nisay dodged, but the sword grazed his shoulder, slashing his skin. Bao swiftly regained his footing, taking a few steps back, a self-assured smile playing upon his lips, savoring the anticipated victory.

"Who will come to your rescue now?" Nisay said, clutching his wounded shoulder. Bao never possessed unwavering confidence when facing Nisay, particularly after their previous encounter. But with

Nisay's injured shoulder, Bao believed he might have a chance. He sprinted towards Nisay, launching himself into the air, delivering a powerful blow. Nisay managed to parry his opponent's sword, but the force was overwhelming, causing him to tumble to the ground.

Rising to his feet, using his sword as support, Nisay saw a smug grin spreading across Bao's face.

"Poor shepherd," Boa said, "Your sword hand is crippled. Even a kitten wouldn't hesitate to kill you."

Nisay could barely move his right hand, it was true. But much to Bao's surprise, Nisay switched the sword from his right hand to his left and smiled.

"They call us Lions because we possess two sword hands," Nisay said. "Never underestimate a lion."

Nisay charged towards his opponent. It took only three deft strikes for Nisay to disarm Bao and position his own sword at the neck of his father's killer. "And now what?" Nisay posed, "Who will come to save *you* now?"

Before Bao could respond, Nisay repeated his father's last words, "Bao, my son Nisay will bring these walls crashing down upon you, and he will sever your head from your shoulders!" He then thrust his sword into Bao's mouth, exerting force until the blade emerged from the back of Bao's head.

As the lifeless body of the King of Turang slumped to the ground, Nisay retrieved his sword, and his ears caught the sound of applause. He turned to behold the person who mattered most to him—Nora, the love of his life – standing a few paces away. She was smiling at him.

Rushing towards her, they embraced tightly, unable to let go. When they released each other, tears streamed down from Nora's green eyes, Nisay whimpered, "Do you think my father will finally rest in peace?"

Nora held him by the arms. "He will find peace, not solely because you vanquished this usurper, but also because he will soon have a new grandson, an heir to carry on his name."

Niday cocked an eyebrow up, and Nora chucked. Tenderly, she guided his hand to her belly and nodded, revealing the new life growing within her.

CHAPTER 27

Nisay was rendered speechless for a moment, trying to grasp the fact that Nora was expecting their child. Despite their seeking the best healers in Solum and Token, their chances of conceiving a child had always seemed slim. They had resigned themselves to the notion that the ancestral line – which had endured for over a millennium – would come to an end, without a successor to carry it forward.

"You're wounded!" Nora exclaimed, her voice panicked as she tore a piece of fabric from her top.

"It's nothing..." Nisay said.

"Shut up!"

A smile crept across Nisay's face, and he followed Nora back to the Arena, where Ali and their companions stood amidst the sprawled Turangy corpses. Nisay took in the sight of hundreds of soldiers, clad in red suits adorned with black and white stripes, scattered across the arena.

"Who are they?" Nisay asked.

"They are a tribe that call themselves the Alinians," Nora replied.

Nisay tightly grasped Nora's wrist, his eyes widening. "Zaya's people?"

Nora turned her gaze towards him, nodding. "Yes, her mother Umali and Queen Aznek seized the opportunity and sent their armies."

Nisay stood frozen in his place, absorbing the weight of Nora's words.

Nora continued, "The Kingdom of Turang is now ours."

It marked the fifth kingdom that Aznek had added to her rule. Not initially part of her plans, perhaps, but when Walid was killed she could not afford to wait and devised a plan with Ali. Nisay's impatience had driven him to act without informing anyone, not even his wife, and it would have cost him his life if it hadn't been for the Lady-Queen's intervention.

Surprisingly, most of the Turangy soldiers had offered little resistance once their gates were breached. Aznek left her prime advisor, Sam, and a thousand soldiers, along with three of her finest commanders, to maintain control. As for Aznek and the rebels, they returned to Solum to savor their hard-earned victory.

On their journey back to Solum, Aznek approached Roulan, who was engaged in conversation with Leah. The queen interjected, asking Leah if she could speak with Roulan alone.

Once Leah had made her way back to Arsalan and Ali, Aznek initiated the conversation. "How does it feel to liberate your homeland?"

Roulan furrowed her brow, "The rightful King of Turang is dead. What kind of kingdom doesn't have a king?"

A faint smile formed on the queen's lips as she answered, "All kings eventually meet their end."

"The man who gives birth never dies," Roulan declared, quoting an old saying from Turang. "That's what I meant, Your Grace."

A silence enveloped them momentarily before the queen spoke again, her tone thoughtful, "Your grandfather is a king, isn't he?"

Roulan felt as though the queen had thrust a blade into her heart with the reminder of her royal bloodline, as it also served as a stark reminder of the oppressive truth in Turang.

"A woman can never rule in Turang," she said.

"Maybe. This law was created by people, and we are people, so we have the power to change it."

Roulan's expression softened. She hesitated a moment before saying, "Thank you, Your Grace."

As the queen arrived at her kingdom and dismounted from her horse, a commander rushed towards her, whispering something urgently. Her face turned pale, and she immediately called for her generals and allies to join her in the council.

"This cannot be good news," Arsalan whispered to Sofia.

As the council members entered the room and took their seats, the queen instructed the commander to provide a briefing to everyone. He forward, approaching Ali and Leah, and knelt on one knee. He struggled to find the words, his voice trembling.

"Lady Leah, Lord Ali... I don't know how to say this," the commander mumbled, unable to continue.

Leah shifted her gaze towards the queen and said, "What is it, Your Grace?"

"Lord Steve!" the queen called out.

"Your son, Noah, has been kidnapped," the commander blurted. He stammered. "I – we –"

Before he could say more, Leah lunged at him, gripping his neck tightly.

Concern spread among the others as Leah refused to release her grip, disregarding the pleas from Sofia and the queen. It was only when Ali placed his hand on her arm that she let go, tears welling in her eyes.

"They took my son, Ali!" she exclaimed.

Ali turned to Steve, urging him to explain how it happened.

"Despite the presence of guards, somehow she managed to sneak out of the castle with Noah," Steve explained.

"*She?*" Nora inquired.

Steve turned his gaze, "It was his nanny. And she left this."

Ali took a rolled parchment from Steve's hands and unraveled it. As he read the words aloud, the room fell silent.

"Noah will go to where he belongs: his grandfather Ceres. Natasha." Announced Ali.

Leah remained silent and abruptly left the council chamber.

A heavy silence hung in the air until the queen broke it. "Lord Ali, I can imagine your anger and frustration. I promise you that I will mobilize the four kingdoms if necessary to bring Noah back."

"Fortunately, Ceres cannot harm him," Nora reassured, "He is his blood."

"This is devastating news for all of us; it is not the right time to make decisions," the queen declared, dismissing everyone from the council.

Ali didn't disagree either, and as he made his way towards the exit, Nora spoke up.

"Lord Ali, Noah is like a son to all of us. Please, whatever plans you have in mind, include us," she said.

Ali nodded once before continuing on his path.

***

Soloman, a young and inexperienced soldier in his junior years of service, found himself stationed by the imposing doors of the council chamber within the last bastion of Ceres' dominion, the kingdom of Toprak. His breaths came in ragged gasps as he struggled to recover from a frantic sprint. Desperate to relay urgent news, he approached the vigilant guards who stood as stalwart sentinels at the threshold and implored for their permission to enter.

The two soldiers burst into laughter, and one of them mockingly inquired, "What do *you* want with the council?"

Soloman didn't appreciate the mockery, but he swallowed his pride. "The fate of our kingdom hinges on the news I bring. Either you let me in, or I will go inform my chief, who will then inform his chief. It will take a significant amount of time for the information to reach His Grace, and by then, it might be too late. If that happens, we will all lose our heads!"

The two guards exchanged glances, and one of them said, "Wait here." He then entered the council chamber to inform the king and returned to allow Soloman inside.

It was Soloman's first time witnessing the proceedings of the Toprak council. He entered the chamber and respectfully bowed, waiting for the king to instruct him to rise.

"What is it that you want, soldier?" inquired the King of Toprak.

Soloman stood up but kept his head lowered. "Your Grace, I know the whereabouts of Izmir."

"Izmir without a title? Isn't she your princess?"

Soloman turned his gaze towards his chief and replied firmly, "My lord, with all due respect, she is a traitor who no longer deserves a title."

"If we weren't in the presence of His Grace, I would sever your head!" the military chief fumed.

Soloman disregarded his chief's outburst and fixed his gaze on the king.

The king gave Soloman a flat stare. "He is right. These accusations could get you hanged, unless you have proof of her treason."

"My father taught me the importance of loyalty to our kingdom, and I am fully aware of the gravity of my words," replied Soloman. "Izmir is in Solum, and she aided the rebels in capturing Turba, Your Grace."

"The treacherous wench!" hissed the king, "You may leave now, soldier. Your reward shall be granted this evening."

As Soloman exited the council chamber, Kemal, the military chief, posed a question, "Do you know what comes next?"

Sakir, the prime advisor, was the first to respond, "Dharatee or us."

"Correct, Lord Sakir. We must prepare ourselves," Kemal affirmed.

The military chief had considered this matter and decided to share his plan. "Your Grace, my lords. My sources in Dharatee informed me that King Anand is desperate to form an alliance with us."

"Aren't we already allies?" questioned the prime advisor.

"On paper, yes," replied the military chief. "But King Anand is willing to join his forces with ours. In my opinion, I believe it would greatly aid us against the impending threat of four armies."

Kemal stroked his beard, lost in thought as he gazed up at the ceiling. The idea of seeking aid from Ceres crossed his mind, but he knew it came at a steep price. Kemal was unwilling to continue paying exorbitant taxes while surrendering all the spoils of victory, if he managed to defeat Queen Aznek.

Regarding King Anand, Kemal's plan remained relatively unchanged. After triumphing over Aznek, he intended to install Suresh, with his royal bloodline, as the new king of Dharatee, leveraging his claim to the throne.

Kemal rose from his seat, signaling the end of the meeting. He instructed the military chief to fortify the walls and prepare the army for the upcoming conflict. Turning to his personal guard, he ordered them to ready his horse and assemble a hundred soldiers to accompany him on the journey to Dharatee. The time had come to set his plans in motion.

CHAPTER 28

Ceres gazed at the boy, searching for any connection beyond their biological tie. Yet, there was nothing. The boy bore no resemblance to his mother; instead, he was a mirror image of his father, Ali. Ironically, Ceres found himself drawn to the likeness, despite the animosity between him and Ali.

"Hello, Noah!" Ceres greeted, "It's nice to finally meet you."

"How do you know my name?" Noah said suspiciously, "I've never seen you before!"

"I'm your grandfather," Ceres said.

Noah approached him and said matter-of-factly, "You must be Ceres, because my other grandfather, Ahmed, is dead."

The boy's astuteness surprised Ceres, considering his tender age. "Who told you about me?" He asked.

"My mother!" Noah exclaimed, prompting Ceres to inquire about what else she had shared with him.

"She said that you're strong and smart!"

Tears welled up in Ceres' eyes as he missed his daughter for the first time since she had left him. He longed for her not only to preserve his image in his grandson's eyes, but also because she was a good person, despite her opinions of him.

Interrupting his thoughts, the little boy expressed his desire to return to his parents. Ceres placed his hand on Noah's head and gently ruffled his hair. "I'm afraid we won't be able to see them for a while. In the meantime, you're welcome to stay here and play with your uncle Phaethon, who is almost your age."

The boy beamed with delight. As he headed towards the door, Thaar entered the room, pausing as she approached Noah.

"Hello, little boy," Thaar greeted him.

Noah's face lit up, and he responded, "Hello, my lady. You're so pretty!"

Thaar's heart melted upon hearing the innocent words from the young boy. "This is my grandson, Noah. Leah's son," Ceres introduced.

A tear slipped down Thaar's cheek, and Ceres inquired about her distress.

"Your Grace, isn't your daughter married to..." Thaar hesitated, unable to utter the last word.

"Ali, you mean—my arch nemesis," Ceres finished her words for her.

Thaar remained speechless, her gaze shifting between the boy and his grandfather.

"I don't care about that rebel or even my daughter. This little boy is my flesh and blood, and his place is here with me and my children," Ceres stated, realizing that Thaar was not involved in politics. He then apologized for his previous assumption and proceeded to take off his shirt.

Thaar, sensing the tension, decided to offer a comforting gesture. She began massaging Ceres' back, her skilled hands easing his stress. In the midst of this moment, she delivered some incredible news.

"Your Highness, I can say with certainty that your illness is no longer fatal," Thaar announced.

Startled, the emperor turned to face her, his expression filled with glee, but confusion also.

Sensing his need for clarification, Thaar continued, "The medicines you've taken have successfully halted its progression. Now, all we need to do is locate the Black Spiders and eliminate them."

With the massage complete, Ceres donned his top and robe, ready to address Thaar.

"Normally, I reward those who serve or assist me with gold. However, your help has surpassed anything I have ever offered," Ceres expressed, gratitude evident in his voice.

"Your Highness..." Thaar began.

But Ceres interrupted, determined to show his appreciation.

"Don't misunderstand me. What you have done cannot be quantified in terms of gold or any material possession in this world. Nevertheless, I am eager to show my gratitude. So, tell me, what is it that you desire most?" Ceres inquired, pointing at her with a playful smile. "And I won't accept 'no' for an answer."

Thaar returned the smile and pondered for a moment. "Well, if you insist, there is something my village desperately needs," she replied, lowering her head. "I want to live in my humble village in peace. I mean, I wish to be far away from the ravages of war."

"Consider it done, Lady Thaar," Ceres assured her. "I will personally request the military chief to establish three barracks around your village. Not even a fly will be able to infiltrate your tribe."

Touched by his promise, Thaar lowered her head in gratitude and excused herself to take her leave. As for Ceres, he made his way to his daily council, his heart uplifted by the exchange.

Despite the loss of his fourth kingdom, Ceres wasn't too concerned. With his newfound leverage of having Ali's son, he believed that Ali would readily trade all four kingdoms for his child's safe return. But truthfully, he desired not only the return of his lands but also the heads of Aznek and Ali. This was the topic he intended to discuss with his chiefs.

"Now that we have Ali's son, how do we reclaim our four kingdoms?" Ceres posed the question to his council.

The financial chief, Robin, was the first to respond. "Either Ali surrenders the kingdoms willingly, or he'll never see his son again."

Filip, the chief of foreign affairs, tutted. "Ali is nothing more than a common soldier. He lacks the authority to even grant a house in Solum. We have no guarantee."

"You're both mistaken!" interrupted Ben. "Lord Filip, Ali is revered as a hero among the commoners. They hold him in the same regard as Queen Aznek."

The prime advisor shifted his gaze to Robin and said, "And as for you, our enemy is astute enough to know that His Highness would never harm his own grandson."

Ceres sighed. "Do you have a strategy, Prime Advisor?"

"Your Highness, we possess considerable leverage. Why should we make the first move?" the prime advisor said.

"You mean we should stand down and take no action?" Ceres asked.

"On the contrary, Your Highness. I suggest that if we choose to negotiate with the queen and Ali, we provide them an opportunity to deceive us. However, if we maintain our inaction, Ali and his allies will unwittingly walk into our trap."

Silence hung in the room as the council members contemplated the proposal.

Ben said, "Believe me, if we dismantle these rebels, the queen will be left more vulnerable than ever before."

Ceres found the idea intriguing, but he refrained from immediately approving or rejecting the plan. Instead, he took the time to ponder the strategy. While trapping the rebels could significantly enhance his chances of reclaiming his kingdoms, he also understood that underestimating Aznek would be a grave mistake. She was a woman to be reckoned with, and he knew it well.

***

Ali gave Leah the necessary time and space to cope with the tragedy while he focused on devising an extraction plan. The echoes of his mother's screams when Unionist soldiers took her away still haunted his memories.

As his friends convened to discuss strategies for rescuing Noah, the queen refrained from endorsing any of their proposals, awaiting Ali's input. On the second day, Ali entered the room dressed in his formidable war suit, greeting everyone with a hand over his chest and a lowered head.

To his surprise, Nora was also present. "Queen Nora, your kingdom is not secure without you and your husband!" he said.

Nora responded with a reassuring smile, "If we were to lose a kingdom, we have the ability to reclaim it again."

Roulan took the initiative and presented her plan. "Lord Ali, I know someone who can assist me in infiltrating the royal residence. I can easily retrieve Noah from there."

Each time a friend volunteered to risk their life for his son, Ali's face lit up with gratitude. "I'm afraid I must go alone," he asserted pre-emptively. "Leah is no longer in her room, and considering Sofia's absence from the council, I suspect they both have gone to the empire."

Arsalan stood up and declared, "Then it seems we have no choice but to pursue them."

"No, Lord Arsalan," Ali responded. " I will go alone."

Interrupting from behind, Nisay interjected, "I understand your concern, Ali, but you cannot ask us to remain idle."

Ali advanced toward Nisay, placing a hand on his shoulder. "No, brother, you are not standing idle. You are pursuing what we started—our cause."

He then began walking among his friends, addressing each one individually. "Nora, do you remember when you initiated the hunt for the highest-ranked soldiers? Arsalan, how many barracks have you razed to the ground? And Roulan, you shook the entire empire when you took down Ramessess."

All eyes were fixed on Ali, and quiet smiles appeared on the faces of his friends.

"Nisay and Aznek, both of you came to fame as wanted individuals. Keita, Alighieri and Sai all sacrificed their lives. Do you know why?" He looked up to the ceiling, "To free our world from criminals like Ceres and his puppets. Nothing should halt us, not even the safety of my own son."

The queen maintained her silence, a smile lingering on her lips as she fixed her gaze on Ali, who took a step closer toward Aznek.

"Your Grace," he said, "I believe it's time to reclaim Dharatee," Ali asserted.

Aznek replied, her smile unwavering. "Great spirits think alike, Lord Ali."

Roulan, however, was quick to voice her objection. "Lord Ali, Dharatee is my son's home. I yearn for its freedom more than anyone. But I don't think the time is right."

The queen shook her head, her tone resolute. "No, Lady Roulan. It's now or never."

A hush fell over the room as the queen continued, revealing the information gathered by her whisperers. "My sources have informed me that Anand and Kemal are joining forces."

Arsalan rubbed his hands down his face. "The emperor isn't expecting us to make a move now, though. He no doubt believes that he holds the upper hand."

"Lord Othman, King Nisay," the queen said, "Prepare your armies. We will convene tomorrow near Lions-River."

As they rose to depart, the gates swung open, freezing everyone in their places.

From the gates, Noah appeared. He sprinted towards his father, embracing him tightly. Leah was beside him, unharmed, with Sofia by her side.

Joy overwhelmed everyone, including the queen, who approached Noah, holding his hand and remarking, "One of your titles should be 'Dharatee Conqueror'!"

Ali, after hugging his wife, said, "How did you manage it?"

Leah smiled and responded, "We did nothing. Someone clandestinely spirited him out of the castle for us."

"Who?" Ali asked, his surprise evident.

"Let's just say we received assistance from within the family," Leah replied.

Roulan recalled David, who had aided her in infiltrating Ramessess' chamber, claiming to be Leah's uncle. "You received help from Lord David?"

Leah nodded, and the queen's plan fell perfectly into place.

Ali pleaded with his wife to stay in Solum with the queen, initially met with resistance. How could she pass up the opportunity to liberate another kingdom, the realm of her friend Sai? However, Ali's argument was compelling. "The only way I can ensure Noah's safety is if his mother remains with him."

Three days later, the three armies arrived at Dharatee, their ranks consisting of over twenty thousand soldiers, standing a mere few hundred feet away from the castle. The sight of the multitude of catapults they brought forth sent chills down the spines of the Dharatian archers.

The military chief of Dharatee issued the order to his commanders, instructing them to prepare for a siege. The commanders complied, rallying their eight thousand soldiers in just a few days.

When it was time, King Anand, adorned in his regal attire, mounted his horse and traversed the ranks, projecting his voice over the soldiers. "People of Dharatee, the enemy has arrived today with the intention to colonize our kingdom and wipe us out. But we will not allow it. Do not fear their numbers. The Unionist soldiers are in their way, and we shall vanquish them before they even make their first move."

Suddenly, a soldier screamed out, "Your Grace! There's a man at the gate claiming to be Ali. He wishes to speak with you!"

In no time, Anand dismounted his horse and ascended the wall via the stairs, reaching the top to confront the intruder.

"What do you want, trespasser?" he said.

"I do not relish war and bloodshed," Ali hissed. " I am here to discuss a way to avert this conflict."

Anand chuckled. "Let me guess, you want me to hand over my kingdom? Too bad. The only blood that will be shed today is yours. So return from whence you came before our reinforcements arrive."

Ali saw through Anand's bluff and said, "I am truly moved by your mercy. We are about to attack you, and yet you warn us! But let's suppose you are right. Do you think we will simply lay siege to this kingdom? A single barrage from our catapults will topple these walls, and we shall claim the kingdom."

"What is it that you want?" Anand said through gritted teeth.

"I want Dharatee to be free. You have until noon to open the gates."

Before Ali returned to his armies, he raised his voice and addressed the soldiers on the wall, "This decision is not his alone, but that of every Dharatian. Remember, we are not here to seize anything from your kingdom. Instead, we aim to liberate your home from the chains of the empire. If you open these gates and surrender, you will reclaim the glory of Dharatee along with its rightful ruler."

Ali departed, leaving Anand with the realization that he had run out of options. He could discern the look of defeat in the eyes of his commanders, and before they turned against him, he issued the order to open the gate.

Ali yearned for Sai to witness this momentous occasion, as he advanced alongside Sai's wife and their companions. Turning to Nora, he spoke, "You are the only queen among us. I believe you should deliver the speech."

Nora smiled as she stepped forward, "The queen insisted that you deliver the speech yourself."

Ali could not defy the command of his queen, and he also felt a desire within him to address the gathered crowd. He ascended the stairs to the balcony and waited until the vast square below, encompassing commoners and soldiers alike, was filled.

Ali cleared his throat and began his address.

"People of Dharatee. Regardless of our color or culture, we are all human beings, united by the common pursuit of freedom and justice. There are always those, driven by greed, who seek to monopolize everything for themselves and revel in the weakness and poverty of others.

We have not come here to take everything from you. On the contrary, we are here to restore your independence and return your wealth to a benevolent ruler."

A tall man with curly hair and black eyes, a true Dharatian, stood silently on the stage. Another elderly man joined him, instantly recognized by all as the highest Speaker, distinguished by his white robe.

The Speaker held two jars—one small, containing a red substance, and the other larger, seemingly filled with water. He summoned one of the commanders onto the stage and posed a question.

Handing the small jar to the commander, the Speaker asked, "Can you determine its contents?"

"It's blood, Your Grace," replied the commander.

"Indeed, it is. But do you know whose blood it is, or rather, whose it was?"

The commander scrutinized the tiny bottle, sealed with the mark of Dharatee. A tag dangled from the bottle, bearing the inscription: "King Ghandy, son of Rahul."

The commander's eyes widened. "This is the blood of His Majesty, our greatest king in history, isn't it?"

A collective gasp reverberated throughout the square. Though none had met King Ghandy, Dharatian manuscripts in libraries recounted his remarkable achievements.

Breaking the seal, the Speaker poured a few drops of Ghandy's blood into the large jar.

"The larger jar contains Aqua Vitae, used for blood analysis," the Speaker explained.

It was an ancient technique used by the Speakers to detect blood relations. Typically utilized during trials for unmarried women who had given birth, it aided in confirming the identity of the father. In the case of a father and child, the liquid turned pink.

As the Ghandy's blood mixed with the tall man's, the liquid transformed into a vibrant pink hue.

The Speaker shifted his gaze toward the man with curly hair and then addressed the palace square.

"People of Dharatee, may I introduce you to Suresh, son of King Ghandy. I hereby proclaim him the rightful King of Dharatee."

CHAPTER 29

Toprak remained the only unconquered kingdom for Queen Aznek to bring under her rule. She understood the daunting challenge ahead, having encountered Kemal once before and recognizing his formidable intellect. The weight of responsibility burdened her, making it difficult for her to find sleep.

While Aznek desired to allow her armies a much-needed respite before attacking Toprak, she knew that stalling would only give Kemal and Ceres an opportunity to strike. Her mentor, King Rajab, had taught her that conquering a kingdom was far easier than maintaining control over it.

Nora and Nisay ensured the safety of Token, while Suresh now ruled over Dharatee, and Othman had brought stability to Turba. Aznek's primary concern was with Turang. Her trusted advisor, Sam, consistently reported conflicts among the leaders of the houses. Disputes like this opened up vulnerabilities the kingdom could not afford.

Roulan, with her royal lineage, would have been the most suitable choice for Aznek to rule Turang. However, the kingdom staunchly rejected the notion of a female ruler. Aznek recognized that forcibly installing Roulan would only spark turmoil, ultimately leading to further instability.

Upon her call, a gathering of over three hundred men congregated within the palace, facing the balcony where Queen Aznek stood, flanked by three Speakers on her left and an elderly man on her right. This elderly man was none other than Sao, the son of the former prime advisor. Remarkably, King Choulou and Bao had spared his life, perhaps fearing a popular uprising.

Sao rose to address the crowd. "People of Turang, my name is Sao. My father, grandfather, and great-grandfather served as council members. But I chose a different path, as I never embraced the rule of the emperor."

Expressing gratitude towards Aznek for their newfound freedom, Sao acknowledged the need for a new ruler. A house leader sought permission to speak, which the old man graciously granted.

He fixed his gaze on Aznek and spoke with determination, his words laced with a mix of gratitude and apprehension. "Your Grace, on behalf of every Turangy, I thank you for returning to us what was rightfully ours. However, rumors have circulated that you intend to name Lady Roulan as the Queen of Turang. While she may possess royal lineage, our people would never accept it. Not because we hold animosity towards women, but because it goes against our religious beliefs. Our God has forbidden such a practice, and we would rather endure ten rulers like Ceres than defy our God's decree."

Aznek recognized this as a false justification fabricated by men to undermine the role of women. "God, in His wisdom, would not create women and deem them lesser," she muttered to herself. While Aznek possessed the power to change such laws, she understood that imposing her will upon the people would be viewed as a form of dictatorship.

"Thank you, my lord," she said, "I find that I disagree. God, in His wisdom, would not create women and deem them lesser. We cannot mold everyone into the same belief, and I choose to respect your law."

A brief silence enveloped the palace before Aznek entered the room, cradling a baby in her arms. "My lords, this is Sai, the son of Roulan, daughter of Ming, son of Feng from House Zhengyi, the family that ruled Turangy for two thousand years."

Another house leader stood and questioned, "How can a baby govern an entire kingdom?"

Aznek responded, "Just like any young king, my lord."

The man could no longer contain his anger and erupted in a fit of rage. "With all due respect, Your Grace, we cannot accept her even as an acting queen!"

"That decision does not rest solely with you, my lord," the queen stated, rising to her feet. "People of Turang!" she called out.

"I am not here to impose anything upon you as Ceres or Bao did in the past. Instead, I am here to assist you in choosing a temporary ruler until King Sai comes of age. Whomever the majority of you select shall be named the Protector of Turang."

Aznek paused, scanning the place with her eyes before she continued, her voice filled with a plea. "Before dismissing Lady Roulan, I implore you to consider the future of your kingdom. Your religion does not explicitly forbid a woman from acting as queen. Think of the best interests of this nation. Who could protect your rightful king better than his own mother? And Roulan is not just any mother; she is the Queen of Arena, renowned throughout the Seven Kingdoms as the Beast-Slayer."

The queen paused again, observing the expressions of confusion on the faces before her. She asked, "Do you know who killed your king and his family?"

Silence echoed in response, prompting Aznek to continue. "It was Ramessess, the same man who kidnapped your orphaned boys and your Speakers; the one who appointed Choulou to rule over you like slaves."

She raised her voice further, commanding the attention of everyone present. "Lady Roulan was the one who severed the head of this criminal and brought justice to your nation and your previous king. Now, I will pose a question to all of you. But before you answer with a simple yes or no, I want you to consider something. Without a strong ruler and strong allies, your kingdom will once again face the risk of falling."

Aznek's words resonated with the audience, and even those who had initially intended to compete with Roulan raised their hands in support of her as the Protector of Turang until King Sai came of age. Thus, Roulan became the first woman to receive such a title in the Kingdom of Turang.

The queen felt a surge of joy, knowing that by placing a new queen in Turang, she would not only stabilize the kingdom but also enable herself to focus on the challenges ahead. While Toprak remained as the only kingdom left to conquer, Aznek was well aware that it would be a formidable task, considering Kemal's resources and the support he would receive from Ceres.

Upon her arrival to Solum, the queen decided to set politics aside for a while and dedicated herself to relaxation. On the second day, she invited all the girls to her residence for dinner, with the exception of Roulan.

Izmir, still relatively new to the group, was not particularly talkative. However, the queen saw it as an opportunity to involve her more. "Lady Izmir, what do you plan to do when you reclaim your kingdom?"

Izmir offered a warm smile and remained silent for a moment, causing the queen to consider withdrawing her question. But then Izmir responded, her voice filled with enthusiasm, "Reclaiming my kingdom? Just hearing those words fills me with ecstasy, Your Grace."

Nora echoed the question, asking, "So, what are your plans?"

Izmir maintained her smile. "First and foremost, I will ensure justice for my father and mother. Then, I will focus on establishing the right council."

Leah chuckled and asked, "Is that all?"

Izmir, perceptive enough to sense that they were looking for something specific, turned her attention to the queen and said, "I feel like this dinner was arranged for me to confess something."

A knowing smile passed between the queen and Nora.

Izmir turned to Nora and asked, "What is it, Nora?"

Sofia laughed, then she looked at Nora and said, "Ask her."

Nora's curiosity burned inside her, and she struggled to contain it. She could sense that her companions were experiencing the same anticipation. Unable to resist any longer, Nora spilled the beans and looked back at Izmir. "Is there something between you and Arsalan?"

"Nora!" exclaimed Leah in a reproachful tone.

The laughter filled the room, causing Izmir to look around, bewildered, trying to grasp the reason behind the mirth.

Silence fell once more, but Aznek quickly composed herself. "It's a personal matter, and you don't have to answer." she reassured Izmir.

"Really?" Izmir queried, and Nora interjected, "No!"

Izmir knew that her companions wouldn't let her off the hook until she satisfied their curiosity.

"There is something between us," she began, "Something more beautiful than anything in this world. Something I never believed in until I saw him. He was undercover, posing as a commander loyal to Kemal. The moment our eyes met, I knew he was pretending. But it was in the execution yard, when he stood against an entire army to save my uncle, that I fell in love with him."

Nora, filled with admiration, commented, "Love at first sight, just like Ali and Leah."

"Not exactly," Izmir clarified, "It started as admiration, but true love bloomed when I witnessed his bravery, strength, and integrity. At that moment, I made the decision to be with this man for the rest of my life."

Her heartfelt words brought back memories for Nora and Leah, reminding them of their own initial sparks of love with their husbands.

The queen raised her mug, taking a few sips before asking, "Is this love mutual or one-sided?"

"I don't know," Izmir replied with a smile, leaving Leah puzzled.

"You haven't spoken to him?" Nora inquired.

"Do you think I should?" Izmir asked, as if she were a lovesick teenager infatuated with a young prince.

Aznek, Leah, and Nora exclaimed in unison, "Of course!"

However, Sofia held a different opinion. "No way!"

They all stared at Sofia, prompting her to join them in the conversation.

In a voice resembling Izmir's, Sofia spoke softly, "Lord Arsalan, I have feelings for you! Do you?"

Sofia then deepened her voice, trying to mimic Arsalan. She cleared her throat twice before saying, "Yeah, I love you like I loved my friends, Ali, Leah, Nora..."

Laughter erupted throughout the room, including Izmir. The discussion continued for a while longer before they retired to their beds.

The queen fell asleep swiftly, only to find Sai appearing in her dreams once more. He wore a white robe adorned with gold, holding a scepter in his hand. Aznek recognized it from a drawing she had seen in the Token Council room. The scepter was made of gold, slim at the base and widening towards the top. Its circular head bore the symbols of all the kingdoms.

"That's King Tamim's scepter," Aznek remarked.

Sai nodded with a smile, and the queen asked, "Is it time?"

"Queen Aznek, you still have a great war to win," Sai replied.

Aznek approached him, her voice trembling. "I'm truly scared. What if I lose?"

Sai reassured her, saying, "That is not what you should be worried about. If you lose, someone else will start anew. The question is, what should you do if you *win*?"

"What any noble lady queen should do!" Aznek said.

Sai offered a smile before disappearing, and Aznek awoke, drenched in sweat as if she had just had a nightmare. She took a drink from a jar, then took a deep breath and declared to herself, "It's time!"

CHAPTER 30

Aznek woke up early in the morning and made her way to a secluded chamber, known only to herself and a select few trusted individuals. Once inside, she locked the door behind her and gazed at the stack of parchments before her. Taking an empty piece, she unrolled it onto her desk. To keep it steady, she placed four stones on each corner. Retrieving a quill from the drawer, she dipped it into a small bottle of blue ink. It was to be the longest letter Aznek would ever write.

To the Usurper Ceres,

It is with immense pleasure that I announce to you that all six kingdoms, and soon to be seven with the resurrection of Grond, are under my rule. Grond will rally with over three thousand Grondies..."

Overwhelmed by her emotions, Aznek's tears began to flow as she reflected on what she had achieved alongside the rebels. The tale of their liberation would be passed down through generations, each kingdom with its own heroic chapter. But the story of Toprak was beyond epic, indescribable with words alone.

A week prior, a letter had arrived for Aznek from her spy within the Union. It informed her that Ceres had rejected Kemal's plea for assistance, which left the King of Toprak with only a few thousand soldiers to face five opposing armies.

This letter served as a catalyst, motivating every Solumy, Token, Turban, Dharatian, and Turangy to march to Toprak. Forty thousand soldiers moved relentlessly towards their destination, determined to conquer Toprak without any gate or catapult standing in their way.

On the second night of marching, they set up camp at the outskirts of Toprak, in a forest known as Inamro. Izmir took the opportunity to speak with Arsalan when he was alone, sitting by a tree with a pensive expression.

Interrupting his thoughts, Izmir asked, "The girls told me you've been waiting for this moment since Afet was taken from you. "Is that true?"

Arsalan stood up and brushed off his hands. "Your Grace..."

"I'm not a queen, and even if I were, I prefer you to call me by my name."

"Alright, Izmir," Arsalan said, "But I promise to restore your title to you."

Izmir returned his smile and rephrased her initial question. "How long have you been waiting for this?"

"Since long before they killed my family," Arsalan replied. "It was before I was promoted to commander, when I learned that I had to swear allegiance to Ceres and serve him with my life."

"So, your wife and child are martyrs, then. They died in the pursuit of justice for your kingdom," Izmir remarked.

Arsalan nodded, and Izmir invited him to sit. "We're all going to die, aren't we?" She said, "But not everyone has the privilege of dying while defending their loved ones. In a way, I envy Afet. Even when they captured her, she died so honourably – I'm not sure I could."

Arsalan remained silent as Izmir continued speaking, but after a moment, he replied, "I made peace with my wife a long time ago."

Surprised by his response, Izmir asked, "Then why are you alone?"

"You think I haven't tried to move on? I have, multiple times. But things never go the way I want. I've never blamed any woman for it. I couldn't commit to anyone because I feel like I want my future wife to be exactly like Afet. It's unfair of me to ask someone to become someone else." Taking a deep breath, Arsalan concluded, "That's why I decided to dedicate my life to my axe."

Izmir rose from her seat, her words resonating through the place like a haunting melody. "You need to move on, just as anyone who has lost their love must," she proclaimed before departing, leaving a lingering trail of unspoken thoughts in her wake.

Arsalan's contemplations on Izmir's advice were brief, soon to be eclipsed by an unexpected interruption. Aznek, the reigning queen to whom Arsalan had pledged unwavering allegiance, gracefully settled beside him.

"Look at her, Arsalan," the queen urged, her eyes fixed upon Izmir. "She is a remarkable woman."

Arsalan's admiration for Izmir was undeniable as he replied, "I couldn't agree more." His voice held a reverence that only heightened the air of uncertainty.

With a hint of urgency, Queen Aznek pressed further, "Then what are you waiting for? She's a Topraki, endowed with beauty and intelligence, and the sole heir to the rule of Toprak."

Arsalan chuckled, a self-deprecating sound, and responded, "You think I don't know that, but I am just a soldier. Who am I to aspire to a woman like her?"

Queen Aznek, her eyes reflecting a knowing wisdom, retorted, "You are one of the rebels, a formidable man who has dedicated years to the pursuit of peace."

Arsalan, deeply moved by her words, stammered, "Your grace..."

But the Queen's intentions were far from vague, and she interrupted him with unwavering determination. "Here is my proposal, Arsalan. I have a plan to reclaim her rightful throne, and it hinges upon her marriage—to a noble man."

The weight of the decision settled upon Arsalan's shoulders, a momentous choice that left him grappling with unfamiliar emotions and considerations. He had never envisioned Izmir in this light, for although he had cherished her from the very moment he set eyes upon her, he had never allowed his thoughts to stray into the realm of romance. Now, with the Queen's proposition, the path ahead was shrouded in uncertainty, and Arsalan found himself on the precipice of a life-altering decision, his own heart an enigma waiting to be unraveled.

The next day, Arsalan joined Ali and the other leaders. The army of Aznek stood in ranks, a few hundred feet away from the Topraki castle. Nora and Roulan led the Turangy and Token armies, positioned in the back, and in the front, Turbans and Dharatians, equipped with twenty catapults.

Ali and Arsalan were positioned on the eastern side. Othman, riding on his horse, moved among the ranks of the Turbans and Dharatians, ensuring that the soldiers were fully motivated for the imminent attack.

He halted next to Nisay and shouted, "What should I call you, Turbans or Dharatians?"

Nisay yelled back, "Neither! Today, we fight as Free People, not defined solely by our nations. We fight to free our brothers and sisters in Toprak. Let us be proud of our identities and histories, today, we unite for a greater cause." He turned to his men, "You will do what no one before you has done. Parents will name their children after you, and those children will grow up following in your footsteps."

Nisay unsheathed his sword, raising it high and screaming, "For our freedom!"

The cheers erupted and continued until Commander Othman raised his hand, signaling for silence before giving the order to shoot.

"Ready the catapults!" shouted one of the Turban soldiers.

The twenty catapults were loaded with large black balls. "Now!" yelled the soldier.

Twenty others drew their swords, cutting the ropes holding the catapult arms. The balls soared through the air, moving like arrows. Instead of aiming for the walls, they were launched high, intending to shatter the inside of the castle. As soon as they landed, they exploded, engulfing the area in flames. Screams echoed.

The screams reached Othman and his armies. He felt a sense of satisfaction hearing the havoc they had caused, and he raised his hands to give the next set of orders. However, Nisay suddenly shouted, "Stop!"

Confused, Othman turned to Nisay and asked, "What's the matter, King Nisay? The assault must continue until they open the gate."

Nisay gestured upwards, prompting Othman to look up at the walls of Toprak. Ununiformed individuals, likely civilians, were throwing stones and screaming in protest. Although their words were indistinguishable, Nisay understood their message. *Get away from our home.*

Othman gritted his teeth and realized Kemal's ruthless tactic. "This criminal has no mercy left in his heart."

Nisay and Othman's assumptions were confirmed, when Ali and Arsalan galloped towards them from the east. Roulan, Nora, and Izmir joined them as well.

"Stop shooting! Kemal has placed the commoners in the front!" He sighed, "He wants to leave us with no choice. We either kill innocents to take Toprak or retreat," replied Arsalan.

Nora seethed, "He's trying to paint us as the villains."

They realized they were caught in a difficult situation. Even a siege would harm innocent lives.

"Lord Ali, what are your orders?" inquired Izmir.

Othman was taken aback by her question. Here was a queen acting like a soldier in front of a man with no noble title or name. And she wasn't the only one. Queen Nora and her husband displayed a similar mindset.

Ali saw an opportunity to outsmart Kemal. "I will take a thousand men with me. We'll use the secret passage to infiltrate the royal residence. We will try to capture Kemal and end this war with minimal bloodshed, just like we did in Token."

"That's an excellent plan, and it would be even better if I led the soldiers myself," stated Arsalan. Before Ali could approve or deny his request, Arsalan continued, "You're our leader in this war, and your orders should not be questioned. However, I'm asking you to let me go in your place, not because you're more important than me, but simply because Toprak is my home. I want the honor of either reclaiming my home or dying while trying."

Ali, understanding Arsalan's determination, had no choice but to grant his wish. Arsalan returned to his army, mounted on his horse, and as he rode away, he glanced back at Izmir, who offered him a smile and a thumbs-up.

Nora whispered to Izmir, "Don't worry, he's a tough man to kill."

"I want him back desperately, just as you would for Nisay," replied Izmir, her voice filled with emotion. "But even if he dies, I would consider myself blessed for having loved a man like him."

The war seemed to come to a standstill as the firing ceased and the Topraki commoners retreated to their homes. Ali and his friends waited anxiously for the bell to ring, a signal of Arsalan's success. They waited in anticipation until a different sound caught their attention—an explosion. They turned their gaze towards the horizon and witnessed men running, the sky above them engulfed in flames.

Without hesitation, Ali and his companions rushed towards the scene, accompanied by a portion of their armies. As they approached, they discovered that these were indeed Arsalan's men. Many had been burned beyond recognition before help could reach them, leaving only a few survivors.

Ali swiftly removed his cloak and used it to extinguish the flames on one of the soldiers' arms. The girls joined him, with Izmir kneeling next to the injured soldier, offering him a bottle of water. Her voice trembled as she asked, "Where is Lord Arsalan?"

The soldier stared at Izmir, then glanced at Ali. "He was at the front when the explosion occurred," he said, coughing on smoke, "I don't think he made it."

Nora held her head, unable to comprehend the loss of one of their most crucial allies even before the war had begun. Roulan went to Izmir, struggling to hold back her tears at the loss of a dear friend. Placing her hand on Izmir's shoulder, she helped her to gain her feet.

Tears welled up in Izmir's eyes as she looked at Ali. "Lord Ali, the explosion claimed Arsalan and our men, but it left a breach in their walls. Please give the orders, and we won't rest until I have Kemal's head."

Ali couldn't approve this idea hastily. Kemal was cunning and likely had set other traps for them. Considering Izmir's emotional state, Ali searched for a delicate way to decline her suggestion. However, Before he could say anything, a horn sound interrupted his thoughts. It was Othman, riding towards them.

"Lord Ali, an army is approaching. One of my men spotted them a few miles away, and they are wearing Union's uniforms."

"Ceres!" Ali exclaimed.

Silence fell upon the group for a moment before Nora spoke up. "Ali, it's your decision."

Ali lifted his gaze towards the horizon, where a cloud of dust billowed towards them. As it drew nearer, the thunderous sound of horse hooves grew louder.

"I suppose we don't have much choice. We shall fight!" declared Ali.

None of the leaders questioned his decision. Instead, each headed in their respective directions to gather their armies and converge at Ali's location. The ranks were formed, and every soldier awaited Ali's command. He remained silent, his eyes fixed upon the enemy before him.

He raised his sword. "For every free man and woman, let us grant them a free world!"

The entire army moved as one, facing the Unionists who advanced in the opposite direction.

The soldiers clashed, and the battle commenced. However, things took an unexpected turn for Aznek's people when eight thousand Topraki soldiers joined the fight as reinforcements for the Union.

On his horse, Ali attacked the enemy riders, skillfully striking from both the right and left. Each hit proved fatal for his opponents.

Nora wielded her bow, swiftly firing arrow after arrow. In a matter of minutes, she had shot forty arrows, each finding its mark and taking down a Unionist soldier.

Roulan brandished both a sword and a dagger, moving among the soldiers with the agility of a snake. She used her sword to disarm her opponents and her dagger to deliver the finishing blow. One strike was all she needed, except for the last soldier. As their swords clashed, he anticipated her next move and blocked her blade. Closing in on her, he attempted to strike, but she foresaw his move. Pushing with all her might, she released her two blades and severed him at the waist.

She screamed, her voice filled with determination, "Fight for your cause, Free People!"

Suddenly, someone leaped at Roulan from behind, and they both tumbled to the ground. With her sword still in hand, she prepared to strike her attacker, but she froze upon seeing who it was—Nisay.

Attempting to stand, Roulan was stopped by Nisay.

"Get your shield and protect yourself!" he shouted urgently.

Roulan remained in place, looking up to witness arrows raining down and claiming the lives of their people. They both crawled towards their shields.

Under the cover of their shields, Roulan asked Nisay, "What's happening?"

"It's Kemal's army!" Nisay replied.

Nora joined them, raising her shield. "Zaya has brought two thousands of her men, and the queen herself has arrived with Leah and around a thousand men."

They were still outnumbered, though. Nora urged Nisay to follow her to a safer location, and they managed to reach a rock where three thousand men, including Aznek and her council members, were gathered.

The war raged on, and Aznek's forces were gradually losing ground. Ali had little time for conversation, but a crucial member of their rebellion had gone missing. He waited until all the rebels had gathered and spoke with urgency, "Some soldiers spotted Izmir on her way to the castle. Whatever she has in mind, it's not good."

Izmir knew that their defeat was imminent, so she made the decision to send King Kemal to his grave before meeting her own demise. With his army occupied in assisting the Unionists, it was now possible for her to reach him within his council.

She successfully evaded the sight of the guards, eliminating them one by one until she reached the council's gate.

To her surprise, Kemal was seated on his throne, as if he had been expecting her arrival.

"Kemal. It's time for you to join Boa and Hosni," she declared through clenched teeth, spitting on the ground.

Unfazed, Kemal remained seated and began applauding. "You managed to sneak into my council without being detected. I'm not sure whether I should feel proud of the daughter I raised or disappointed."

"How about dead?" Izmir asked, her grip tightening on her sword.

Kemal burst into laughter and replied, "My dear Izmir, it would take more than a sword to kill a king." Just as Izmir was about to retort, he shouted, "Now!"

Two doors swung open, and about forty men entered the room, encircling Izmir. Kemal smirked, saying, "I'm not as foolish as your father. I always have a backup plan."

"Not this time, usurper!" a rough voice echoed from the entrance.

Izmir turned her gaze and almost dropped her sword when she saw who it was. Arsalan stood before her, unscathed and wielding his axe, resting the hilt on his shoulder.

But Arsalan wasn't alone. He was accompanied by Aznek, Leah, Sofia, Roulan, Nora, and Zaya.

Kemal erupted into laughter. "I've always considered you a clever man, Arsalan. Instead of bringing real soldiers, you brought six women to protect you."

Queen Aznek sheathed her sword and corrected him, "Five women. I'm here merely to observe and pass judgment at the end."

"Kill them all!" Kemal screamed, expecting to relish in the sight of his enemies' blood.

He was wrong – and in the end, he was petrified. His forty men were swiftly dispatched by the five formidable women and Arsalan.

Frantically, he called for more soldiers, hoping others would come to his aid. But his castle was empty, devoid of any remaining loyalists.

Arsalan approached him, and Kemal raised his sword to fight, only to lose it in their first clash. Arsalan then pressed his axe against Kemal's neck, demanding him to move.

"Lady Queen, what is your command?" Arsalan asked, hoping for the order to execute him.

But Queen Aznek had a different plan. She saw Kemal as leverage to secure the safety of Ali and his armies, who had suffered heavy losses but continued to fight, clinging to the hope that Ali's plan would succeed. And it seemed their wish was granted when the sound of a Topraki horn echoed through the air.

One of the Topraki commanders began shouting, "Retreat! The king is in the enemy's hands!"

Word spread among the soldiers as they battled, and both armies ceased their onslaught, retreating in opposite directions.

Ali seized Kemal's crown and strode with deliberate steps towards the no-man's land, the muck squelching beneath his boots.

Two Union commanders and one from Toprak approached him. The Topraki commander spoke, "Lord Ali, release the king immediately!"

"Or?" Ali countered, toying with the crown in his hands. "Come on, you can do better than that."

Realizing that Ali held the upper hand and knew how to use it, the commander narrowed his eyes. "What are your terms?"

"For starters, tell the Unionists to depart, and I give you my word that no further blood will be shed."

It was a reasonable request, and Ali was known for keeping his word. The Topraki commander turned to relay the suggestion to the Unionists, but before he could speak, one of them impaled him with a sword thrust to the heart.

The Unionist commander turned to Ali and sneered, "The only ruler who matters in this world is His Highness, Emperor Ceres. The rest are just puppets we place to enforce our rule."

Ali remained unfazed by the blunt statement, his expression unyielding. The Unionist commander's words hung in the air, laden with both threat and a hollow promise. "Surrender and give us our four kingdoms," the commander demanded, his voice dripping with arrogance, "and I promise, you and your foolish queen won't be harmed."

Ali's gaze remained fixed on a distant point, his mind racing with thoughts of strategy and resilience. He refused to succumb to fear or let the commander's words shake his resolve. Ignoring the commander's attempt to provoke a reaction, Ali maintained his composure.

The Unionist commander, sensing Ali's steadfastness, felt compelled to further assert his authority. "I will grant you time to discuss this matter with your queen and friends," he declared, a hint of impatience seeping through his tone, "but be aware that time is not on your side."

Izmir was the first to speak up upon learning of the Unionists' disinterest in having Kemal back. Addressing the Lady Queen with determination, she expressed her belief in the importance of justice prevailing, regardless of the war's outcome. "Lady Queen, we cannot predict the end of this war, but justice must be served. Since our enemy has no interest in reclaiming Kemal, the man who murdered my family and stole our home, I wish to pass sentence on him."

A knowing glance was exchanged between Aznek and Ali, their shared understanding evident. Aznek smiled and affirmed, "He's all yours, Your Grace."

Izmir reached into her pocket and retrieved a small object, making her way towards Kemal, who was bound to a nearby tree. His eyes widened in terror as he saw what she held in her hand—a needle, the very same murder weapon he had used to kill her mother.

"I took this from your drawer," she stated, her fingers twirling the object.

Kemal pleaded, "No, please, not this one!" His gaze then turned to Ali, his voice trembling, "Lord Ali, the Creator prohibits such executions. Beheading is the only permissible method according to his law."

Ali smiled in response and calmly replied, "You have misunderstood, my friend. It is written in all the holy books that a killer must be put to death in the same manner they took a life."

Before Kemal could utter another word, Izmir swiftly plunged the needle into his neck. The gruesome scene unfolded, causing some of the watching soldiers to move away to vomit. Kemal's face turned red, foaming at the mouth. Blood flowed from his ears and eyes.

Despite the long-held grudges in her heart, Izmir found herself unable to derive satisfaction from Kemal's suffering. She made the decision to end his torment, driving a dagger into his heart.

Aznek approached Izmir, tapping her shoulder with pride. "I am so proud of you. Let us go and reclaim your throne."

Izmir surveyed the remaining few thousand Toprakies from the initial battle who decided to join her, as well as the other armies. Exhaustion marked their bodies, and she knew they were ill-prepared to stand against the Unionists. Nevertheless, she raised her sword and spoke with determination, "I may not regain my throne, but I refuse to surrender. I will fight, and so should all of you, Toprakies!"

The Topraki soldiers cheered in response, joined by the other armies, recognizing that this battle would be their last. However, Ali held a different belief. He had a winning card up his sleeve, and it was time to reveal it. With a powerful voice, he declared, "None of us will die, not today at least. I understand your frustrations completely. We may be outnumbered and weary, but we possess someone who can tip the scales in this war. Sir Albert!"

Sai's apprentice emerged, his face filled with anticipation. He clapped his hands, summoning four men who rode towards him, pulling a carriage behind them.

All eyes were fixed on the carriage, curiosity piqued. What could be concealed within? The soldiers pulled out small catapults, each with a black ball encircled by a thick red line in its bucket.

Ali beckoned Nora over, knowing her remarkable archery skills. Nora approached, unaware of what these miniature catapults were intended for.

"Queen Nora, I have fought for over two decades, and I can say with certainty that I have never witnessed anyone – man or woman – shoot like you," Ali said.

Nisay and Roulan shared Nora's confusion, eager for an explanation. Perplexed, Nora looked at Ali and asked, "What do you mean?"

"It's quite simple, Queen Nora," Ali explained. "We will launch these balls with the catapults, and all you need to do is shoot them within the red lines before they land. Can you do that?"

Nora prepared her quiver and winked, "With my eyes blindfolded."

Ali urged the soldiers to release the catapults, and the balls soared through the air. As Ali had anticipated, Nora didn't miss her mark.

Everyone expected explosions upon impact, but instead, the balls unleashed a fine dust that cascaded like rain upon the enemy forces.

"What in the world is happening?" Izmir questioned.

"That, my friend, is the Tears Dropper," Albert answered.

Nora understood the effect this powder could have on individuals, but she couldn't fathom its application on a mass of people. Blinding every soldier in such a vast army seemed implausible.

Nora turned to Albert, who chuckled and clarified, "The Tears Dropper is inspired by the onion. Its effects occur when we smell it, not when it comes in contact with our eyes."

He wasn't mistaken, as screams erupted from the enemy ranks. Ali gave the order to attack.

With their adversaries left vulnerable and disoriented, the united Free People, their blades glistening under the unforgiving sun, moved with ruthless precision through the chaos. The enemy, their vision impaired by the blinding powder thrown upon them, could hardly see their relentless foes.

The cacophony of screams continued to pierce the air, and the battlefield bore witness to a gruesome tapestry of blood splattered across shields, horse hooves, and gleaming blades. The realization soon dawned upon both the Union and Topraki forces that victory was unattainable. They reluctantly began their retreat, and the Free People, having achieved a decisive triumph, showed little interest in pursuit.

This glorious moment marked the long-awaited liberation of the last kingdom held in colonial shackles.

CHAPTER 31

..And that's how we have regained our last Kingdom, Toprak.

Aznek concluded in her letter to Ceres. She left no detail unmentioned. Her intentions weren't merely informative; they were meant to stoke anger in Ceres' heart.

As Ceres finished reading the letter, he tore it into shreds and immediately called for his council to convene. The generals were taken aback, witnessing a side of him they had never seen before—red-faced, with furrowed brows.

Ben, the prime advisor, spoke up first. "What are your orders, Your Highness?"

Rather than answering the question, Ceres shifted his gaze to the military chief and inquired, "How many soldiers do we have left?"

"Approximately a hundred thousand men!" Lord Filip responded.

Ceres rose to his feet, his voice resolute. "Prepare all the soldiers for attack. Gather our weapons and catapults. We shall reduce Solum to rubble. Can you do that?"

The military chief stepped forward, bowing as he declared, "Consider your walls already adorned with the heads of rebels, Your Highness."

The prime advisor coughed twice before voicing his opinion, "Your Highness, I don't believe that launching an attack now is the right course of action."

"Why not?" the military chief blurted.

Before Ben could reply, Ceres cut him off. "Lord Ben, I understand your concern. If we strike now, we will lose the element of surprise. However, if we delay, our enemy will grow stronger, and they might be the ones to strike first. It's either us or them."

The military chief added, "Our craftsmen have discovered a way to breach their walls. With our catapults and new weapons, they stand no chance."

Although Ceres and Filip presented compelling arguments, Ben remained unconvinced. However, he understood that he couldn't sway Ceres from his decision. Thus, the plan was agreed upon.

Ceres faced further complications when he began to feel the return of the pain in his back. He had thought it had disappeared, so he summoned Thaar, the Turban healer.

Thaar entered the room, visibly concerned, and noticed Ceres' pallid complexion. "Your Highness, you don't appear well."

"You bet, Lady Thaar. I lost a third of my army, and the pain has returned, just like the first time," Ceres replied in a subdued tone.

Thaar approached him cautiously and spoke, her eyes fixed on him. "I am deeply sorry for your soldiers, Your Highness. But don't dwell too much on their loss. They perished fulfilling their duty. Instead, focus on the future and how you can bring justice in their name."

Ceres gazed at her silently, his expression unchanged.

She continued, "As for your pain, you should be glad about it!"

Ceres shot her an angry look, but she persisted. "It signifies that your body is responding to the latest treatment, the treatment that will eradicate all remnants of the Black Spiders."

Ceres' expression remained stoic as he inquired, "How much longer until this pain subsides?"

"Two weeks at most," Thaar replied. Ceres dismissed her, but before she reached the exit, he called out to her.

"Lady Thaar, I will go to war. I won't be with the main army; instead, I'll camp a few hundred feet away from the battlefield, and you will accompany me."

Thaar turned and lowered her head as she responded, "Your Highness, you won't require my constant care, so there is no point in me joining you. Please, spare me from that. It's not that I refuse, but I simply don't feel comfortable going to war."

"That is an order, Lady Thaar," Ceres said, and before she could reply, he added, "Close the door on your way out."

***

Usually, Aznek would celebrate each conquest, but this time, she had no time to revel in her victory. Instead, she took Ali and Izmir with her to Toprak, the kingdom they had just freed from Ceres' rule.

For the first time in history, Toprak remained without a ruler for a week. Nonetheless, things were stable there, thanks to Judge Ayden. He wasn't an ordinary judge; his influence over the people was akin to that of a king.

Izmir briefed her companions about Ayden and revealed his corrupt nature. She even suspected him of being involved in the conspiracy to usurp her father's throne.

They entered the kingdom during the day. Some Toprakies cheered upon seeing Aznek and knelt in her presence, while others hurled insults and labeled her a usurper.

The queen and her companions remained composed, paying no heed to the insults and compliments alike. They proceeded to the council room, where Judge Ayden and his consultant awaited their arrival.

The three of them approached the throne where Ayden was seated, but they did not bow.

"Good day, Judge Ayden," Aznek greeted him.

Ayden returned the greeting and invited them to take a seat. "Your Grace, I am glad the war is over."

Ali took it upon himself to respond. "There is only one way to end this war, Judge Ayden, and we both know how."

Ayden's displeasure was evident as he attempted to silence Ali. "Lord Ali, I believe I was addressing Queen Aznek."

"Ali is one of my most trusted advisors, and his words carry the weight of my own," Aznek retorted.

Ayden remained silent on the matter and decided to get straight to the point. "Your Grace, we have agreed to acknowledge your title as Lady Queen. However, we need to choose a new king for Toprak first."

"I am not concerned about my title, Your Honor. I know it is rightfully mine, but I am here to ensure that Toprak gets the right ruler," Aznek stated.

Ayden was a shrewd man and understood the implications behind her words. "Your Grace, if you are planning to name Princess Izmir as queen, I'm afraid it is not possible. Despite her royal blood, our centuries-old law has never allowed a woman to rule."

Ayden had no power to force Aznek, and he knew she could easily name Izmir as the queen. However, he also understood that such a decision would not be well-received by the people of Toprak, who were deeply attached to their laws and traditions. They would not hesitate to revolt against that choice.

"I am not planning to name Izmir, Your Honor," Aznek declared, surprising Ayden. He refrained from jumping to conclusions and instead invited the queen to explain further.

Aznek, however, did not provide any additional information. Instead, she retrieved a rolled parchment from her pocket. "In my hand, I hold the official document of Kemal's nomination as king, signed by you. He was not elected by the Toprakies; instead, he was named as if it were his birthright." Aznek revealed.

She unrolled the parchment and continued, "As you justified in your document, Your Honor," she began to read, "*according to Topraki law, marrying a woman with royal blood grants any male Topraki the right to rule.*"

One of Ayden's consultants stood up, shouting, "This is madness! There is no such law!"

Ali exchanged a knowing smile with Izmir.

Aznek pressed on, disregarding the consultant's outburst. "I won't debate that with you, my lord. My knowledge of Topraki law is limited," Aznek shifted her gaze back to Ayden. "You have two choices. You can either deny the existence of this law, and we can proceed to the election of a new king..."

"Of course, we're going to do that," the advisor sitting next to Ayden interrupted.

"Lord Ali, if this man interrupts again, behead him!" the queen asserted firmly, continuing her ultimatum. "Or, If you choose to deny the law and go through with the election, Lord Ayden, you will be held accountable for manipulating the law when you named Kemal as king. Such an act of treason is punishable by death."

Ayden's face turned pale, and he swallowed nervously. The queen smiled as she continued, revealing her alternative proposition. "But I am not a woman who seeks trouble. I have a way out for you," Aznek declared.

Ayden's eyes widened, eagerly awaiting her solution.

"Just as you named Kemal, you will name Izmir's future husband: Lord Arsalan. In exchange for your compliance, you and your team will be offered land with a house in Solum and a monthly wage until the end of your days," Aznek proposed.

The consultant attempted to intervene, but Ayden shot him an angry look and whispered, "It's either that or the chopping block."

CHAPTER 32

Ali and the council members were positioned along the walls of Solum, patiently waiting for the enemy to appear. Aznek's spies had provided them with detailed information about Ceres' army, including their massive numbers and formidable arsenal of weapons.

Ali had never felt more confident. He recalled the moment when Lady Bianca had given him his freedom certificate. Back then, he was just one man standing against an empire and seven kingdoms. With no military or political background, he had made the bold decision to fight under the banner of taking down Ceres, no matter the cost.

He had lost friends like Keita, Alighieri, and Sai along the way, but he had persevered. Now, only one battle remained, and he firmly believed that victory was within their grasp.

Aznek, with her keen judgment of character, saw the fire of triumph burning in Ali's eyes. She looked at him and said, "Lord Ali, it will be you who delivers the final speech."

Ali hesitated, feeling overwhelmed by the magnitude of the moment. "I wouldn't dare, Your Grace," he replied humbly.

A smile played on Aznek's lips as she responded, "You started this rebellion, you should be the one to finish it."

Nora and Roulan, standing nearby, exchanged smiles and nodded. Ali felt cornered, with no other options but to obey his queen's command.

He looked down at the soldiers gathered in the courtyard, thousands of them standing at attention, their gazes fixed upon him. Ali took a deep breath and began to speak.

"Five years ago, we stood in this very place, facing an enemy three times the size of our army. With our meager resources, we fought as one, and we drove the invaders back to where they came from. Today, we face an army three times our size, but nothing has changed. We can still emerge victorious from this battle."

Ali paused, surveying the soldiers' expressions. Fear still lingered in their eyes, and he pressed on, determined to instill courage within them.

"In fact, there is one thing that will change. If we win this war, it will be the last war. The life of peace that each and every one of you deserves will be restored. So fight for your lives and fight for your kingdom. And even if you sacrifice your lives in the process, rest assured it will not be in vain. You will live on eternally in the memories of all the generations to come."

Lifting his sword high, Ali let out a resounding cry, "For a free world!"

The soldiers erupted in cheers, the echoes of their voices filling the air, until the sound of the enemy's horn pierced through the cacophony.

Aznek gazed out at the vast army amassed before them, a sense of terror gripping her heart. The sheer size of the enemy's forces was overwhelming, and she found herself unable to discern the end of their ranks.

"Is that what a hundred thousand soldiers truly look like?" she whispered to herself.

Nora stood beside Ali, her mind racing to find a strategy to defeat such a formidable force. "Do you have a plan, Lord Ali?" she asked, desperation creeping into her voice.

Leah, standing on Ali's other side, took a deep breath before responding, "Beyond fighting until the very end, I see no other recourse."

Ali placed a reassuring hand on his wife's shoulder and spoke with unwavering conviction, "Trust in Arsalan's plan. I give you my word that it will succeed."

Leah offered a faint smile, not wanting to delve further into the matter. She didn't wish to disappoint Ali, who had placed great hope in Arsalan's plan, even though she believed it to be nothing short of suicidal.

The Union forces had yet to initiate their attack. They continued their taunting song about Ceres, attempting to provoke the people of Solum before launching their assault.

Meanwhile, Ceres had set up camp a few hundred feet away from his army, filled with anticipation of seeing Aznek and Ali's heads impaled on his soldiers' spikes. He had stationed around a hundred men to guard his camp against any potential enemy incursion. Only Thaar and his personal guard were allowed inside his tent.

"You appear to be in good spirits, Your Highness," remarked Thaar.

"Damn right I am!" Ceres exclaimed. "It's not every day I get to learn that my enemies are cowering like rats behind their walls. They think these foolish fortifications will shield them, little do they know that we have found a way to breach them."

Thaar handed him a mug and replied, "I am a woman who values peace, but after witnessing what they have done to your men, I find solace in the fact that justice will prevail."

Curiously, Ceres examined the contents of the mug and asked, "What is this?"

Thaar responded, "It is a medicinal concoction mixed with your favorite juice. It will alleviate any pain you may be experiencing."

Ceres downed the contents of the mug in a single gulp and continued sharing stories about how he and his father had established their empire. Thaar listened attentively, savoring each word he spoke.

Suddenly, Ceres began rubbing his throat and wiping sweat from his forehead with his forearm. "Lady Thaar, why am I sweating? It's cold in here," he inquired.

"It is the effect of the medicine I administered, Your Highness."

Ceres felt a sense of relief and asked, "How long will it last?"

Thaar approached him, whispering, "It depends on your body, but it will persist for at least a full day."

Confusion etched across Ceres' face as he stared at Thaar. She smiled, "The duration is precisely the amount of time needed to transport you to Her Grace, the Lady Queen."

A look of shock washed over Ceres' face, and before he could call for help, Thaar swiftly placed a piece of fabric in his mouth and secured it tightly with a rope. Struggling to resist, Ceres found his limbs heavy and unresponsive. He glanced at Thaar, silently questioning her actions.

"You have every right to be afraid, Your Highness. You have indeed been deceived," Thaar stated calmly.

Ceres began to mumble as he locked eyes with his guard, who removed his mask and relished in the terror reflected in the emperor's eyes.

"This is King Arsalan, the new ruler of Toprak, and it was he who proposed your arrest, Emperor," Thaar declared, signaling to Arsalan, who approached to remove the cloth from Ceres' mouth. Despite his attempts to scream, Ceres could barely move his lips.

Thaar positioned herself in front of him and began to elucidate, "I have been developing this poison for months, which you willingly consumed from your mug. It has a unique effect—it paralyzes the entire body while allowing the person who ingests it to remain fully conscious, able to see and hear everything happening around him."

The tent's curtain was abruptly pulled aside, causing Arsalan to instinctively place his hand on the pommel of his sword. However, his hand froze in mid-motion as he recognized the unexpected visitor—Zaya.

She entered the tent, her expression dark, and delivered the startling news: all the Union guards had been slain by the Alinians.

Turning to Thaar, Arsalan spoke, "We are ready to proceed."

"Not before I explain everything to His Highness," Thaar retorted, "Do you know what Thaar means in the ancient language?"

Thaar smiled mischievously before continuing, "Vengeance. You probably assumed it was just a fabricated name. In reality, I have used many names, one of them being Umali."

She relished the look of shock on Ceres' face, and she didn't hold back. "Yes, I am Umali—the leader of the Alinians. I am the same woman who sent David, the man you believed to be your loyal guard, who had been deceiving you for years." She paused, "Tell me, Ceres, how does it feel to be defeated and powerless?"

Ceres couldn't respond, knowing that the question was rhetorical. He simply waited for her to continue.

A tear trickled down Thaar's cheek as she spoke, her voice filled with emotion. "You did the same thing to me when you took my only son away. You didn't care about the feelings of a helpless mother. But that was the mistake you made—you provoked a mother and attempted to harm her child. And let me tell you, that is the worst enemy you could ever make."

"Lady Umali, we must hurry," Arsalan interjected.

Ignoring Arsalan's urgency, Umali maintained her gaze on Ceres and proceeded, her voice filled with intensity, "Umali is actually two words in the ancient language: 'Um' and 'Ali.' Do you know what it means?"

Arsalan exchanged a startled glance with Zaya, whose tears continued to flow. Umali carried on without pause, "It means *'the mother of Ali'*—the same Ali who turned your life into a living hell and took your daughter away."

Umali's words momentarily faltered as she wiped her eyes, before resolutely continuing, "I left my tribe while pregnant with my daughter, Zaya. Fortunately, I encountered kind-hearted individuals who assisted me in giving birth to her. And now, after twenty-six years, I have returned to bring justice to all the free people, and at last, I have the opportunity to meet my son."

Arsalan was taken aback, his eyes fixed on Zaya, who offered a smile, "He is my brother."

A few miles away, Ali remained stationed on the wall, anxiously awaiting news from Arsalan, who had promised to capture Ceres—the only leverage they had to secure victory in the war and dismantle the empire. Unbeknownst to Ali, he had no idea that his own mother was involved, nor was he aware that she was still alive.

"Lord Ali," a voice called out from downstairs, and Ali could hardly believe his eyes when he saw who it was—his comrade, Arsalan.

Without waiting for him to ascend the stairs, Ali hurriedly descended, placing his hand on Arsalan's shoulder. "Please, tell me you have some good news."

A smile spread across Arsalan's face as he replied, "I have Ceres."

All the council members gathered, brimming with excitement upon hearing the momentous news. Aznek urged them to expedite the negotiations before the enemy began launching their catapults.

"King Arsalan, since it was your idea, you have the privilege of ending this war," Ali said.

But Arsalan shook his head, "No, Lord Ali You started this rebellion, so you should be the one to finish it."

Ali turned his attention to the queen and asked, "Is this some new protocol you've all adopted?"

Aznek remained silent, instead directing her gaze towards Nora, who grinned and said, "I came up with that statement. Consider it a token of gratitude for the one you devised for me. 'You're a queen, you're meant to be served.'"

Ali mounted his horse and departed from the castle, heading towards an army of one hundred thousand soldiers. He rode alone.

Although the army had yet to mobilize, Ali knew deep down that the war was already over. He pressed on until he reached the forefront of the Unionist forces.

A commander rode towards him and warned, "Speak, or you shall utter your last words."

"I need to speak with the prime advisor," Ali shouted.

"Speak your mind. I am a commander, and I can relay your message even to His Highness."

Ali paid no attention to him and said, "Do not waste my time, soldier. Fetch your prime advisor. I have valuable information for him, and if you delay any longer, you will surely lose your head for it."

The commander did not argue and swiftly disappeared amidst the soldiers. A short while later, he returned, accompanied by two men.

The military chief grinned as he approached Ali. "Ila, in the flesh. It's good to see you here. I will finally have the pleasure of severing your head."

Ali smiled and responded, "I understand I was tough on you, Lord Filip, but I was simply doing my duty. I see, you've risen to become a prime advisor."

Filip corrected him, stating, "I am the military chief, and this is Prime Advisor Ben."

Ben glared at Ali with a scowl before questioning, "Why do you insist on speaking with me?"

"I wished to converse with the most powerful man in the Union," Ali replied.

Ben exchanged a bewildered look with Filip and quickly corrected himself, "His Highness, Emperor Ceres is the most powerful figure within the Union and the seven kingdoms."

"Not for the moment, Lord Ben," Ali responded calmly. With purpose, he reached behind him and retrieved the crown of Ceres, then tossed it onto the ground beside Ben's horse. The metallic thud echoed through the air, the weighty symbol of power now lying discarded before them.

Filip and Ben couldn't conceal their astonishment as Ali's words sank in. "He's in our custody now, and unless you wish for him to meet his demise, I suggest you gather your soldiers and vacate our lands," Ali declared firmly.

With a tug of the reins, he swiftly turned his horse and galloped away.

As Ali approached the gate, the jubilant sounds of cheering and exultation from the Free People reached his ears. Turning back, he beheld the Unionists beginning their retreat, leaving the premises.

Hugs and tears of joy flowed ceaselessly throughout the night. The news of Ceres being in their custody resonated deeply with the people. The people understood that the tide had shifted in their favor, and relief washed over them, dispelling the shadows of conflict.

The following day, Aznek summoned everyone to the council chamber. Ali arrived last, greeted by the smiles and admiring gazes of those present. Pausing in the center of the room, he addressed the assembly.

"Don't look at me as if I were the sole bringer of this victory," Ali chuckled, "It was Arsalan and the queen who played pivotal roles. There was also a third woman who aided us," he continued, his gaze shifting towards the queen. Ali suspected it was Zaya's mother, Lady Umali, who had lent her support.

A sob caught Ali's attention from the left, and he turned to see Zaya in tears. She was not alone; the other girls beside her wept as well. Curious, he approached Leah.

She walked towards him, softly speaking as she held his hand. "Umali was the woman who assisted me in rescuing Noah when he was kidnapped," Leah revealed.

Ali was captivated by this revelation. He turned his gaze to Aznek, questioning whether she had known about this, and she nodded in affirmation. Feeling a mixture of gratitude and bewilderment, he asked, "Why didn't you tell me? I could have personally expressed my gratitude to her."

A soft voice emerged from behind, stating, "Why do you need to thank a woman who was simply taking care of her grandson?"

Ali turned towards the source of the voice, and his heart seemed to stop as his eyes met Umali. Time stood still as he beheld her familiar features, realizing that she had not changed much over the years. Her broad smile and expressive brown eyes remained unchanged, evoking a flood of memories within him.

For over two decades, Ali had longed to see his mother. Not a day had passed without him thinking of her, yearning for her presence, and cherishing the memories of her bedtime stories, kisses, and warm embraces. The absence of her love and guidance had left a void in his heart that nothing could fill. Every time he ventured to the Blessing Tree, he fervently prayed for just a fleeting glimpse of her, but the Thinkers had never granted his wish.

The longing in his soul intensified as he stood there, frozen in the moment, unable to believe that his mother was standing before him once again. The depth of his yearning and the pain of their separation surged through him, compelling tears to well up in his eyes. In that instant, he silently vowed to cherish every precious moment with his mother, for he knew the love between them was eternal, transcending time and distance. The room was filled with a bittersweet mixture of joy and sorrow, as the reunion of mother and son ignited a shared sense of longing and the understanding of time lost.

Overwhelmed with emotion, Ali found himself unable to utter the two syllables he hadn't spoken in twenty-six years.

"Mother!" he finally managed to say, and he rushed towards her, falling to his knees. Holding her hands, he kissed them while tears cascaded down his face.

Halima assisted Ali to stand and embraced him tightly. He had no intention of letting go, and she shared the same sentiment. Tears flowed freely from everyone present in the room, including Arsalan, as the weight of their experiences and the joy of reunion washed over them.

CHAPTER 33

Ali and Halima spent the entire night awake, catching up on the events of the past twenty-six years. No one dared to interrupt their conversation, not even Zaya, who could finally address him as her brother.

Ali was astounded when Halima revealed that she had been the midwife who assisted in Aznek's birth, as well as Nisay's. They were the last babies she delivered before mysteriously disappearing from her home tribe.

Ali had so much to say, but what consumed him the most was her sudden disappearance. "The moment Lady Bianca gave me permission, I rushed to Okorom to find you, but they told me you had left the tribe right after I was taken," he explained.

Halima took a deep breath before continuing, "You were my special boy, Ali. Everything about you was extraordinary—strong, intelligent, and compassionate. Aznek's father once told me that these qualities were only found in iconic figures like King Tamim. And then one day, soldiers came and took you away from me."

Ali held her hand tightly, "Why did you leave Okorom? People told me that you threw yourself down a well. But I couldn't believe it."

Halima let out a sigh and replied, "I didn't leave home to seek death, but rather to rescue my son. I was fortunate to find kind-hearted people who took care of me and helped me give birth to your sister, Zaya. I made numerous attempts to infiltrate the empire and bring you back, but I failed each time. Eventually, I gave up, until I met a noble man named Rio."

Ali was taken aback by the mention of that name and interrupted his mother, "Rio, the gardener? Leah's friend?"

Halima smiled and nodded, saying, "Yes, he's the one who helped me get in touch with Lady Bianca. I offered her a substantial amount of gold to purchase and free you, but she selflessly agreed without accepting any payment from me."

"She was a remarkable woman," Ali said, but then confusion filled his voice, "But why didn't she tell me about you?"

"That was my request," Halima explained. "When I learned about your plan to confront Ceres, I asked her not to reveal my existence to you so that you wouldn't be distracted from your mission."

Ali felt as if he were in the presence of a skilled storyteller, narrating a tale of adventure and intrigue. But Halima wasn't finished.

"Instead of meeting you directly, I decided to support you from the shadows. That's when I joined David's tribe, and a few years later, I became their leader."

Ali inquired, "Did anyone else know about you?"

Before Halima could respond, there was a knock on the door. It was Aznek, Leah, and Zaya. Halima smiled and said, "Speaking of which, these three ladies were the only ones who knew about me."

Aznek spoke up, "I learned about her from the Thinker."

Zaya added, "And mother told me the night before my wedding."

Ali turned his gaze towards his wife and uttered, "You knew, and you kept it hidden from me."

Leah chuckled and responded, "She made me swear not to tell, and I learned from you to never break an oath."

Laughter filled the room, but it quickly subsided as the queen urged Ali to accompany her to speak with Ceres. They made their way to the dungeon where Ceres was being held. The effects of Halima's poison had worn off, and he had been provided with food and drink.

As they opened the door to his cell, Ceres greeted them. "Queen Aznek and Lord Ali, the two individuals who captured the most powerful man in history."

Aznek rolled her eyes, "Shut up, or I'll make sure Lady Thaar comes and silences you once again."

Ceres burst into laughter and then turned his attention to Ali. "I thought we were going to have a man-to-man conversation, but you disappointed me by bringing a woman to discuss political matters."

Ali gazed at the queen, seeking her approval, and she nodded.

"Do I have to remind you, Ceres, that if it weren't for a woman, you would still be sitting on your throne right now?"

Ceres began to respond, but Ali interrupted, raising his voice, "I'm not here to play games with you."

Confused, Ceres stared at Ali and asked, "Then I assume you want to execute me. You could avoid the trial and kill me."

Ali's tone was laced with sarcasm as he replied, "You're my father-in-law. I would never kill you. Instead, I would like to set you free."

Ceres looked at them with disbelief.

Aznek spoke up this time, saying, "We decided to spare your life."

Ceres gazed at both Aznek and Ali, but they remained silent, the tension palpable. Taking a deep breath, Ceres finally spoke up. "Alright, this is where you tell me what you want in return."

Aznek's response was simple and direct. "Your gold."

Ceres looked at Aznek, surprised by her request, and she continued. "I have no use for your head, but your gold would make a significant difference in my kingdoms."

Curiosity piqued, Ceres asked, "How much do you want?"

Aznek exchanged a knowing smile with Ali before replying, "Everything you have."

Ceres' face turned red with anger, and he stood up to respond, but the queen interjected, rejecting his immediate retaliation. "You have three days to consider this proposal, please think carefully about it. It is this, or death."

Three days later, Aznek and Ali returned to Ceres. The sarcasm that once laced Aznek's tone was now absent, replaced with a firm resolve.

"I have decided to grant you what you desire," Ceres said, resigned. "In exchange for my gold, I want my daughter and my grandson."

Ali smiled at Ceres. However, the queen's reaction was one of rage as she screamed, "Guards!"

The guards swiftly arrived, and Aznek addressed them coldly. "Prepare the execution yard."

Desperate to regain control of the situation, Ceres cried out, "Wait! Ali, restrain this woman! We can negotiate!"

Ali's smile vanished, and he approached Ceres, his voice stern. "There is no negotiation with criminals like you. Give us the gold if you wish to leave this place with your head intact."

Reluctantly, Ceres asked, "How much do you want?"

The queen glared at Ceres, issuing a final threat. "This is your last chance. Disclose the locations of your gold, and you will be set free. Refuse, and the consequences will be dire."

Defeated, Ceres interjected, "Fine. You win."

He proceeded to divulge the locations of his hidden gold. It took them four days to retrieve every last coin, the total amounting to over six-hundred thousand gold pieces. It would be enough to boost the economies of all the kingdoms.

Before Ceres was set free, Leah visited him—a surprise that brought him joy, despite what she had done to him in the past.

Sitting next to him, Leah stared at the ceiling and spoke, "You see, Father, if only you hadn't succumbed to your ego, you could have achieved greatness. But instead, you chose the easy way, and now you find yourself ashamed and imprisoned."

"I'm leaving it, and I will hit back," Ceres declared defiantly.

Leah shot him an angry look. "Don't you ever learn from your mistakes?" She softened her tone and took his hand. "There's always time for redemption."

Ceres smiled, "The only regret I have in this entire war is that my elder daughter isn't by my side. But apart from that, I will continue pursuing your husband and your so-called queen until my last breath."

Leah stood up, disappointment evident in her eyes. "Farewell, Father."

The following day, the prime advisor arrived at Solum, to retrieve the emperor.

On their journey back to the empire, all Ceres could talk about was revenge. The prime advisor shared his excitement, unaware of what awaited him. However, their spirits dampened when they realized that Ceres had given all his gold to Aznek.

Ben, the prime advisor, pulled the reins of his horse and couldn't contain his bewilderment. "Your Highness, why did you do that?"

Ceres, with a hint of sarcasm, retorted, "Oh, should I have politely requested to be set free? I had to give them what they wanted in order to secure my release."

"But why did they demand such an exorbitant ransom of gold from us as well?"

Perplexed, Ceres asked, "What do you mean?"

"After your arrest, Arsalan approached us, demanding a payment of five hundred thousand gold coins as ransom."

A wave of shock washed over Ceres as he began to unravel Ali's intricate game. "And you actually gave them that amount of gold?" he asked, his disbelief evident.

"It was either that or losing you forever, your highness," Ben replied, his voice irritated.

Ceres shook his head, his expression reflecting disbelief. "But you don't have all this gold."

Ben sighed, acknowledging the truth. "You're right. Our treasury only held a hundred and eighty thousand coins, so we resorted to forcibly collecting the rest from the commoners," he explained, revealing the desperate measures they had taken in their attempt to meet the ransom demand.

As feared, the situation rapidly deteriorated, plunging the empire into chaos and despair. Poverty and starvation became pervasive, fueling the anger and desperation of Ceres' people.

Ceres, burdened by the weight of his decisions, realized the extent to which he had been played by Queen Aznek and her allies. Instead of executing him, they had stripped him of his wealth, leaving his people destitute and resentful. Many sought refuge in neighboring free kingdoms, seeking a better life away from the crumbling empire. However, others harbored deep-seated resentment toward Ceres himself, unable to forgive him for the suffering he had caused.

In the depths of the night, Ceres lay in his chamber, consumed by relentless contemplation of the tragedy that had befallen him. His once-vast empire, rule, and wealth had all crumbled into the abyss of history. Yet, amidst this sea of losses, what tormented his heart most was the haunting memory of murdering his own wife and the painful knowledge that his own daughter had abandoned him to join his most bitter adversary.

In a desperate quest for solace, Ceres sought refuge in the embrace of sleep, hoping to escape the weight of his remorse. However, his fragile respite was abruptly shattered. Under the cover of darkness, five relentless assailants, fueled by the unrelenting rage that had come to define the fallen empire, descended upon him. In an act of brutal retribution, they coldly and mercilessly slit his throat, extinguishing the flickering embers of his life.

CHAPTER 34

It took Leah days to come to terms with the loss of her father. Many people condemned her for mourning the passing of such an evil man, but Ali was different. He understood the significance of a father, even if he couldn't remember his own. His mother had taught him that a parent is sacred, second only to the Creator.

Leah admired her husband for his wisdom. However, she felt disappointed when she discovered that Commander Othman had been named king in Ali's place. She knew that Aznek would only make such a decision if Ali had declined the title.

She had initially refused to attend the grand coronation organized by Aznek, but the queen insisted on her presence. Reluctantly, Leah made her way to the square palace. As she arrived, she saw a gathering of over a thousand men and women from different kingdoms. Sofia informed her that they were the leaders of the noble houses from the seven kingdoms.

In the center of it all, Queen Aznek sat among two women and four men. Leah and Sofia took their seats on the left side, while Sam, Nisay, and Izmir occupied the right side.

The cheers and screams continued until Aznek rose to her feet and raised her hand. The noise subsided, and a hush fell over the crowd as Aznek began her speech.

"Our dream has come true—a world with seven kingdoms and seven rulers. This would not have been possible without all of you, from the humblest servant who prepared our meals to the skilled blacksmiths who armed our great warriors; to those who fearlessly fought for glory and freedom."

The crowd erupted in applause and cheering, prompting Aznek to pause momentarily before she resumed speaking.

"But we must remember that traitors and evil will always exist. Our journey is not yet over. To maintain this hard-won peace, we need honorable rulers, and we have them. King Arsalan for Toprak, Queen Nora for Token, Queen Roulan for Turang, King Othman for Turba, King Suresh for Dharatee, King Seydou for Grond, and myself, Queen Aznek for Solum." she paused, her voice rising in intensity. "Three queens to govern our world. Isn't that mesmerizing?"

The crowd erupted once again, with a dominant female voice resonating above the rest. Aznek had to raise her hand three times before the screams subsided.

"I was raised by a man named King Rajab. He was my idol, and if it weren't for him, I might have become a slave in some distant land. Our worth as individuals is not defined by our gender but by the goodness in our hearts and our will to help others."

Aznek paused, locking eyes with each of her five council members, before continuing.

"Queen Roulan played a significant role in weakening the empire by taking down their prime advisor. Nisay bravely conquered Token on his own, and I liberated Solum from our enemies. However, it is important to acknowledge that we accomplished these feats when we became strong and had the support of our allies. Despite the greatness of our collective achievements, they pale in comparison to what our hero, Lord Ali, accomplished. He was once a slave when he made the audacious decision to stand against seven kingdoms and an empire. He had no military background, no powerful allies, yet he refused to submit to Ceres' tyranny. He never uttered the words, 'This war is too big for someone like me.'"

Aznek paused for a moment, her eyes filled with a mix of admiration and anticipation. She then turned to the attentive audience and posed the question, "Do you know what he always said?"

Nora's voice trembled as she shouted, "Free the world from the chains of the empire or die trying!"

Aznek nodded, her expression filled with admiration. "He gathered half of the rulers you see around this table, individuals who were defeated and broken from within. He instilled hope in their hearts and led them with unwavering determination. Despite the countless lives we lost, Ali never wavered in his resolve. He lived in constant danger, risking everything to help us achieve this moment of glory."

Aznek's voice softened as she continued, "His heart was so pure that the daughter of our enemy, against all odds, abandoned the wealth and power her father had amassed. She believed in Ali's cause and dedicated herself to pursuing his dream.'

The rulers and allies gathered were unsure of the queen's intentions, but they were moved by her epic speech about their friend Ali. And Aznek was not done yet.

"Despite my bloodline and my right to be the Lady Queen, I have chosen to step aside and cast my vote for the rightful candidate," Aznek declared. She looked from right to left, addressing the kings and queens gathered before her. "It is now up to all of you to decide whether to support this decision. If there is disagreement, we can initiate a new election."

A wave of shock washed over every face in the palace as the realization sank in. Some individuals stood up, their voices filled with astonishment and conviction, "You're the legitimate lady queen, Your Grace!"

Aznek raised her hand, a gesture commanding attention and restoring order to the room. Gradually, the voices subsided, and a profound silence settled over the gathered assembly.

Aznek spoke with unwavering determination, her words carrying the weight of conviction, "Ceres may be gone, but his ideas will continue to deceive weak hearts. Believe me, there will be those who follow in his footsteps. The Lord King or Lady Queen must be someone capable of thwarting these traitors—a person who can serve as an example to soldiers and inspire rulers. And I see no man or woman better suited for this role than Lord Ali."

Othman, unable to contain his enthusiasm, rose from his seat and exclaimed, "My vote is for Lord Ali!"

His declaration reverberated through the room, followed by resounding agreement from Suresh and Seydo, their voices joining in unison to support Ali's candidacy.

In unison, Nora, Roulan, and Arsalan stood and declared, "May the Lord King Ali be blessed."

Aznek glanced at Leah before leaving the royal table. The other rulers followed suit, taking their seats next to the Solumy council members. The entire venue fell silent for a moment, anticipation hanging in the air.

Finally, the new Lord King appeared on the balcony above them, donning a white robe adorned with golden stripes. His beard was trimmed, and his hair reached his shoulders. Standing at the center of the royal table, he observed the joy on the faces of his comrades. Cheers erupted from the palace, bringing him delight.

Aznek leaned in close to Leah and whispered, "You won't allow another queen to take your place!"

Leah responded, "I am not dressed for the role of Lady Queen."

Aznek smiled and replied, "Trust me, when you appear next to Ali as the Lady Queen in that brown dress, the highborn ladies will rush to their tailors, demanding similar attire."

Leah had no words but walked toward her husband. Standing beside him, she could hardly believe that he was no longer the ailing man he once was.

"I thought you wanted to be a Thinker," she whispered.

Ali smiled, replying, "Not before ensuring that our son is prepared to be the next Lord King."

Leah placed her hand on her belly and asked, "Our son as the Lord King, or perhaps our daughter as the Lady Queen?"

Ali's eyebrows shot up. "Of course, my love. Of course."

***

Everything in the empire underwent a profound transformation, as if Ceres and his father had never existed. The empire he had once ruled was now depleted, with many seeking refuge in their preferred kingdoms. Ali seized this opportunity to establish it as the capital, where he and his council members resided.

Capitalizing on the strength of its structures and the vast training grounds, Ali transformed it into a hub for both scientific advancements and military excellence. It became a place where knowledge and strategic prowess thrived.

Leah persuaded her sister, Emily, to live with her along with their younger brother, leaving behind the burdens of the past. Emily agreed under one condition: she would take on the responsibility of caring for their little brother. Leah saw no issue with this arrangement, trusting her sister's dedication.

While Emily and her five-year-old brother were together in their room, he spoke up with innocence in his voice, "I miss my father."

"He is gone, and it is best for us to move forward and leave the past behind," Emily gently reassured him. She leaned forward to embrace him tightly. She continued, her tone filled with determination."But, we will never forget what these traitors did to us. I promise you, little brother, that one day you will reclaim what rightfully belongs to you."

Printed in Great Britain
by Amazon

74108aba-b90e-4a62-8bd0-712e95323f6eR01